PRIME SUSPECTS

A RAIN CITY LEGAL THRILLER

STEPHEN PENNER

INKUBATOR
BOOKS

Published by Inkubator Books
www.inkubatorbooks.com

ISBN (eBook): 978-1-83756-474-3
ISBN (Paperback): 978-1-83756-475-0
ISBN (Hardback): 978-1-83756-476-7

1

"Daniel Raine, attorney at law," Rebecca Sommers threw her arm wide to their host for the evening, "may I present Alexandra Pruitt, the queen of Seattle real estate."

Alexandra laughed at the introduction, then stepped to the side to allow Raine and his sometimes-investigator into her penthouse condominium. "Welcome to my humble abode, Mr. Raine. I'm so glad you could make it. Rebecca has told me absolutely nothing about you."

The 'humble abode' was anything but, as might be expected for the residence of Seattle's real estate monarch. A cascade of stairs led down from the entry to a sunken living room and dining area wrapped in floor-to-ceiling windows framing a panoramic view of the surrounding skyscrapers, their randomly lit windows creating a star-like effect against the night sky.

Spread across the luxurious furniture were the other invitees and, where applicable, their plus-ones. Sommers had listed off their names on the way over, but Raine had never been great at remembering names, especially without seeing the faces they were attached to. He was going to need a round of introductions. And judging by what little Sommers had divulged in the car, he was probably also going to need a drink.

"Dan isn't my date, Alexandra," Sommers defended her lack of information about her companion. "He's a business associate. I would never bring a romantic interest to a professional event."

"Professional event?" Alexandra questioned. She was certainly dressed more for a social evening than a business meeting, Raine thought. She wore a champagne-colored evening dress, trimmed in lace and sequins, and an assortment of jewelry made from what Raine guessed might be real pearls. Her thick gray hair was up and perfectly styled. She looked ready for an evening at the opera or a lavish fundraiser featuring Seattle's rich and famous. "This is a party."

"A retirement party," Sommers countered. "That's professional."

"Not retirement," Alexandra insisted. "At least, not simply retirement. An ending, to be sure, but a new beginning as well. I have a big announcement, and it affects each one of you."

"Each one of who?" Raine asked. He was just there because a friend asked him to tag along, and he didn't have other plans that night. His kids were with his ex, and his girlfriend was out of town. It was either the swanky real estate party or whatever movie was the top recommendation on his streaming service.

"The Fab Five," Sommers answered. "Alexandra took each of us under her wing at some point and showed us enough of her secrets to become successful businesswomen ourselves."

"The Fab Five." Alexandra laughed, creasing her face at the corners of her eyes and mouth. "I love that you call yourselves that. So, yes, tonight is professional, but it's also personal. But we can be both colleagues and friends, can't we?"

"You and I can, Alexandra," Sommers answered. "I'll give you that much. No promises after that. Now, where's the champagne?"

"Follow me, Rebecca, Dan." Alexandra began descending the steps. "I have to check in with the caterer. And find Ernest, wherever he's disappeared to. But I can certainly guide you to the bar on my way to the kitchen."

Raine and Sommers followed Alexandra down the steps and into what Raine feared might be an exceedingly polite lion's den. Then again, the weapons would be words, and he was a trial attorney—words were his stock and trade.

"The bar is just over there if you're looking for a cocktail." Alexandra pointed to a small setup against a wall near what appeared to be a cloakroom. "There are also servers walking around with trays of champagne. Or at least, there are supposed to be. If you'll excuse me, I need to find someone to yell at."

And with that Alexandra swept away, her gown glittering behind her.

"She seems nice," Raine commented.

Sommers laughed. "She's Alexandra. She's whatever the moment needs. She was nice to us, but I wouldn't want to be the caterer in charge of champagne." She gestured toward the bar, with its single, nervous-looking caterer standing behind it. "Buy a girl a gin and tonic."

"And an old fashioned for the gentleman," Raine approved.

Once the drinks were in hand, and tip was in the tip jar, Raine and Sommers ventured into the party proper.

"Come on," Sommers encouraged. "I'll introduce you around. Keep your guard up."

Raine smiled at the warning. It sounded fun. And he'd thought the evening would be boring.

The first of the women they encountered, in no particular order other than their proximity to the bar, was standing next to the fireplace with a man in a dark suit and open collar. She wore an emerald dress with her ginger hair teased up into a cascade or curls. She was probably in her late thirties to early forties, but it was hard to tell under the makeup and dimmed lights.

"Caroline," Sommers greeted her contemporary as they reached the couple, "this is my friend, Dan Raine. Dan, this is Caroline Howard."

"Another of the Fab Five?" he ventured, mostly because he wanted to say the phrase.

He expected Caroline might wince at the kitschy nickname, but instead her face lit up.

"Absolutely!" Caroline flashed a broad smile, revealing unnaturally white teeth—and the wrinkles hidden in her previously relaxed expression. "Rebecca and I are practically sisters. Pruitt sisters."

Sommers turned to Raine. "We are not sisters," she declared. "We are colleagues. At most."

Caroline's expression dropped slightly, but she fought to maintain it. Raine felt bad for her, so he changed the subject. He extended a hand to Caroline's companion. "Dan," he offered.

The man hesitated, then shifted his drink to his left hand and shook Raine's hand. "David. Nice to meet you."

Raine was about to ask him if he was also in real estate, but before he could Caroline brought the conversation back to her sister, and their mother.

"What do you think Alexandra's big announcement is?" Caroline asked Sommers. "I think she's going to sell everything and move to Mexico." She leaned in closer. "And give us each a fat check as a thank you."

"Thank you for what?" Sommers laughed. "We're the ones who should thank her."

"Well, maybe." Caroline shifted her weight and tucked a stray strand of hair behind her ear. "But we're not in the same position as her to just give money away."

Sommers grinned and tipped her head slightly. "Alexandra doesn't just give money away," she said. "And speak for yourself."

Caroline gasped and prepared a reply, but Sommers cut her off before she could say anything.

"Always good to see you, Caroline," Sommers said. She nodded to Caroline's date. "David." Then a second nod to Raine. "Come along, Dan. There are more people to introduce you to."

Raine complied and offered his own regards before hurrying after Sommers.

"That was," Raine hesitated—he didn't want to call his compatriot 'rude'.

"That was fine," Sommers cut him off with a hiss over her shoulder. "Caroline has always been the least successful of us. She's Alexandra's biggest disappointment, or she should be anyway. It's just gross to be speculating about Alexandra giving us money. She's given us all more than enough to succeed on our own. It's not Alexandra's fault Caroline couldn't figure it out."

Raine's eyebrows shot up. He expected some good-natured rivalry among Sommers and her peers, but it was already more entertaining than he could have hoped. "Who's next?" he asked.

"Julia Kim," Sommers stopped short as they reached the next couple, seated on a white sofa across the room from the fireplace, "this is my friend Dan Raine. Dan, this is Julia and her husband, Tommy."

"Tom is fine." The husband grinned as he stood up and offered Raine his hand.

Julia followed her husband to her feet. She wore a red body-con dress that stopped just below her knee. Her silky black hair hung loosely at her shoulders, parted by large gold hoop earrings. Ruby-red lips parted in a welcoming smile. "Nice to meet you, Dan. Are you Rebecca's latest beau, I hope?"

Raine returned, "I'm afraid not. We're business associates. Nothing more."

"Nothing," Sommers confirmed, a little too quickly, Raine thought.

"Oh, are you in real estate, too?" Julia asked. "I don't know if I've heard your name before."

Raine shook his head. "No, I'm a lawyer. Rebecca helps me out on cases sometimes."

Julia turned her grin to Sommers. "Oh, Rebecca, that is interesting. You'll need to fill me in on those cases. I'm not surprised you have a side hustle. You were always the hardest working among us."

"Oh, Julia." Sommers shook her head. "You always were the biggest flatterer among us."

Julia's smile grew. "A valuable skill in our line of work."

"Indeed," Sommers agreed.

Then Julia leaned forward. "Any idea what Alexandra has planned for us tonight? I can't remember the last time we were all in the same room together. It must be something big."

Sommers shook her head. "No idea at all. I'm not even worrying about it. I'm here to celebrate her retirement. Her big announcement could be what type of cake we're having, for all I care."

Julia's perma-smile chilled slightly. "Of course," she agreed unconvincingly. "Me too. Just curious. Only natural, I suppose, right?"

"Totally," Sommers confirmed. "And Alexandra loves building things up and the big reveal. I'm sure whatever she has planned will be a surprise to all of us. Something we never even thought of."

Julia nodded. "I'm sure that's right."

"Nice to see you again, Tommy," Sommers ended their interaction. "I want to show Dan the view of the bay from the dining room."

Another round of departure niceties and Sommers was pulling Raine toward the windows.

"They seemed nice," he observed.

"I like Julia," Sommers replied. "She has the most flair out of all of us. Her face is all over Seattle, but honestly, I'm not sure how she affords the advertising costs. I've never noticed her make any big sales and she's never listed in the trades as one of the top agents. Still, she drives a Bentley and is always jetting off on some luxury vacation. She was the only one to ignore Alexandra's advice about not getting married, but I don't think her husband is how she affords everything. He's a veterinarian. Nice guy, but not rich. Handsome as hell though, so he fits her image. My guess is that they're deep in debt."

Raine looked back at the couple they had just left. "Wow. Do you all know everything about each other?"

"Not quite everything, but a lot," Sommers admitted. "It can be annoying sometimes."

That reminded Raine of a question he had been meaning to ask her since she'd first invited him to join her that evening. "Speaking of which, why am I here tonight? To prove your side gig is real?"

Sommers stopped and faced her companion. "Three reasons. One, I would never bring an actual boyfriend to this. Two, I would never come to this alone. And three," she reached out and straightened his tie, "you look good in a suit."

Raine couldn't help but grin at the compliment. But he didn't get a chance to thank her. She grabbed his arm and pulled him up the small set of steps leading to the dining area, and the next of the Fab Five. "Come on. Let's catch Meredith before she disappears again. She's always the hardest to pin down. She never stops moving,"

The woman in question was staring out the window, hugging her arms tightly around her torso and bouncing a foot on the marble floor. Sommers called out to her, and she turned around. She had long blonde hair like Sommers, but it was golden, not platinum. Her purple dress was bare on one shoulder and longer at the back than the front. A single gold chain decorated her throat.

"Meredith, this is my friend, Dan Raine," Sommers introduced them. "Dan, this is Meredith Beauchamp."

"Nice to meet you." Raine extended a hand which Meredith shook sharply.

"You too," she replied. "How do you know Rebecca?"

"We work together sometimes," Sommers answered for him. "Dan is a lawyer. I help him if he needs real estate expertise."

"Oh, wow, how interesting," Meredith said, in a genuine tone. "How did you two meet?"

"Long story," Raine answered. "Interesting, but long."

Meredith just nodded and smiled at his response. She looked at Sommers. "It's nice to have everyone together again. It's been too long."

"It has," Sommers agreed, although Raine doubted her sincerity given her comments after their last two interactions.

"I wonder what Alexandra's big announcement will be," he ventured.

He was more interested in what Meredith's guess was, and how Sommers would respond to it once they were walking away. Meredith didn't seem terribly interested either.

She shrugged. "It seems pretty obvious to me. She doesn't want to work anymore but she has this huge business empire to run. She's going to offer to make us partners, then leave it to us to run the business while she draws a healthy salary and travels the world with Ernest."

Raine considered for a moment. "That does make a lot of sense."

"More sense than liquidating everything and just giving us each a fifth of the proceeds," Sommers agreed.

"Well, whatever the announcement is, I hope we get to it

soon." She pressed a hand against her stomach. "I'd like to have dinner before I get too hungry."

Raine could agree with that sentiment. The bourbon and simple syrup were filling his stomach for the moment, but he was going to be hungry soon. His curiosity about Alexandra's announcement turned to curiosity about her dinner offerings.

"Are you here by yourself?" Sommers asked, with a quick glance around the condo.

"Oh, um, yeah," Meredith answered. "I'm kind of between relationships right now."

Sommers nodded. "I can understand that."

Meredith didn't reply. Raine knew not to try.

"If you'll excuse me," Meredith said after a moment, "I need to attend to something. It was nice to meet you, Dan. Good to see you again, Rebecca. Maybe we can sit next to each other at dinner."

Sommers offered a noncommittal reply and Meredith departed toward the kitchen.

"She seemed nice," Raine opined. "Or are you going to tell me I'm wrong about that?"

Sommers laughed. "You're not wrong. Meredith is very nice. She was the quiet one who did her homework and built her business slowly and steadily. She doesn't need anything from Alexandra, and it shows."

Raine could only agree with that based on what he'd seen. "So, who's left? Counting you, I've met four of the Fab Five."

Sommers sighed, then nodded toward the woman standing by herself on the opposite side of the room from everyone else. "Fiona Mendoza."

Fiona was dressed simply, in a nice but plain floral dress,

and her brown hair twisted into a simple bun behind her neck.

"Shall we go talk to her?" Raine expected.

"I don't think so." Sommers rolled her eyes and sighed. "Fiona is the worst. Just the worst. It's hard to explain why. I don't think I can handle talking with her just now. Or ever, really."

Raine looked again at the solitary woman across the room. "Really?"

"Really," Sommers confirmed. "Come on, I'll show you that view I mentioned earlier. Even through the rain, it's a hundred times better than talking with Fiona."

The view was in fact spectacular. Up close, the sea of lights from the windows of the neighboring buildings parted to offer a view of Elliott Bay, black in the night, with wave crests illuminated by the lights of the waterfront. The cycling colored lights of the Ferris wheel at the center of the boardwalk reflected off the water in an undulating rainbow.

Raine enjoyed the last of his drink as he took in the view. It was nice to slow down sometimes. The party was Sommers's event. He could let her stress over whatever she felt compelled to stress over. His job was to not be her boyfriend and look good in a suit. He was confident in his ability to do both of those things.

"I'm getting hungry," Sommers finally broke the trance. "I wonder if any of these waiters have hors d'oeuvres, or just champagne."

Raine turned to survey their offerings. When they had arrived, there were no waiters to be seen. Now it was hard to see through them all. Whatever fire Alexandra had lit under the catering staff, it was raging.

"I only see drinks," Raine observed. "Way more than any of us could drink."

"Speak for yourself," Sommers responded, reaching for a glass of sparkling wine from the nearest waiter. "Come on. Let's see if we can find Alexandra. I'm dying to know what her big surprise is."

"Do you really think she'll tell you in advance?" Raine questioned.

"Tell me? No," Sommers admitted. "But maybe you can pull it out of her with a series of expertly crafted questions. You are a lawyer, right?"

Raine cocked his head at Sommers. "Is that the fourth reason I'm here?"

Sommers smiled but didn't answer his question. "Come on. I bet she's in the kitchen. It sure looks like no one else is."

A quick scan confirmed all of the other guests and far too many caterers were crowded in the living room. Raine acceded to Sommers's direction. He didn't have any contrary plans of his own, and he was curious how nice the kitchen was. He guessed it was to die for. He was a little too correct.

He and Sommers walked through the swinging kitchen door, and both immediately stopped in their tracks. There, in the center of the kitchen floor, lay Alexandra Pruitt. A broken bowl of soup was near her feet, and a spoon lay inches from her outstretched hand. Her other hand was clutching her throat, but her tongue protruded between her lips and her eyes were dull and glassy, staring lifelessly at the ceiling.

They both rushed over but Raine pulled Sommers back from disturbing the body.

"It's too late, Rebecca," he said. "She's dead."

2

"What happened?" Sommers's voice cracked at the sight of her dead mentor.

They were alone in the kitchen, although 'kitchen' was perhaps too small of a word for the opulent food preparation facility in her luxury penthouse condominium. Stainless steel pots hung from racks over several stovetops and marble counters. Banks of refrigerators and pantries filled the walls between the two sets of swinging doors, one leading to the back hallway and the bedrooms, the other to the dining room full of guests who had no idea, yet, that their host was dead.

"Poison," Raine hazarded. "The toxicology will tell us for sure. But I'm deducing from the position of the body and the broken soup bowl. She dropped the bowl in distress, but it wasn't from choking. You can't choke on soup."

Sommers leaned forward and sniffed at the spilled soup.

"What does it smell like?" Raine asked.

Sommers frowned. "Tomato, with a hint of basil. And almonds."

"Almonds?" Raine questioned. "Was she allergic to almonds?"

"No." Sommers shook her head. "But cyanide smells like almonds. It's also one of the only poisons that acts almost instantaneously."

"Where would someone get cyanide?" Raine questioned.

"You can make it yourself," Sommers answered. "From apple seeds."

"How do you know all that?" Raine asked.

"I was a girl scout," Sommers replied.

Raine frowned at her. "They teach poison-making in the girl scouts? Is there a cyanide merit badge?"

"They teach poison recognition," Sommers defended. "And maybe I had a morbid curiosity and looked into the darker things on my own. Why do you think I like working with you?"

Raine supposed there was some truth to that.

"We need to figure who did this, Dan," Sommers practically pleaded.

"Isn't that the police's job?" Raine posited.

"Since when do you trust the cops?" Sommers challenged.

"Good point," Raine admitted. "But the first step is to avoid being accused of the murder ourselves. Someone is going to walk in on us any second."

"It's okay. You're a lawyer," Sommers responded.

"I'm a lawyer, not a cop," Raine answered. "It's not even like I'm a prosecutor. Those guys like to pretend they're cops. I'm just a businessman with a law degree. I sell speeches and stationery. I have no more authority over this body than you do."

"Then we better figure it out fast," Sommers said, "before we get found here with—"

"Ms. Pruitt, ma'am? I'm terribly sorry, but Rico can't find the cake knife and—" A young woman walked into the kitchen from the dining room, eyes downcast. Raine deduced she was part of the catering staff, judging by her crisp white shirt, dark pants, and apparent anticipation of a berating. When none was immediately forthcoming, she lifted her eyes and took in the scene of her client dead on the floor, surrounded by two guests outwardly unbothered by her condition. "And, and, and—"

Raine wasn't a prosecutor, but he had gone up against enough of them that he could act like one in a pinch. He glided swiftly to the shaken food server and began talking before she thought too much.

"I need you to do exactly what I say," he told her in his most serious voice, the one he used for closing arguments in murder cases. "The integrity of the investigation is absolutely dependent on it. Can you do that for me?"

The young woman nodded. She couldn't have been more than twenty years old, with doe eyes, large glasses, and a reddish ponytail.

"Good," Raine encouraged. "I need you to go back out there and make sure everyone sits down at the dinner table and no one leaves. Okay? The police are on their way. Do you understand? If anyone leaves, don't try to stop them, but I want you to write down their name, if you know it, and if you don't, then exactly what they were wearing. Do you understand?"

The young woman didn't reply. Her eyes were fixed over Raine's shoulder at the dead woman on the other side of the room.

"Do you understand?" Raine repeated.

The woman's gaze snapped back to Raine. "Right. Yes. Understood. Everyone sits down. No one leaves. Names and clothes. Got it."

Raine reached out and gently but firmly grabbed the woman's shoulders. "Good. You may be the reason justice prevails tonight."

The corner of the woman's mouth curled into a smile at that, despite the circumstances. "You can count on me," she assured, then she spun around and marched back out to the dining room.

Raine turned to face Sommers again. "That bought us five minutes, tops. Who do you think did this? We'll have time to confront one person and one person only."

Sommers thought for a moment. "I can't believe anyone here would have done this."

"Well, someone here did it," Raine answered. "Caroline, for the money? Julia, for the same reason? Meredith, for some reason? Fiona, because everyone hates her? Those four plus you make the Fab Five, and obviously you didn't do it. That means we have four prime suspects."

"Five." Sommers frowned. "Ernest."

"Ernest?" Raine repeated.

"Alexandra's long-time boyfriend, Ernest Poplowski," Sommers explained. "They've been together for as long as I can remember. A decade, at least. But she would never marry him. She was too successful and too distrustful. I remember she told me never to get married. If he's good enough to stick around, he will. If he wants half, he can earn half and keep his own. Ernest never made nearly as much as her and maybe he was finally tired of playing supplicant."

Raine rubbed his forehead. "Five suspects is four too

many. We only have time to confront one. And we're running out of that."

"Ernest," Sommers decided. "We all had our issues with Alexandra and with each other, but I can't believe any of us would harm the woman who gave us the chance to be successful. Ernest's relationship with Alexandra is different in kind."

"Ernest it is." Raine nodded, then pulled out his cell phone.

"Who are you calling?" Sommers asked. "I thought you said we were running out of time."

"The police," Raine answered, "and we are. I want them to get here before all hell breaks loose. Caterer girl won't be able to stop the rats from fleeing for the exits, but the cops will."

He held up a finger and turned away slightly to speak into the phone. "Hello? 911? I want to report a murder."

After giving the dispatcher the address and a brief recitation of the facts known to that point, which were precious few, Raine and Sommers emerged from the kitchen into the dining room, intent to find Ernest wherever he was hiding, but immediately sidetracked by the argument being screamed across the dining room table where all of the guests had quickly gathered. Raine wasn't thrilled about walking into the middle of someone else's argument, but it might offer them extra time. And information.

"You're pathetic, Julia!" Caroline shouted. "You always wanted to be Alexandra's favorite, but you never were. She tolerated you. That's it."

"Oh, be quiet, Caroline," Julia replied calmly. "You're just jealous because you were never as successful as the rest of us, despite Alexandra giving you twice as much help."

"Twice? Ha!" Caroline scoffed. "More like half. I had to do more on my own than any of you ever did."

"And look how far it got you," Julia laughed. "Living with a failed screenwriter and wearing Gina Caren knockoffs."

"David is not a failure!" Caroline shrieked. "It's a difficult industry to break into. He's very talented. And my dress may be fake, but not as fake as your boo—"

"Ladies! Ladies!" Meredith interjected. "Don't do this. Not here. Not now. This is Alexandra's retirement celebration. We should all be thanking her and wishing her well, not ruining her big day with petty grievances."

"Her big day is already ruined," Raine whispered to Sommers.

Sommers frowned back disapprovingly.

Raine and Sommers had stopped directly in front of the door to the kitchen, effectively blocking the door. No one who wasn't already in a back bedroom was getting into the kitchen.

"Stay out of this, Meredith," Caroline huffed. "You'll take whoever's side you think will win the argument so you can feel good about yourself. Do you feel good about yourself? Are you the hero for telling us to shut up?"

"Don't attack Meredith." Fiona stepped forward from the wall to defend Meredith. "She's just trying to help."

Caroline, Julia, and Meredith all turned to their floral-garbed colleague. "Shut up, Fiona," they said in unison.

"Nobody likes Fiona," Sommers whispered.

Raine scanned the condo, filled with the five fabulous women, a couple of plus-ones, and a team of catering staff. But no dead woman's boyfriend. "Where's Ernest?"

Before Sommers could answer, the young woman who

had walked in on them in the kitchen stepped up to Raine. "How am I doing?" she asked in a lowered voice.

"With what?" Raine replied. She didn't seem to be doing anything at all.

"With keeping everyone here," she answered. "I told Ms. Howard that I overheard Ms. Kim say she had no business being here tonight. And I told Ms. Kim that Ms. Howard said she was dressed like a ten-dollar whore."

"Whoa." Raine's eyebrows shot up.

"Yeah, the argument happened pretty fast after that," the young woman said proudly. "And no one wants to leave in the middle of a show."

"Nice," Raine admired. "Does this sort of thing come up a lot in the catering industry?"

"I'm sorry?" The woman cocked her head at him. Then, "Oh. I'm not—"

Before she could say more, Sommers interjected. "Do you know where Mr. Poplowski is?"

"Yes, we need to speak with him right away," Raine added. "The police will be here any moment."

The young woman shook her head. "No. I haven't seen Ernest for a while now. I don't know where he is."

A scream from the kitchen pierced the condominium and all eyes turned to the door behind Raine and Sommers.

Raine frowned. "I think I know where he is."

3

Everyone rushed into the kitchen, led by Raine and Sommers, if only due to their proximity to the door. Inside they found Ernest, sitting on the floor cradling Alexandra's lifeless body. He was rocking back and forth, tears streaming down his face, sobbing, "No, no, no..." over and over again.

"I don't think he did it," Raine whispered to Sommers.

"Not unless he's one hell of an actor," Sommers agreed.

The crowd started to converge on Ernest, but Raine jumped ahead and put up his arms. "Stop! This is a crime scene. Don't touch anything. The police are on their way."

In truth, Ernest had already contaminated the crime scene sufficiently that any further kicking of the soup spoon across the floor likely wouldn't have mattered. But his command wasn't what bothered the other guests.

"Who called the police?"

"Did you know about this?"

"Why didn't you say anything?"

"Did you do it?"

Thankfully, before Raine could decide how, or even whether, to try to explain the events of the previous ten minutes, the aforementioned police made their entrance. Caterer woman held the door to the kitchen open for the officers who spilled into the room.

"Police! Nobody move!"

Several of the guests put their hands up. Raine wondered if that was life experience or too much television. He suspected the latter.

He also raised his hands, but in an open greeting to the arriving officers, and especially the one at the center of the group with the stripes on his arm. "Thank you for coming, Sergeant. I was just telling everyone—"

"Who are you?" the sergeant demanded. He was a large man, even taller than Raine's 6'3", and probably fifty pounds heavier, although it was hard to tell how much of that was the bullet-proof vest. Short salt-and-pepper hair and a gray mustache spoke to his years of experience.

"I'm Daniel Raine," he answered. "I'm an attorney and—"

"Are you a prosecutor?" the sergeant interrupted.

"Uh, no," Raine admitted, "but—"

"Do you represent the killer?"

"We don't even know who the killer is yet," Raine answered.

"Then you're not an attorney," the sergeant harrumphed. "Not as far as I care. You're a witness. And this is a crime scene. Which means you're in my way. Just like everyone else in here."

He turned his attention to the assembled guests. "Ladies and gentlemen!" he bellowed. "My name is Anthony McCollum. I am a sergeant with the Seattle Police Department. We are responding to a report of a murder. This is an active crime scene and all of you are witnesses. I need you to leave this room immediately. Please walk in an orderly fashion to the living room and find somewhere to sit down. None of you are free to leave until I say so."

"How long?" came a question shouted from the crowd.

"I have other places to be tonight!"

"Will I get paid overtime?"

"As long as it takes," Sergeant McCollum answered. "But you can expect to be here for several hours. Your other plans are cancelled. And Seattle Police will not be paying anyone overtime except my officers."

Grumbling rippled through the group, but McCollum headed off any further pushback.

"Those are the last questions I will be answering tonight," he informed them. "A detective will be arriving shortly, and they will be the ones asking the questions. I suggest you answer them completely and honestly if you want to help us figure out who committed the crime."

A chorus of agreement came from the crowd, but Raine couldn't help but hold back his acquiescence. If a legal career that included defending accused criminals had taught him anything, it was don't talk to the cops. Especially if you're the one who found the body and didn't tell anyone. On the other hand, he was the one who called the police, which was generally rare for murderers. Raine decided to wait and see how things developed. Hopefully the detective would realize he and Sommers were witnesses, not suspects.

It took nearly an hour for the detective to arrive, and another hour of her talking with her officers and the forensics team before she was ready to speak to any of the guests. And even then, Raine and Sommers weren't the top priority.

They may have been the first to find the body, but Ernest was the boyfriend. The cops always start with the boyfriend.

"What do you think Ernest is telling them?" Sommers whispered.

They were sitting in two small chairs pushed into a reading nook in the far corner of the living room. The wooden chairs weren't terribly comfortable, but all of the good seats had been taken by other guests. And Raine didn't want to sit too close to any of them anyway. He may not have been a prosecutor, but he was in full lawyer mode. Everything you say, to anyone, can and will be used against you.

"My guess? The truth," Raine answered. "At least the truth as he perceived and recalls it. That's the problem. That's always the problem. Everyone's observations are filtered by emotion, vantage points, biases, and prejudices. Ten people could see the same traffic accident and you'll get ten different versions of what happened."

"Well, they'll all agree there was an accident," Sommers argued.

Raine shrugged. "Yeah, and everyone here will agree Alexandra's dead. After that, it gets murky. I am not looking to go to jail tonight, or ever again for that matter."

"Well, me neither," Sommers replied with some trepidation in her voice. She ran her hands down her gown. "Would I get a chance to change clothes first?"

"You get a change of clothes at the jail," Raine answered. "I hope you like red. Murderers get red."

"Murderers?" Sommers shook her head. "They won't think we're murderers. We don't look like murderers."

"No one here looks like a murderer," Raine responded, "but one of them is."

Sommers frowned. She glanced out at her assembled

colleagues and competitors. "Okay, super lawyer. Who did it?"

"That depends," Raine answered while gazing out at the same guests, "on what Alexandra was planning to announce, and whether anyone found out in advance."

"And what happens now that she didn't get to announce it," Sommers added.

Raine nodded. "Exactly."

He already had his suspicions, and enough experience to doubt those suspicions already as well. But before he could share his thoughts, the person whose job it was to actually identify the culprit walked up to them.

"Mr. Raine, Ms. Sommers, I'm Detective Olivia Kahale," she introduced herself.

She had silky black hair pulled into a long ponytail and bright white teeth set against smooth brown skin. She was tall, with a well-worn blazer and a tired countenance. It was getting late, and she had hours of work ahead of her.

"It's my understanding that you two were the first ones to find the body. Is that correct?"

"Correct," Raine confirmed.

"And you didn't tell anyone," Kahale followed up. "Is that also correct?"

Raine sighed. "That is also correct," he admitted.

"We did call 911," Sommers defended. "Well, he did. But I was there, and I approved."

The corner of Kahale's mouth curled into a smile. "Good for you. Any reason you didn't tell the others right away?"

"Well, we wanted—" Sommers started.

"We didn't get the chance," Raine interjected. "We came out to the dining room, and everyone was already engaged in a discussion. Before we could interrupt, Ernest found the body and called out. Then everyone rushed into the kitchen and your officers arrived."

There was a lot of information in that apparently short answer. Raine wondered whether Kahale would pick out the important bit.

"What was the discussion about?" she asked after a moment.

Raine had to suppress his own smile. He liked Kahale. Maybe the police would actually be able to identify Alexandra's killer after all.

"You should probably ask them," Raine answered. "We walked into the middle of it."

Kahale rubbed her chin for a moment then looked to Sommers. "Do you recall, Ms. Sommers?"

Sommers took a beat, then shrugged. "I agree with Dan. You should talk to them directly. I don't want to repeat hearsay."

Kahale tipped her head slightly. Raine was glad to see that too.

"It's not hearsay to report what someone else said," Raine explained.

"It's not?" Sommers questioned.

"Well, it is if you want someone to believe what the person said was true," Raine answered, "but it's not if you're just reporting what was said. It depends on your intent in reporting it."

Sommers frowned. "That seems silly."

"A lot of the law is silly," Raine allowed.

"This is serious," Kahale interrupted the evidence lesson. "What you heard might be the difference between catching your friend's killer or letting them get away with murder."

Sommers looked again to Raine, her expression betraying concern Kahale might be correct.

"And if we guess and get it wrong," Raine answered the detective, "you might act based on inaccurate information and arrest the wrong person. We don't want to be responsible for that."

Kahale frowned. She was used to being in charge of the crime scene. That was difficult with a lawyer in the middle of it. "Maybe I should speak with each of you separately."

Sommers's eyes widened slightly. But Raine's narrowed. "That won't be possible, Detective. Ms. Sommers is my client for the purposes of this investigation. She has a right to have me present for any questioning. I'm afraid you're stuck with the both of us."

Whatever residue of a smile was still on Kahale's lips evaporated. "Is that correct, Ms. Sommers?"

Sommers hesitated, but only for a moment before she grinned and gestured to Raine. "I'll defer to my attorney."

Kahale sighed. "I see." She called out to the nearest uniformed officer and pointed at Raine and Sommers. "These two leave last," she instructed. "Understood?"

The officer acknowledged the order.

Sommers's jaw fell open, but Raine just pushed himself deeper into his chair. It was going to be a long night.

A long night turned into a long morning. Generally, witnesses were allowed to leave after providing a written statement, but when all the witnesses were also suspects, no one got to go home early. Raine didn't think he or Sommers were seriously suspects, but they had defied a police officer, so they were being punished by watching the dawn break through Alexandra's picture windows. A rhythmic morning rain beat against the glass.

Sommers leaned forward and stretched. "How much longer is this going to take? This dress wasn't made to sleep in."

Raine wasn't particularly comfortable in his suit either after spending the wee hours in a small chair. A hot shower and a warm bed had rarely been more inviting.

"Honestly, I have no idea," he admitted. "They seem to have talked to everyone multiple times. Except us, of course. Maybe that's why it feels like it's taking so long. We've just been sitting here the whole time."

"It feels like it's taking so long because we've been in this condo for over twelve hours," Sommers replied. She stood up and repeated the stretch, with a series of audible pops up her spine. "Maybe we should talk to that detective after all. She might let us go after that. We could strike a deal."

Raine shook his head. "They can do this without us. The one they talk to the most is the one they probably end up arresting. We don't want to be that person."

"Really?" Sommers asked. "Why is that?"

"It shows they're interested in you and your actions," Raine explained, "and every conversation leads to increased interest because your story will change, at least a little bit, every time you tell it—even if you're telling the truth. You leave out a detail one time, then add it the next time. The first time you told the story you said there was a car. The next time you add that the car was blue. Well, why didn't you tell us the car was blue the first time, you liar? It's just how humans communicate, but you can seize on little differences to make it look like someone is lying."

"How do you know that?" Sommers questioned.

"Because that's what I do whenever I cross-examine a witness." Raine grinned. "There's their original statement to the cops. A lot of times there's a follow-up statement. I may interview them at least once before trial. Finally, they give a full direct examination before I even stand up to ask my first question. By then, I have at least four separate versions of the same event, each with slightly different details. I stick the tip of my spear into that tiny crack, then pop their entire story open."

"That's devious," Sommers observed, no judgment in her voice. "Is that why we didn't talk with the detective more?"

"That's one reason," Raine confirmed.

Then Sommers realized something. "Oh my God, you've been counting, haven't you? You know who they've talked to the most, don't you?"

Raine nodded.

"Who is it?" Sommers dropped back into her seat and grabbed Raine's knee. "It's Caroline, isn't it? She always was jealous of the rest of us. Or maybe Julia? No, not Julia. Definitely Caroline, right?"

Before Raine could answer, Detective Kahale returned to the living room and called out, "May I have your attention, please?"

"Are you finally going to let us go?" Caroline called out. "We have lives, you know."

Raine glanced around the room, searching for clues as to what was about to happen. Caroline and her boyfriend were in armchairs on one side of a large glass coffee table. Julia and her husband were on the other side of the table, taking up two of the three seats on an overstuffed leather couch. The third couch seat held Meredith. And Fiona stood off by herself near the fireplace, her hands behind her and leaning against the wall. The catering staff was all seated around the dining room table, except for the woman who had walked in on Raine and Sommers and the dead body. That woman was standing on the other side of the room, right next to the highbacked chair where Ernest was seated, face in his hands.

The forensic technicians had finished documenting the scene hours ago and the body had been removed by the Medical Examiner staff an hour or so after that. The only law enforcement left were Detective Kahale and a cadre of uniformed officers who were spreading out to cover the exits, save two who took up positions directly behind the detective. No one was getting out of that living room until Detective Kahale was finished talking. And then one of them was likely leaving in handcuffs.

Raine wondered if he had guessed the suspect correctly.

"We appreciate everyone's patience," Kahale responded obliquely to Caroline's complaint. "These sorts of investigations can take longer than anyone might like. We've now had a chance to speak with everyone."

Almost everyone, Raine thought with an inner grin.

"And, crucially," Kahale continued, "we've also had a chance to review the security video."

Everyone, including Raine and Sommers, looked at each other in surprise. No one had considered they were being recorded. Least of all the murderer, Raine suspected.

Kahale stepped forward and pointed at the couch. "Meredith Beauchamp, you are under arrest for the murder of Alexandra Pruitt."

4

Raine left immediately after Meredith was taken into custody, who protested her innocence even as they handcuffed her. There was nothing Raine could do to stop it and he, along with everyone else, had been up all night. He needed a nap and a shower. And maybe a drink, although he supposed he should wait until at least noon for that.

When he finally made it into his office the next afternoon for a quiet Saturday of catching up on work, he found Sommers waiting for him, leaning against the locked door, arms crossed and face compressed into a scowl.

"You just left," she accused. "How could you just leave?"

Raine considered for a moment. "I drove?"

"You know what I mean." Sommers uncrossed her arms and took a step toward him.

Raine put up his hands. "Look, there was nothing we could do. The police made their decision. We were free to go. So, I went."

"But Meredith is my friend," Sommers protested. Then,

she qualified, "Or at least my colleague. She was one of us. We should have been there for her."

"Did you want me to fight the cops?" Raine questioned. "That's its own crime. You know that, right? The Bar Association frowns on assaulting law enforcement officers. Detrimental to the image of the profession, or some nonsense. It also wouldn't have worked. I'm not about to risk my license to utterly fail to prevent a lawful arrest."

"Well, you could have said you were her lawyer," Sommers suggested, "like you did with me when they wanted to question us separately."

"That's different," Raine answered. "For one thing, that was just questioning, not a murder charge. For another, I knew you would be okay with it. I had no idea whether Meredith would even want me to be her lawyer."

Sommers pulled out her cell phone and held it up. "Well, she does."

"What?" Raine cocked his head at Sommers and her phone.

"Meredith wants you to be her lawyer," Sommers repeated. "She used her one phone call to call me. She wants to hire you."

Raine ran his hands through his shortly cropped hair. "Damn it. Another criminal case. I am so tired of criminal cases." But then he remembered why he kept taking those cases. "Can she pay?"

It was Sommers's turn to cock her head. "She's one of the Fab Five, Dan. She has money. A lot of it."

Raine considered the situation. He was as rested as he could expect to be and whatever was waiting on his desk could wait a few more hours. "Then it looks like you and I are going to do a jail visit."

Sommers smiled. "Thank you, Dan."

Raine offered a nod in reply, then pulled the keys to his office out of his pocket. "Just let me print out a copy of my standard criminal fee agreement. But double the fee."

"Double?" Sommers questioned as Raine pushed the door open. "Why?"

Raine smiled over his shoulder. "Because she was the one I thought they would arrest."

5

The King County Jail was just far enough away from Raine's office to make the walk a bit of a chore, but not far enough away to justify driving. There was no parking anywhere near it anyway. By the time they had traversed the six-block, uphill journey, Raine was more out of breath than he would have liked. He needed to work out more, he knew. He wasn't getting any younger. But it was hard to find the time. Maybe the occasional lunch hour?

"I said, do you really think she could have done it?" Sommers half-shouted as they reached the pedestrian plaza in front of the jail. "Are you even listening to me?"

Raine shook his head to get it back in the game. "Of course I'm listening to you. And of course she could have done it. There's a reason she's in jail."

"Maybe the reason is that the cops made a mistake," Sommers argued.

Raine nodded. "That's also possible." He pulled open the door to the jail lobby. "Let's see if we can figure out which one is true."

All jails have set visiting hours for family and friends. No jail could possibly staff a system where any visitor could visit any inmate at any time. But attorneys were exempt from those limited hours. The courts had ruled that the jails had to staff a system where any lawyer could visit their client at any time, at least between breakfast and lights-out. Raine didn't need an appointment; he just needed his bar card and his client's name.

"Meredith Beauchamp," he informed the guard behind the bulletproof glass. "Currently held on investigation of murder."

It was "investigation of murder" because she hadn't been charged quite yet. The prosecutor had up to seventy-two hours to file charges before Meredith would have to be released. That meant they had the whole weekend to put the case together and file charges first thing Monday morning. Raine knew it was unlikely the prosecutor wouldn't rubber-stamp Kahale's arrest decision, but if there was any information that might change the prosecutor's mind, it would come from the conversation he was about to have.

"Have a seat," the guard instructed with a nod toward the row of yellowing plastic chairs bolted to the floor. "We'll let you know when she's in a visiting booth."

That could take a while, Raine knew. Just because he could visit her whenever he wanted to, within the bounds of civilized hours, didn't mean she was just sitting around waiting for him to arrive. She probably didn't even know he was coming, unless Sommers had promised her he would take the case—a possibility he neither discounted nor felt compelled to confirm. Either way, given the time of day, Meredith could be anywhere from the cafeterias eating an early dinner to the library reading a 30-year-old paperback donated by some do-gooder non-profit, to sitting in her cell hoping her cellmate(s) didn't start a fight with her.

"How long will this take?" Sommers asked. Her leg was bouncing, her voice irritable. Raine had never really seen her stressed like that before.

"The wait or the consultation?" Raine asked.

"Both, I guess," Sommers answered.

Raine shrugged. "Hard to say. It'll take as long as it takes."

Sommers shook her head. "I still can't believe this is happening. I've never had a friend charged with murder."

Raine mentally went through their cases together so far. "A first time for everything, I suppose."

Sommers frowned. Then she looked up at Raine with the closest thing to pleading eyes he had seen from his normally stoic partner. "Do you really think she could have done it?"

Raine could tell it was no time for a flippant answer. But it wasn't time for an uncritically comforting one either. "Ask me again after we talk to her."

In the event, it took a little over twenty minutes before Meredith Beauchamp was placed in one of the attorney-client visiting booths. Raine traded his bar card for an elevator access badge, and they took the elevator to the third floor. Meredith was already inside Room #3. She was wearing those red jail scrubs Raine had mentioned to Sommers. They made her look even more exhausted and frightened than she certainly was. They were separated by a plexiglass window with a metal grate embedded at chest level. Sound could travel through it, but not easily. It required everyone to raise their voices so much that the privacy supposedly afforded by the booth was undermined by the shouts audible by anyone standing outside. But

Raine wasn't going to be able to fix everything at once. He wasn't sure he could even fix the one thing they were there for.

"Can you get the charges dropped, Mr. Raine?" Meredith asked immediately. "I'm innocent, I swear."

"Well, technically, you haven't been charged yet," Raine began lawyering. "Although I think we can expect the charges to be filed first thing Monday morning. It's unlikely the prosecutor will go against the detective. They have to charge you within seventy-two hours of the arrest or let you go."

Meredith's face lit up with the faintest glint of hope.

"And it's even less likely they will let you go," Raine continued. The glint extinguished. "You can expect to be arraigned Monday afternoon. That's also when bail will be set."

"Bail?" The hope returned. "So, I can just post bail and get out?"

Raine shook his head. "It's not that easy. This is a murder case. Premeditated first-degree murder. The prosecutor will ask for a bail so high that you can't post it. The judge will be tempted to go along. No one wants to be the one who let a murderer out on the street."

"But I'm not a murderer!" Meredith protested.

Raine was glad for that reaction. It was what an innocent person would say. A guilty person would have asked how high the bail was going to be. But she asked that next.

"I have substantial financial resources, Mr. Raine," Meredith said. "I may well be able to post the bail. What kind of number are we talking about?"

"The bidding on a murder one usually starts at a million," Raine answered. "If they know you have substantial financial resources, it'll be higher. So, let's keep that between us for right now."

Meredith nodded. "A million dollars?" She frowned. "Does that have to be cash?"

"Cash is best," Raine answered. "If you post cash, you get it all back at the end of the trial. If you go with a bonding company, they'll charge you at least a hundred grand, and you never get that back. But honestly, there aren't a lot of bonding companies that want to be on the hook for a million dollars. If they post that and you use your substantial financial resources to fly to some Pacific island without an extradition treaty with the United States, then they lose their money. I don't know of a lot of businesses that can afford to just lose a million dollars for no good reason."

Meredith's frown deepened. "I don't have a million dollars cash. But I could start liquidating some assets." She turned to her fellow Fab Five member. "Rebecca, do you have any clients who are looking to buy some commercial real estate on the Eastside? Someone who could close quickly?"

"Let's not get ahead of ourselves," Raine cut off the conversation. He hadn't come to talk real estate. "Whatever bail gets set, you'll still be charged with murder. If you're convicted of that, you can't post bail for your prison sentence."

"Shouldn't we address the first things first?" Meredith challenged.

"Let's address the most important things first," Raine countered. "If I can start to develop strategies of attack against the underlying charge, that will help me when I try to convince the judge to set a lower bail. Almost everyone in this jail is guilty of what they got arrested for. But not everyone. The judges know that. I need to plant some doubt in the judge's mind as to your actual guilt. That will do more to lower the bail than any speech about your ties to the community or how you being in custody will seriously hamper my ability to prepare and present a proper defense."

Meredith thought for a moment. "I guess that makes sense."

"I told you he was good," Sommers said.

Raine smiled slightly. He appreciated the vote of confidence. But he also wanted to be worthy of it. "So, let's start with why you're here," he oriented his potential client—she hadn't signed the fee agreement quite yet. Raine knew he was also auditioning for the part of her lawyer, and the fee that came with it. He wanted to be worthy of that as well.

"I don't know why I'm here," Meredith protested. "I'm innocent."

Raine nodded. "Those two things are unrelated. You may be innocent, but the cops think you're guilty. We need to figure out why they think that. Did they tell you anything after they arrested you? I assume they interrogated you. Please tell me you asked for a lawyer and didn't say anything."

"Wouldn't that have made me look guilty?" Meredith questioned. "Of course I talked to them. I told them I didn't do it."

Raine pinched the bridge of his nose. He hadn't actually expected Meredith to have been wise enough to lawyer up, but he had allowed himself to hope. Whatever story she had told them then, while she was exhausted and scared and being led around by a professional interrogator, that was the version Raine was stuck with. He might be able to add to it, but he couldn't deviate too much without making Meredith look like the liar he made other witnesses look like whenever they changed their stories.

"What did you tell them?" he asked. Then, before she could answer, he raised his palm. "No. What did they tell you?"

Meredith thought for a moment, then shrugged. "I'm not sure. They were asking questions, and I was answering. I don't remember them telling me anything."

"They told you things in the questions they asked," Raine explained. He was eventually going to get a transcript of the interrogation, but that would arrive days, maybe even weeks after the arraignment, along with the rest of the police reports. "The detective mentioned the security video when they arrested you. What did they say about it? Did they tell you what was on it that made them think you committed the murder?"

Meredith's mouth tightened shut and she looked away. Raine knew that wasn't good.

"What was on the security video, Meredith?" he pressed.

"I didn't do it," she insisted, without looking back at him.

Raine sighed. "If it's anything less than you pouring the poison down her throat, I can deal with it," he said. "But I need to know, and I need to know now."

Meredith sighed and turned back to face her visitors. "It shows me taking something out of the refrigerator in the kitchen, leaving out the back door, then returning a few minutes later and putting something back in the refrigerator. I leave and a few minutes later, one of the cooks takes the soup out of that same refrigerator and puts it on the stove to warm up. He leaves and a few minutes after that, Alexandra comes in, takes some of the soup and eats it and dies."

Raine looked at Meredith, then at Sommers, whose jaw

had dropped open again, then back to his client. "I can see why you were arrested."

"But I didn't do it!" Meredith cried. "It wasn't even the soup that I took out of the refrigerator. You just can't see what I was carrying."

"Why not?" Raine questioned.

Meredith hesitated. "Because I was hiding it under my jacket."

"You realize that's not a good thing, right?" Raine asked.

"What's going on, Meredith?" Sommers interjected. "Is it happening again?"

Raine turned and raised an eyebrow to his partner. "Is what happening again?"

Sommers didn't answer, but Meredith did. "Yes. And I was too ashamed to tell the police. So, I just insisted it wasn't me on the recording and there must have been something wrong with the cameras."

"I can see why you were booked after the interrogation," Raine added. "And I think you can expect an astronomically high bail Monday. What is happening that could possibly explain this in any way that doesn't include you poisoning your friend and mentor?"

"CHSP," Meredith answered, eyes downcast.

"Chew and spit disorder," Sommers translated. "It's an eating disorder. It's similar to bulimia but you don't swallow the food. It's pretty much what it sounds like."

Raine had never heard of it, but a part of his brain knew he should be sensitive about it. Another part of his brain knew it might make a good defense. "How long have you struggled with this? Or any eating disorder? And are there any medical records for past treatment?"

"Dan!" Sommers scolded. "Back off a little, okay? This is difficult to talk about."

"Okay," he allowed, "but going to prison for the rest of your life is also difficult to talk about. Maybe we can talk about how one of those things might help me prevent the other thing."

"It's okay, Rebecca." Meredith waved a weak hand at her friend. "Mr. Raine is right. We need to focus on the big picture. And the big picture is that I'm going to be charged with murder because I snuck some potatoes before dinner, spit them out in the toilet in the back bathroom where there were no cameras, and then lied to the police about it."

"The lying to the police isn't great," Raine replied, "but I can explain that away. They wouldn't have believed you anyway. Still, this is why you never talk to the cops. Talk to your lawyer, and only your lawyer."

Meredith looked to Sommers.

"And his investigator," Sommers added with a weak grin.

"This is a good start." Raine tapped a finger against his lips. "They're still going to charge you, but we have two things to work with now."

"Two things?" Sommers questioned.

Raine nodded and raised his fingers. "One, you have an explanation as to why you aren't the murderer. And two, that means someone else is. The CHSP may end up being a good defense. But the best defense will be catching the real killer."

6

As expected, the prosecutor's office filed charges first thing Monday morning. Raine downloaded a copy of the criminal complaint from the court's online portal. One count of murder in the first degree in the case of *The State of Washington versus Meredith Ann Beauchamp*. Arraignment was scheduled for 1:00 that afternoon. The prosecutor who signed the complaint was named Kevin Scarborough. Raine thought the name was familiar, but he hadn't had a case against him before. He tried calling him but of course he had to leave a message, and of course Scarborough didn't call him back.

Raine arrived at the arraignment courtroom fifteen minutes early. That was enough time to check in with Meredith before the hearing. Any earlier and she wouldn't have been brought by the guards yet anyway. There were a couple dozen arraignments all scheduled for 1:00. Every felony committed over the weekend—or at least the ones where they caught the perpetrator. And at least one where they arrested and charged someone other than the perpetrator. Maybe. Raine was willing to believe his client's claims of innocence. Then again, he hadn't had a chance to read all of the police reports yet. It wouldn't be the first time a client lied to him.

"How are you holding up?" was Raine's first question when the guard put Meredith into the even smaller attorney-client meeting closet next to the holding cells behind the courtroom.

"Okay, I guess," she answered.

Raine thought that was an honest answer. She looked a little rougher than when they had met on Saturday but a couple of days in jail will do that to a person. Especially if they're facing murder charges and the prospect of an unattainably high bail.

"Good," Raine replied. Then he got down to business. "When they bring you into the courtroom, come directly to where I am and stand next to me. Look up at the judge but don't say anything. Let me do the talking. Don't react to anything the prosecutor says and especially to anything the judge says, no matter how bad it seems. Like we talked about, your bail is likely to be high. Any show of disrespect for the court or the process will only make it higher. Understood?"

Meredith nodded. "Of course. I may not be a lawyer, but I understand how people work. We're asking the judge to trust me. I need to appear worthy of that trust."

"Exactly," Raine agreed. He was maybe going to like working with Meredith Beauchamp. "Is there anything I should know before we go out there? Anything at all?"

Meredith thought for a moment. "Only that I'm innocent. I did not murder Alexandra."

Raine offered a lopsided smile. "If only that mattered."

Raine ended their conversation then. He needed to get back into the courtroom before the judge came out. He didn't want to walk in after court had started; that would be disrespectful. He also wanted to be there when Scarborough arrived. He wanted a minute to size up his competition, and pump him for any clues as to what bail he would be requesting and his arguments in support of it.

The courtroom had filled up in the few minutes Raine had been with Meredith. Those two dozen arraignments each had a prosecutor and a defense attorney attached, and even with some duplication of attorneys—that day's assigned public defender would handle at least half of the cases—there were still almost twenty professionals in suits milling around waiting for the judge to appear. Raine looked for someone he didn't know. There were several, but only one man wearing the dark suit and humorless expression of a prosecutor.

"Mr. Scarborough?" Raine ventured, approaching the man with a hand extended. "I'm Dan Raine. I represent Meredith Beauchamp."

Scarborough was tall and thin, with red hair cut short and combed away from his face. His suit was black, his shirt was white, and his tie was a forgettable shade of yellow. He had wire-framed glasses with small, square lenses, and a neatly trimmed red beard. Raine guessed his age at somewhere in his early forties. He shook Raine's hand with a firm grip.

"Mr. Raine," Scarborough replied. He reached into his file and extracted copies of the charging paperwork: the complaint Raine already had, and the supporting document called a Declaration for Determination of Probable Cause. It was a summary of the police reports; the judge would review it to confirm there were sufficient facts to support the charge. It wasn't a finding of guilty, but it was the first step on that path. The judge had to find probable cause in order to set bail pending trial, and in doing so the judge was supposed to assume everything in the probable cause declaration was true. Theoretically, Meredith was presumed innocent. Practically, the jails were filled with presumptively innocent people awaiting their trials.

Raine accepted the documents. He had about two minutes to read the Declaration for Probable Cause before the judge came out and Meredith's case was called. They would call the murder case with the homicide prosecutor and the private defense attorney first. The car theft cases with the junior prosecutors and public-defender-of-the-day would go last.

"What bail are you asking for?" Raine asked even as he started to skim the declaration.

"Three million," Scarborough answered. He seemed to be a man of few words so far.

"That seems a little high, don't you think?" Raine replied. "She has no criminal history. She has extensive ties to the community. She's hired a private attorney and has a successful business to run. She's not going to flee, and she doesn't pose a threat to anyone."

Scarborough listened with intent eyes, then replied, "She murdered someone."

"She's presumed innocent," Raine reminded him.

"That's why she's even allowed to post bail. There's no bail for prison. She might as well start accumulating credit toward her sentence."

"You'll have to convict her first," Raine challenged.

Scarborough nodded. "I'll let the bailiff know we're ready."

Before he got the chance, the bailiff stood up and announced, "The King County Superior Court is now in session, The Honorable Henry Brenner presiding!"

Raine nodded. Brenner was a good judge. He'd been on the bench long enough to know how things worked, and more importantly, how they should work. He was in his early sixties, with dark skin, white hair, and kind eyes. But he was also going to set bail at whatever the prosecutor asked. You don't get to be a judge that long without getting reelected several times, and you don't get reelected if you let murderers out on low bail.

Judge Brenner took the bench and advised everyone, "Please be seated." Then asked, "Do we have any matters ready?"

Scarborough spoke up. The prosecutors always spoke up first. "The Beauchamp matter is ready, Your Honor."

A nod from the prosecutor to the jail guard at the side door was enough for the officer to open the door to the holding area and call out, "Beauchamp!"

Meredith scuttled in a few moments later as Judge Brenner called the case for the record. "This is the matter of The State of Washington versus Meredith Ann Beauchamp. Will the attorneys please state their appearances for the record."

"Kevin Scarborough on behalf of the State of Washington." As dry as that sentence was, Scarborough managed to deliver it with even less emotion than Raine thought possible.

"Daniel Raine on behalf of the accused, Meredith Beauchamp, Your Honor," Raine rang out with what he hoped was the proper balance of enthusiasm and decorum. The tone was intended to communicate comfort, even confidence. The term "accused" instead of "defendant" was meant to remind everyone that Meredith was presumed innocent. It might not work, but Raine needed to make a show of it, even if just to make sure his client was satisfied with his representation. This was his first chance to demonstrate how he handled the case in court. A satisfied client is a paying client, Raine knew.

Brenner recognized the tone. Raine wasn't the only lawyer in town who needed to keep his clients happy. The judge offered the slightest of nods to Raine, then a larger one to the prosecutor. "Please proceed, Mr. Scarborough."

"Thank you, Your Honor." Scarborough handed the originals of the charging documents to the bailiff. "With this complaint, the State charges the defendant, Meredith Ann Beauchamp, with the premediated intentional murder of Alexandra Pruitt. We ask the defense to acknowledge receipt of the complaint, waive a formal reading of the charges, and enter a plea."

The arraignment was a formalistic dance, almost anachronistic, a holdover from the early days of attempting to create a fairer criminal justice system. The prosecution having begun the dance by advising the defendant of the charges against her—not consistently the practice in other systems—the defense took up the dance by acknowledging the advisement and, more often than not, protesting their innocence.

"The defense acknowledges receipt of the complaint," Raine responded, "waives a formal reading, and submits a plea of not guilty to the charge of murder in the first degree."

"A plea of not guilty will be entered," the judge declared.

That effectively ended the arraignment. The important part
came next. "I will now review the declaration for determination of probable cause."

That gave Raine a chance to do the same. He didn't have
access to the police reports yet, so this would be the first
summary of the evidence against his client. He hoped he was
a faster reader than the judge.

"What's happening?" Meredith interrupted with a
whisper.

Raine stifled a sigh. The judge didn't have anyone interrupting him. "The judge is reading a summary of the
evidence against you so far to determine whether there are
facts sufficient to set bail."

"Are there?"

"Probably," Raine answered, "or they wouldn't have filed
charges. But I don't know for sure because I haven't had a
chance to read it yet either."

"You should probably read it then," Meredith suggested.

Raine smiled tightly. "Yes. Thanks."

But the judge was a faster reader than Raine would have
liked. "I do find fact sufficient for a finding of probable cause for
the charge of murder in the first degree," Brenner announced.
"I will hear from the parties regarding conditions of release."

Raine let out that stifled sigh. He'd have to read the probable cause declaration later. He already knew the relevant
facts anyway; he'd been there for some of it and Meredith
had already explained the seemingly damning security
video. Part of being a trial attorney—a large part of it—was
the ability to roll with the punches and move on to the next
thing. The next thing was "conditions of release," even if that
term was a bit of a misnomer.

There were several possible conditions of release, but only one of them mattered, and it was the one that prevented release. A judge could order a criminal defendant to have no further law violations, to have no contact with certain people or places, to abstain from alcohol and drugs, and a number of other directives designed to reduce the risk to the community posed by the defendant. But before any of those would matter, there was the threshold issue of bail. A defendant wouldn't be able to contact a victim, return to the scene of the crime, or consume drugs if they remained locked up in the county jail.

"Thank you, Your Honor," Scarborough began. He got right to it. "The State is asking the Court to set bail in the amount of three million dollars."

Raine shook his head. That was a lot of money.

The judge's eyebrows shot up. "Three million dollars?"

"Yes, Your Honor," Scarborough confirmed. "The defendant has significant financial resources. We believe she is likely to post a lower bail and could then use her remaining wealth to flee the country."

Raine looked to Meredith. "You don't have a million dollars in cash, do you?" he asked in a low voice.

Meredith shook her head incredulously. "Of course not. That would be crazy. Sitting in a checking account, not even earning interest?"

"So, you do have three million, but not liquid," Raine leaned in to whisper as quietly as he could. That wasn't something he wanted either the prosecutor or the judge to hear.

"Three?" Meredith thought for a moment. "No, not that much. I have some accounts I could drain, some assets I

could sell, but that would take time, and cost a lot in penal-
ties. Maybe if I sold my house too..."

"As the Court can see from the probable cause declaration," Scarborough continued, "the murder was motivated
by financial gain. There is no reason to believe she feels any
sense of remorse for her actions, or would feel in any way
obligated to answer for her crime."

"Motivated by financial gain?" Raine muttered to
himself. He really needed to read that probable cause
declaration.

"Your Honor," Raine interjected with a raised hand. "I
was only provided the probable cause declaration moments
before Your Honor took the bench. I haven't had a chance to
thoroughly review it. May I take that time now, in order to
respond to the prosecutor's assertions?"

The afternoon arraignment calendar—and in truth,
every non-trial criminal calendar at every hour of every day
—was a high-volume calendar. They could only get to every
case if every case was handled expeditiously. If every lawyer
insisted on actually reading every pleading and being fully
prepared, the calendar would run until midnight. On the
other hand, it was a murder case. The car-theft lawyers
would have to have a few minutes shaved off their
arraignments.

"Please be quick, Mr. Raine," Judge Brenner allowed.
"We have a lot of cases this afternoon."

Raine was already reading before the judge replied. He
was going to read it no matter what Brenner said; it had only
been a question of whether he would get chastised for
doing so.

"What—?" Meredith started to ask another question, but
Raine held up a finger to her. She needed to wait.

Raine read the document as fast as he could, skimming over the parts about dead bodies and poisons to find the part about motives and money. He found it. He read it. Then he turned again to his client and placed his lips against her ear.

"Did you," he whispered in as quiet a voice as he could manage, "sign a partnership agreement with Alexandra immediately before her murder that would result in her entire business empire transferring to you upon her death?"

Meredith started to answer, but Raine cut her off.

"And were you the only one of the Fab Five to sign it before she died, even though there were signature lines for each of them as well?"

"I can explain," Meredith squeaked.

"No," Raine hissed.

She didn't need to. Or rather, Raine needed her not to. Not then. Not there. Not yet. But soon.

"The defense would like to reserve argument on the issue of bail," Raine told Judge Brenner. "I will need additional time to respond."

Another part of being a trial attorney was knowing when one of those rolling punches was going to knock you out, and stepping back just enough to avoid the blow.

"The defense having reserved argument," Judge Brenner announced, "I will set bail in the amount requested by the State: three million dollars. In addition, the defendant is to have no contact with the family of the victim, is to have no further criminal law violations, and, in the event she posts bail, is to return for all future court dates. When will the next court date be?"

"The pretrial conference will be two weeks from tomorrow," the bailiff answered.

"Would you like to add the bail hearing to that date, Mr.

Raine?" the judge asked. He'd reserved argument, but he hadn't waived it. Two weeks might be enough time to figure out what the hell Meredith actually did and whether he had any chance to prove she didn't.

"Yes, Your Honor," Raine answered. "Thank you."

"This matter is concluded," Brenner declared. "Next matter, please."

Scarborough made a beeline for the exit. Raine stepped away from the bar as well, even as the jail guard stepped forward to take hold of Meredith's shoulders and guide her out of the courtroom.

"I can explain," Meredith repeated.

"And you will," Raine answered, "but not until I've done enough investigation to know if there's anything else you aren't telling me."

7

I t took Raine three days to get the first round of police reports. And then only after personally delivering his Notice of Appearance and Demand for Discovery to the prosecutor's office and then constantly nagging them for whatever reports were ready. He spent Wednesday morning sitting in their lobby and staring at the receptionist in the hope that she would develop a personal interest in getting the reports to him so he would leave. It worked and Wednesday afternoon he had what he needed and shoved it across his desk at Sommers.

"Have you ever seen this before?" he asked her.

She had agreed to move her 1:00 meeting up to noon and skip lunch so she could meet Raine at his office before her 2:00 appointment. She was dressed to kill—or rather to close, whatever deals were at stake at those two appointments, and the ones likely scheduled for later in the day as well. That was good. She was in a business mindset, and the document Raine had given her was all business.

"A partnership agreement?" She picked it up off the desk

and leaned back in her chair to examine it. "For Alexandra's company? Where did this come from?"

"The prosecutor," Raine answered. "Look at the signature page."

Sommers flipped to the last page of the document. Her eyebrows shot up. "Meredith signed this?"

"And Alexandra," Raine pointed out. "And no one else."

"It's dated the night of the murder," Sommers realized.

"Exactly." Raine frowned. "This was the big announcement. Alexandra was going to make you all partners in her business. When she retired, you'd all get an equal share of her empire, and with no estate taxes even. She had a good tax lawyer. But the rest of you never got the chance to sign it. Meredith signed it..."

"And then Alexandra was murdered," Sommers finished the sentence and looked up from the document. "So, Meredith gets everything?"

"Not if she murdered her," Raine answered. "Murderers don't get the benefit of their crimes. The courts will invalidate that agreement."

"Who gets the business then?" Sommers asked. "Ernest?"

"Depends on her will," Raine answered. "Whoever it is, they'll be our top suspect."

Sommers set the document back down on the desk. "What did Meredith say? Did she explain how she signed it when none of the rest of us even knew about it?"

"I haven't asked her yet," Raine answered.

"Why not?"

"Because I need to know what really happened first," Raine explained. "So I'll know whether she's telling me the truth when she answers."

"How do we do that?" Sommers wondered aloud. But then the light bulb went on. "Ernest."

Raine nodded. "He's the only one who doesn't have a signature line on that agreement. And he's the only one who might have known what Alexandra had planned. Or how Meredith found out about it."

Sommers checked her phone. "I can't move my two o'clock, but I should be free by five. Should we call first or just show up on his doorstep?"

Raine grinned. They both knew the answer. "I'll meet you on his doorstep at five."

———

ERNEST'S DOORSTEP was the same doorstep Raine and Sommers had departed across when the police finally let them go four days earlier. There was the possibility that Ernest wasn't home, but Raine guessed the poor man hadn't left the condo since the murder, rattling around lost in his robe and despair. Unless he was actually the murderer, in which case he was probably already out of the country on that non-extraditable island in the South Seas.

Sommers was waiting outside the door when Raine stepped off the elevator.

"Did you close your deal?" Raine asked in greeting.

"Of course," Sommers answered. "Well, the first part of it anyway. There's more to be done."

"There always is," Raine agreed. He nodded toward the condominium door. "Ready?"

Sommers grinned. "Always."

Raine appreciated both the answer and its accuracy. He knocked sharply on the door. He expected it might take a few knocks before Ernest heard them and cinched his robe sufficiently to open the door.

Raine raised his fist again to knock, but the door swung open and he was genuinely surprised by what—or rather, by whom—he saw inside.

"Caterer woman?" he stammered.

The woman squeezed her eyes shut and pinched the bridge of her nose. "I'm not a caterer. My name is Caitlin Kennedy and I'm—"

"Caitlin Kennedy?" Sommers repeated. "Aren't you Alexandra's new secretary?"

"Personal assistant," Caitlin corrected. "And yes."

"We've talked on the phone, right?" Sommers said.

"More than likely," Caitlin answered. "I've talked to a lot of people. Especially since Alexandra's... death."

"You were going to say murder," Raine jumped in. "That's okay. Go ahead. It definitely was a murder."

"But you represent the murderer," Caitlin offered, "so I thought—"

"Oh, I'm not claiming it wasn't a murder," Raine told her. "I'm just saying Meredith Beauchamp isn't the one who did it."

"Because you're being paid to say that," Caitlin suggested.

Raine had to grin. "In part. But also because she didn't do it. Probably."

"That's why we're here, actually," Sommers explained. "We came to see Ernest."

Caitlin's expression twisted. "Um." She threw a glance inside the condo, the entrance to which she was still blocking with her body and the half-closed door. "Now isn't really a great time to see Ernest."

"We should have called first," Sommers said to Raine.

Raine didn't agree. "Sounds like it's the perfect time to talk with Ernest. No time to prepare his story."

"Story?" Caitlin questioned. "What are you suggesting?"

"I'm suggesting that people lie," Raine answered. "And the lies are harder to identify if the person has time to prepare them."

"You don't think Ernest—" Caitlin started.

"Actually, no, I don't," Raine answered. "But I do think he has information that might lead us to the real killer. Even if that real killer is Meredith."

"You said Meredith didn't do it," Caitlin said.

"I said 'probably,'" Raine clarified. "Now, can we come in or am I going to have to come back with a subpoena?"

That was actually a nonsensical threat. A subpoena ordered someone to appear in court. But he figured Caitlin might know only a cop could "come back with a warrant". A lawyer could probably come back with a subpoena, even if she didn't know what that would mean exactly.

"I, uh, I mean—" Caitlin stammered.

"Let us in, Caitlin," Sommers soothed with a gentle smile. "It won't take long, and it might help us discover the truth about Alexandra's death. Don't you want that?"

Caitlin hesitated, then pulled the door all the way open. "Okay, you can come in. But I'm really busy." She held up a list of tasks, written in neat block letters, the vast majority of which had not been checked off yet. "And I'm not sure he's up to seeing visitors. He's been pretty distraught since Alexandra's death."

"Murder," Raine corrected again as he and Sommers stepped inside.

Cailtin nodded. "Right." She gestured toward the living room. "Have a seat. I'll get him."

Caitlin disappeared down a hallway and Raine and Sommers sat down on the couch their client had been sitting on a few days earlier when she was first accused of Alexandra Pruitt's murder.

"What do you think?" Raine asked.

"About what?" Sommers replied.

Raine nodded toward the hallway Caitlin disappeared down. "About her. And about Ernest being too distraught to talk to us."

Sommers shrugged. "I don't know. That seems entirely possible. And she seems nice enough."

"Why is she here though?" Raine asked. "Her boss is dead."

"Probably to deal with wrapping up the business side of things," Sommers ventured.

"Like that partnership agreement," Raine suggested.

Sommers's eyes widened. "Oh, yeah. I bet she knew about that."

"I bet she did," Raine agreed. "And she might know more. Like why Meredith is the only one who signed it."

"Well, then, it's a good thing she's here," Sommers said.

But Raine shrugged. "I wouldn't go that far."

"Why not?" Sommers asked.

Before Raine could reply, Caitlin reappeared and provided the answer herself. "I'm afraid Ernest isn't up to seeing visitors today."

"Because she's an obstacle," Raine whispered, "even if she means well."

"Maybe if you come back next week," Caitlin suggested. "And call first."

Raine stood up and clapped his hands. "Well, we tried."

Sommers looked askance at him. She stood up slowly and whispered, "That's it? Really?"

"Small talk," he whispered back. Then, in a normal volume to Caitlin, "Could I use the bathroom before we go?"

"Of course." Caitlin pointed down the hallway. "First door on the left."

Raine took a moment to catch Sommers's eye then darted his glance to Caitlin and back, hoping Sommers would understand.

Sommers raised an eyebrow in response. "So, Caitlin," she called out. "Tell me more about you and Alexandra. When did you start working for her?"

Raine scurried past Caitlin as she answered, "Not very long. Six months or so."

The first door on the right was definitely a guest bathroom. Raine walked right past it. The next door was the back door to the kitchen—the one Meredith used to sneak to the bathroom for her taste of potatoes. Probably. If she was telling the truth. Raine walked past the kitchen door as well. The hallway turned 90 degrees to the left, back toward the bedrooms, Raine deduced. He also guessed that the master bedroom was probably the last one, so he passed the rest of the rooms until he came to the final door at the end of the hall.

There was nothing on the outside of the door to indicate what lay within. He considered knocking, but likened it to calling first. Who knew what valuable information he might discover if he opened the door without warning. All with the cover of looking for the bathroom. 'Oh, I thought you said the *last* door on the right. Sorry.'

He grabbed the doorknob and began turning it slowly,

hoping it wasn't locked. Happily, it spun smoothly and steadily in his hand and he both heard and felt the mechanism dislodge from the door frame. A soft click, but unmistakable. He began to push the door open ever so slowly.

His right hand was still firmly grasping the doorknob, so when Ernest yanked the door all the way open from the inside, Raine stumbled forward off balance and barely had time to raise his other hand as Ernest slashed at his face with the largest kitchen knife Raine had ever seen.

A flash of pain seared across Raine's palm. "Arrgh!"

He instinctively shoved his wounded hand into his opposite armpit and fell back into a crouch to square up against his attacker. His hand was throbbing, blood running down his arm. "What the hell, man!"

Ernest was dressed, barely, in a silk robe that was very much not tied closed. He waved the knife, now bloody, in front of him menacingly. "Who are you? How did you get in here? Why are you here?"

Those were all good questions, Raine supposed. And he would be happy to answer them, after the threat to his life was eliminated. His eyes darted to the area immediately around him. There were plates and food scraps all over the floor, along with dirty clothes and various other personal items. One such item was a still-damp towel. Raine discovered its dampness when he grabbed it and wrapped it loosely around his injured limb. He had a moment to hope there was nothing infectious on it that might enter his bloodstream via the gash on his hand, but then Ernest lunged at him again, knife first.

Raine raised his towel-wrapped arm to deflect the strike. It was only partially successful. Had Ernest slashed at him again, the blade likely would have glanced off the layers of

Egyptian cotton. Instead, Ernest stabbed point first. The towel absorbed some of the thrust, but not all of it, and the tip of the knife managed to tear through the fabric and drive a half inch into Raine's forearm.

Raine's reaction was instinctual, immediate, and decisive, not least because Ernest was some twenty years his senior. Raine's left arm occupied with the knife imbedded in it, he used his right arm to throw a roundhouse punch that landed squarely against Ernest's ear.

The old man crumpled, dropping the knife and falling into a half-naked pile of fear and regret.

Raine pulled the knife from his arm and threw it across the room then jumped on top of Ernest and raised his fist again in case he encountered any further resistance.

"What the hell is going on?" Caitlin's screech pierced the bedroom. She was standing in the doorway, her expression managing to combine shock, anger, and betrayal in equal measures.

"This isn't what it looks like!" Raine insisted.

"It looks like you lied to me about needing to use the bathroom," Caitlin shouted at him, "forced your way into Mr. Poplowski's bedroom, and attacked him."

Raine considered the scene. "Okay, it is what it looks like. Well, some of that anyway. But there's also the part where he attacked me with a knife." He held up his bloody hand. "I was defending myself."

"Can you defend yourself after you break into someone else's room?" Caitlin demanded.

Raine took a moment to consider the law of self-defense. "Not generally, no," he admitted, "but I can explain."

"Dan!" Sommers sprinted up behind Caitlin and stopped short in the doorway. "What the hell are you doing?"

"You're the two who found Alexandra," Ernest whimpered. "You killed her, didn't you? And you came back to
finish the job and kill me too."

"We're not here to kill you," Raine insisted, still sitting
astride Ernest. "And we didn't kill Alexandra."

"No, you just represent her killer," Caitlin accused.

"Meredith isn't the killer," Raine replied. "Probably." He
pushed himself off Ernest, wincing at the pain that shot
through his left hand in doing so. "Look, maybe we can just
start over. Can we go into the living room and talk about that
partnership agreement? Ernest, you know what Alexandra
was thinking, and Caitlin, you know what she drafted. I just
need to know why only she and Meredith signed it."

"You should ask her," Caitlin dismissed Raine's inquiry.

"I'm asking you!" he shouted back. "Your boss is dead.
Your girlfriend is dead. Meredith didn't do it but someone is
sure making it look like she did. Why is that? And who really
did it? Don't you want to catch her real killer?"

No one answered. Then Sommers said, "Dan. Your
hand."

With the towel discarded and the adrenaline pumping
through his veins, blood was running down the side of
Raine's clenched fist and onto the floor.

"You need to see a doctor," Sommers added.

"You need to stop bleeding on the carpet," Caitlin added.

"You need to get the hell out of my home!" Ernest
shouted from the floor.

Raine took a deep breath. He allowed himself to feel the
throbbing in his hand again. He supposed all three of them
were right.

"Okay," he conceded. "Fine."

He glanced down at the dark wet spot next to his left foot. "Sorry about the carpet."

He turned to look at Ernest, still lying on the floor, his open bathrobe leaving nothing to the imagination. "Sorry about your ear."

Then he looked to Sommers. "Just sorry."

Sommers stepped into the room and put her arm around Raine. "We'll show ourselves out," she told Caitlin. "I think Ernest could use some help getting up."

Caitlin stepped forward to help her late employer's life partner, and Raine and Sommers stepped away and toward the exit.

Once they were outside and the door to the condominium was safely closed behind them, Raine looked down at his bleeding limb, the palm cleaved, the forearm perforated. "This really hurts," he admitted. "Did it work?"

Sommers grinned. "Did your felonious attack on a sixty-seven-year-old man distract Caitlin sufficiently to allow me to sneak into Alexandra's office two doors down and rummage through her desk before she noticed I wasn't right behind her?" She held up a shiny black thumb drive. "Yes."

8

"How did you know where to find the thumb drive?" Raine asked Sommers several hours later.

The first stop had been urgent care. There, the medical staff took one look at his hand and pushed him back out the door, with instructions to go to the emergency room. Urgent care was for bumps and bruises. Gashes that exposed tendons and bone needed to go to the emergency room. Of course, once he was there, his laceration had to wait behind the gunshots and heart attacks.

Eventually a nice doctor who was distressingly younger than him stitched the hand closed and an even nicer and even younger nurse covered his left hand in a bandage that would prevent him from using it as anything but a paperweight for several weeks. They attended to the wound on his forearm arm as well, but that only needed some antiseptic and a butterfly bandage. It was his hand that made him look like he'd lost a fist fight with a blender.

So, it wasn't until they got back to Raine's office at nearly

9:00 p.m. before they could open the thumb drive and see what was on it.

Sommers pushed the drive into his laptop. "Alexandra gave us advice about everything. And she wasn't one to give advice that she didn't follow herself."

"So, you have a backup of all your important records in a thumb drive taped to the underside of your desk?"

Sommers thought for a moment. "Well, not after this. I'll be moving it."

Raine nodded admiringly. "Not a bad idea. Was the tape black too? No way you'd find that if you didn't know where to look."

"Exactly," Sommers confirmed. "Now, let's see what she was up to."

"Hopefully there's a copy of that partnership agreement on there." Raine leaned in closer to read over Sommers's shoulder.

"I'm sure it's here somewhere," Sommers replied, "but there's a lot more than just that. It has documents for all of her businesses, all of her accounts, all of her money."

"I bet it's a lot of money," Raine ventured.

"For sure," Sommers agreed.

"Is there a will somewhere?" Raine asked. "I'd like to know where the money will go if Meredith is convicted."

"You think she's going to get convicted?" Sommers laughed. "You don't think too highly of yourself, huh?"

"On the contrary," Raine smiled sideways at her, "I think very highly of myself. Because I know that whoever gets the money if Meredith is convicted has a motive to frame Meredith. Assuming no other surprise partnership agreements, and the one in existence being rendered void by a murder conviction, Alexandra's money will pass through her will."

"What happens if she didn't have a will?"

"Does she have any living relatives?" Raine answered. "If so, they would get it. If not, it escheats to the state."

"Escheats?" Sommers wrinkled her nose. "Is that a real word?"

"It's a lawyer word," Raine confessed. "It means it gets forfeited to the state."

"Well, that might be what happens." Sommers gestured toward the screen. "Alexandra didn't have any relatives, and I don't see any will. I think maybe she didn't have a will."

"What?" Raine was surprised. "Someone with that much money. Why not?"

Sommers shrugged. "A lot of people with money never get around to writing a will. It's one thing to amass wealth while you're alive. It's a completely different thing to think about what to do with it when you die. It can be hard to face the inevitability of death. Alexandra may have been guilty of whistling past the graveyard. I know she never mentioned any will to me."

"Why would she?" Raine questioned.

"I don't know," Sommers answered, "but she didn't."

Raine wasn't convinced. He squinted at the screen, but that only confirmed no folders that obviously contained a last will and testament. But a different folder caught his eye.

Raine pointed at the screen. "Click on that folder. 'P.H.'"

Sommers followed Raine's direction, and a pop-up window filled the screen. "There's almost a hundred files and subfolders in this."

"Open the folder named 'Articles'," Raine suggested.

"Articles of incorporation," Sommers knew. She clicked on the folder, then on the document marked 'AOI'.

"Pruitt Holdings," Raine read the name of the business

Alexandra had incorporated only two weeks before her death, "a Limited Liability Corporation."

"Owned by up to six partners," Sommers scanned the document that set out the form and structure of the proposed business. "Alexandra and the Fab Five. Only there are no signatures on this one."

"That makes sense," Raine observed. "She printed it out to get the signatures but died before she could."

"At least before she could get all of them," Sommers suggested.

Raine frowned. "That kind of talk doesn't help our client." He pointed again at the computer screen. "Does that folder say 'Randall'?"

"Yes." Sommers cocked her head. "Who's Randall?"

She didn't need Raine to tell her to open the folder. But when she clicked on it, there were no files inside. 'This folder is empty,' the pop-up window informed her.

"Why create an empty folder?" Sommers wondered.

Raine thought of a different question. "Or why delete what was in it?"

"What do you think that means?" Sommers asked.

Raine raised his own hand to his mouth. "I don't know." Then, "So let's go with what we do know. Print out those articles of incorporation for Pruitt Holdings and the unsigned partnership agreement."

"Okay," Sommers replied, "but why?"

"Because we can't take a laptop into the jail," Raine answered. "We're going to confront Meredith first thing in the morning."

9

It was probably a different visiting closet from the last time Raine spoke with his client, but the rooms all looked the same, so it felt like a repeat of their first conversation. But this time, Raine was determined not to allow the lies by omission to continue. He brought Sommers again, in part to be a witness, in part to call bullshit on the bullshit he might not otherwise know. He had a fee agreement with Meredith, but Sommers had history.

"Where have you been?" Meredith demanded as soon as she sat down. Then, seeing the bandage on Raine's hand, "What happened?"

"Long story." Raine didn't feel like recounting it just then. It would be a distraction.

"Ernest stabbed him," Sommers explained. "But he kind of deserved it."

"I did not," Raine defended. "And the hand was more of a slash. The stab was on my arm." He pointed to the bandage hidden under the arm of his suitcoat.

Meredith frowned, then returned to her original

complaint. "I've been calling your office for days, but no one will accept the calls."

"I told my receptionist not to answer your collect calls until I was ready to talk with you," Raine explained.

"Oh, and so now you're ready?" Meredith crossed her arms.

Raine shrugged slightly. "Ready enough. The case is moving forward, whether we like it or not."

"And I'm stuck in this jail," Meredith complained, "because you didn't ask for anything lower than the three million dollars the prosecutor wanted."

"Because you didn't tell me the prosecutor had a rock-solid motive for you to murder Alexandra," Raine countered. "I only get one shot to argue bail. I wasn't going to attempt it when I didn't have all the facts. I'll be able to ask for a lower bail at our pretrial hearing next week."

"I told you I could explain," Meredith reminded him with a petulant frown.

"Okay." Raine crossed his arms and leaned back in his chair. "Explain. Explain to me why you signed a partnership agreement that allows Alexandra's entire business empire to transfer to you, tax free, on her death, and explain to me why she died between the time you signed it and the time anyone else could do so, which would have diluted your shares. Explain to me how the jury is not going to convict you as soon as they hear that. Please, Meredith, please. Explain that to me."

Meredith drew herself up as much as she could manage in her current situation and attire. "Simple. I didn't sign it."

Raine's eyebrow shot up. "I'm sorry?"

"I never signed that partnership agreement," Meredith repeated. "The first I ever heard of it was in court the same time you learned about it. I have no idea what it is or why they think I signed it."

Raine glanced over at Sommers, who only offered an equivocal frown in return. He reached into his file and extracted the copy of the signed partnership agreement he'd received from the prosecutor. He turned to the last page and held it up for her to see. He pointed to one of the two signatures—the one that didn't read 'Alexandra Pruitt.'

"Is that your signature?"

Meredith leaned forward and squinted at the document. "That looks like my signature," she allowed, "but I never signed that. That's a forgery."

Raine leaned back again and let out a long, deep sigh. That was the worst possible explanation Meredith could have given. Even if it were true, it wasn't believable.

"A forgery?" he questioned.

"Yes," Meredith confirmed.

"You want me to tell the jury," he leaned forward again, "that the signature on what I'm going to call the Motive Document, the signature that looks exactly like your actual signature, and the signature that no one else would benefit from being on this document—that signature is a forgery?"

"Yes," Meredith repeated, "because that's the truth."

"It doesn't matter if it's the truth," Raine returned, "if no one is going to believe it."

Meredith threw her hands up. "What do you want me to say?"

"Well, part of me wants you to say that you did sign it," Raine answered, "but you expected everyone else was going to sign it too. Say that you just thought she was going alphabetically, and Beauchamp was first on the list. Say you only signed it because she asked you to. Say you didn't even need the money, and you don't want it now."

Meredith's head dropped to one side. "But none of that is true."

Raine sighed. "That's the problem. The other part of me —the one who wants to keep his bar card and knows he can't suborn perjury—wants you to tell the truth. But the part of me that wants to win this case thinks that's a terrible idea."

There were several moments of awkward silence.

Finally, Sommers spoke up. "I believe you, Meredith. And if I do, the jury can too. The truth shall set you free, right?"

Meredith smiled. Raine didn't.

"If it were that simple," he said, "I wouldn't have a job."

10

Of course, Raine did have a job. And moreover, he had a specific job to do. The next milestone in the case of *The State Washington versus Meredith Beachamp* was the pretrial conference. Just Raine and Scarborough—and a hundred other criminal lawyers milling around in a crowded conference room, negotiating cases like a night of speed dating. There were too many cases and too few lawyers to justify any different system.

Raine was lucky. He only had one case that morning. Scarborough likely only had one case as well; homicide prosecutors had smaller caseloads. One homicide case was equal to twenty car-theft cases, give or take. But everyone else in the room had multiple cases and multiple clients.

Raine found a seat amidst the hurricanelike game of musical chairs and waited for Scarborough. He had arrived a few minutes early because Scarborough struck him as the sort of person who would appear exactly on time. Not early, not late. Precisely on time. Sure enough, as the clock on the far wall rolled over from 8:59 to 9:00 a.m., Scarborough broke the plane of the entrance door, his rigid frame and awkward gait visible through the crowd like streetlights through a crack in the curtains.

Raine stood up and waved to him as if calling over a friend to his table at a Parisian street café. Except they were anywhere but Paris. And Scarborough was anything but a friend.

"Mr. Raine," Scarborough greeted his opponent as he reached the table. Then, nodding to Raine's hand. "Did you injure yourself?"

Raine looked down at his hand. He had graduated from a full-hand wrap that had immobilized his left hand for several days to a gauze square held against his palm by a few loops of medical tape. A small amount of blood had oozed into the center of the pad. "It's nothing," he assured. "And you can call me Dan."

Raine offered the familiarity mostly because he knew it would make Scarborough uncomfortable. "Can I call you Kevin?"

Scarborough looked visibly pained. "That is my name," he practically conceded.

The purpose of the pretrial was to negotiate the case and see whether a plea bargain could be reached. Most cases, almost all cases in fact, settled short of trial. Upwards of ninety-five percent. Most car thieves were caught in the car and confessed at the scene. That wasn't a trial; that was an argument about exactly how much prison time the defendant would accept and feel like they got some modicum of representation from their public defender. The cases that went to trial were the ones where the punishment was too severe to agree to and where there were at least some evidentiary issues to play with. Something a jury might bite off on. Something better than "I didn't sign that document I obviously signed."

"I don't imagine this will take very long," Scarborough continued. He had declined to sit down despite the empty chair across from Raine. He reached into his file and produced a formal written offer sheet. "My offer is to recommend the low end of the sentencing range if your client pleads as charged to murder in the first degree."

Raine accepted the paper and frowned at it. There was a logical progression of homicide charges. At the bottom was manslaughter in the second degree—killing someone negligently and more than just a typical accident. Then came manslaughter in the first degree—killing someone recklessly, like pointing an "unloaded" gun at a friend and pulling the trigger as a joke, because of course it was loaded. Next was murder in the second degree—killing someone intentionally, but not with any sort of premeditation. You go to the bar to celebrate your birthday and get into a fight with some jackass who spilled your drink, so you pull out your gun and shoot them. You didn't plan it, but you intended it. Then there was murder in the first degree—premeditated murder. You kill that guy at the bar because he spilled your drink last week and you needed time to buy the gun and dig the grave.

Finally, there was aggravated murder in the first degree. That was the one that used to get you the death penalty before the state supreme court struck it down for being unfairly applied. After that, it just gave you life in prison without the possibility of parole. It was premediated murder plus something else that supposedly made it even worse—

committed during the course of some other serious felony like robbery or burglary, or the victim was a cop on duty or a judge, any time (you could tell who wrote the laws).

Meredith wasn't charged with aggravated murder one, but the sentencing range for regular murder one was twenty to thirty years. At her age, thirty years was the same as life without parole.

Raine had been hoping for a manslaughter one offer. The sentence for that could be as low as ten years. Raine would have to counsel Meredith to consider accepting an offer like that, even if she were innocent. It was the difference between dying in prison or stepping out of prison and breathing free air at least once before she died.

Scarborough's offer was twenty years. It was fifty-fifty Meredith would ever get out of prison on that sentence; life expectancy was a lot lower for people in prison than for the general public. It wasn't the healthiest place to spend your golden years, or even your pre-golden years.

"That's not much of an offer," Raine replied. "I can ask for that even if she's convicted at trial."

"You can," Scarborough admitted, "but you won't get it. No judge will give a defendant a low-end sentence after trial. Doing that discourages pleas."

"And not doing that penalizes a defendant for exercising their constitutional right to a trial," Raine returned. "You're not saying you intend to violate my client's constitutional rights, are you?"

Scarborough exhaled long and loud through his nose. "That's my offer, Mr. Raine. If you accept it, we can schedule the guilty plea next week. If you reject it, we call this hearing complete, schedule the trial date, and get back to our offices."

Raine raised a finger and offered a lopsided grin. "Ooh, not quite. If my client rejects it—and I'm going to advise her to reject it—then we have to go in front of the judge to finish the bail argument."

Scarborough repeated his nose sigh, this time with eyes pressed shut. "I had forgotten about that."

"I hadn't." Raine jumped to his feet. "Let me just run this so-called offer past Ms. Beauchamp, and then we can go in front of Judge Brenner again. I won't be but a minute."

Raine would have preferred to just reject Scarborough's offer right then and there, but it was technically Meredith's call. That only made sense; she was the one who would face the consequences of it. Maybe she wanted to die in prison and was eager to get started. Unlikely, and he would advise strongly against it, but ultimately clients were allowed to make bad decisions.

In order to accommodate the conversations necessary for the acceptance or rejection of plea offers, the negotiating room had a row of attorney-client closets on the far wall. They were nicer than the ones in the jail, but the holding cell they crammed all of the morning's defendants in was considerably less comfortable than the common room in the jail the inmates got to use during the day. Meredith was visibly relieved to enter the relatively cooler and more spacious conference chamber to meet with Raine when he asked the guard for his client.

"It's so hot back here," she panted through the plexiglass, a dozen pencil-sized holes drilled in it to allow conversation. "Haven't they ever heard of air conditioning?"

"I haven't found the jail staff spends a lot of time worrying about their inmates' comfort," Raine replied.

"They're pretty focused on controlling locations, not making those locations pleasant."

Meredith shrugged. Despite the stuffiness of the holding cell, most inmates found a change of pace, any change of routine, to be at least a little invigorating. She seemed more buoyant than during their last conversation. That wouldn't last. "I suppose so," she allowed. "Anyway, am I getting out soon?"

"Does twenty years sound soon?" Raine asked.

Meredith's expression collapsed. "Twenty years?"

"That's the prosecutor's offer," Raine explained. "Plead guilty as charged and get twenty years in prison."

"I won't last twenty years in prison!" Meredith called out.

"That's probably true," Raine agreed. "Accordingly, I would advise you to reject the offer."

Meredith hesitated. "What happens if I reject it?"

"We go to trial," Raine answered. "And do everything we can to win."

"And if we lose?" Meredith understood. "Do I get more?"

Raine had to nod. "You're not supposed to, but yeah, probably."

"How much?"

"Thirty years," was the answer.

Meredith's eyes bulged. Raine thought he saw them start to glisten as well. "Thirty years," she repeated weakly.

"That's why we do everything we can to win," Raine said. "If we win, it's no years in prison."

"If," Meredith whispered the key word, almost to herself.

"In a way, this is better," Raine tried to raise the mood, to the extent possible under the circumstances. "This is an easier decision than if they offered you a reduction to manslaughter. That would be ten years in prison, and we would have to talk about accepting that, even if you are innocent."

"I am innocent!" Meredith insisted a bit louder than necessary.

"Again, easy," Raine replied. "We reject the offer, set a trial date, and ask to lower your bail." He paused. "Well, actually, we should probably address bail before choosing the trial date."

"Why?"

"Because if you can't make bail," Raine answered, "then we'll want the soonest possible trial date. You don't want to sit in here on bail for months and months."

"Months?" Meredith shook her head. "No, I have a business to run. I have to get out of here. I'm innocent. I didn't murder Alexandra. I shouldn't be in here."

"Well, then, let's try to get you out." Raine stood up. "I'll meet you in the courtroom. The guards will bring you in when the judge is ready for our case."

"Mr. Raine!" Meredith stood up. "Dan. I really am innocent. You believe that, don't you?"

Raine took a moment before he answered. It was important to tell the truth. "I don't care. Either way, I have a job to do. And I intend to do it to the best of my ability."

Meredith's face betrayed a mix of emotions. Raine could discern disappointment, but he was pretty sure he could see some appreciation in there too. One ruthless professional to another.

"I guess that's enough," she said.

"It'll have to be," Raine replied. "Now get ready to look like the kind of defendant who will definitely come back to court if released on bail."

Raine exited the conference booth and walked across the

crowded room toward the entrance to the courtroom. As he did, he caught Scarborough's eye and provided two gestures. A thumbs down for "Offer rejected" and a point toward the courtroom for "Let's go".

Scarborough provided no discernible reaction but did walk toward the courtroom as well.

Raine hoped they wouldn't have to wait too long. It was early still. Maybe they could slip in immediately after whatever mini-hearing the judge was dealing with just then.

With all of those pretrials being negotiated in the adjoining conference room, there were bound to be small issues that the parties couldn't agree upon, the most common of which was the trial date. If the defendant was in custody, the defense would want the soonest possible trial date, both to prevent their client from sitting in jail any more than necessary and also to try to jam up the prosecution and hope they couldn't get their evidence together quite that fast. The court rule said a defendant being held pending trial had a right to a trial within 60 days of their arraignment. They had already burned over two weeks of that, and if he lost the bail hearing, he would use the court rule as a weapon against Scarborough.

On the other hand, if a defendant had posted bail or been released on their own personal recognizance, it would be the prosecutor who would be trying to set the trial sooner rather than later. The defense would be happy to set the trial a year or two out if they could get away with it. Raine knew a defense attorney who called delays "temporary dismissals."

As a result of this dynamic, Judge Brenner spent his mornings mostly back in his chambers, prepping for the daily afternoon arraignment calendar and being called out to the bench by his bailiff only when his services were needed. Raine stepped into the courtroom to see that he and Scarborough would be the first attorneys to need those services that morning.

"Good morning," Raine greeted the bailiff, a woman in her fifties with curly gray hair and half-lens reading glasses attached to a beaded cord around her neck. "Would the judge be available to hear a case? We need to finish a bail hearing and select a trial date."

The bailiff frowned slightly at the mention of a bail hearing. They both knew that would take a lot longer than just picking a trial date. Like everyone else, the bailiff had more than enough work to do and could get some of it done between hearings. When court was in session, she had to pay attention to the proceedings and her email would start to back up again. "You're a defense attorney, right?"

"On this case, yes," Raine confirmed. "I'm trying to cut back on criminal cases, but—"

"Where's the prosecutor?" But before Raine could answer, Scarborough entered the courtroom. The bailiff took one look at the socially awkward state's attorney and rolled her eyes ever so slightly. Like most court staff who sat quietly while the lawyers and judges did all the talking, she knew everyone in the courthouse, and had opinions about each of them. She picked up her phone. "I'll call the judge."

It only took a few moments for Judge Brenner to appear.

"All rise!" the bailiff called out, but the only lawyers in the front chamber were Raine and Scarborough, who were both already standing.

Raine gave a nod to the guard. "Beauchamp."

The guard nodded back and called for Raine's client.

A minute later everyone was ready to proceed: Brenner on the bench, Scarborough at one end of the bar, Raine and

Meredith at the other, and the bailiff silently thinking her thoughts about all of them.

"The is the matter of The State of Washington versus Meredith Beauchamp," Brenner announced for the record. "Will the attorneys please make their appearances for the record?"

"Kevin Scarborough on behalf of the State, Your Honor." Scarborough seemed to want to stand up even straighter to deliver his reply, but his posture was already fully extended.

"Daniel Raine on behalf of Meredith Beauchamp, Your Honor," Raine put in. "Thank you for taking the bench to hear this case—"

"The bail hearing, correct?" Judge Brenner interrupted. "Are we ready to conclude that now?"

"We are," Raine confirmed.

"We also need to select a trial date, Your Honor," Scarborough added. "We were unable to reach a settlement agreement this morning."

The judge suppressed a knowing smile. "You don't say. Well, then, let's pick that trial date first. That should take less time than the bail argument."

"I might like to know the bail amount before selecting a trial date, Your Honor," Raine ventured a protest.

Brenner smiled again, just as knowingly. "I'm sure you would, counsel. But let me ask you this: if your client is unable to post bail, you'll be ready to try the case in six weeks, won't you?"

Raine did manage to pull himself up a bit straighter. "Yes, Your Honor."

"Exactly," the judge answered. "And I expect you'll be doubly prepared if Ms. Beauchamp posts bail and can meet with you at length at your office for trial preparation."

Raine couldn't claim that wasn't true.

"How about you, Mr. Scarborough?" Brenner turned his attention to the prosecutor. "You're probably ready to try the case today, aren't you?"

"No, not quite, Your Honor," Scarborough answered.

"Can you be ready in six weeks?" the judge followed up.

"If the Court tells me to be ready in six weeks," Scarborough responded, "then I will be ready in six weeks."

Raine suppressed his own eye roll. He stole a glance at the bailiff to see if she agreed, but if she'd rolled her eyes, she'd done it quickly enough that he missed it.

"Well then, that's settled," Judge Brenner announced. "The trial date will be in six weeks. Six weeks from yesterday, to be exact. I think a Monday is the best day to start a trial."

Raine wasn't sure about that, but the judge didn't seem to be inviting any disagreement on the point.

"Shall we discuss bail now?" Brenner suggested. "I believe when we left off, it was your turn to speak, Mr. Raine. Whenever you're ready."

Raine took a deep breath. There were the laws, then there were the facts. There were the rules, then there were the equities. There was what a judge should do, and then there was what a judge was afraid to do. There were criminals, and then there were human beings. Search engines could produce the law. Prosecutors could apply the law to the facts. But true lawyering was blending the cold lifelessness of the law with the vibrant human experience that summoned laws into existence in the first place. Laws and rules should serve humans, not the other way around. In the sterile and formal rooms of a courthouse, it was easy to forget that. Raine's job was to make people remember.

"Meredith Beauchamp," he began with the most important piece of information for both his presentation and the judge's decision—his client, a living, breathing human being, "was born at Swedish Hospital in Seattle, not ten blocks from this very courthouse—"

"I'm going to interrupt you, counsel," Judge Brenner interjected. "I don't care that your client is a native Seattleite. I don't care that she started a business here in our fair city, or that she employs a dozen of our fellow citizens who depend on her to pay their rent and feed their children. I don't care about her family, her charitable giving, her hobbies, or her favorite color. I care that she's charged with murder, and I care that she comes to court for her trial and doesn't hurt anyone else between now and then."

The judge gestured at Meredith. "If I keep bail at an amount she apparently can't post, judging by her continued custodial status, there won't be any reporters up here asking me why I made that decision. But if I lower her bail and she gets out and hurts someone, I and my decision to reduce her bail will be the lead story on the six o'clock news. So, don't tell me about her, Mr. Raine. Tell me about me. Tell me why I should take a risk on someone who, at least according to the materials filed by the prosecutor's office, had the means, motive, and opportunity to commit the crime of murder in the first degree. Why her, Mr. Raine? Why, out of all the hundreds of defendants I see every week, why is she the one I should take a chance on?"

Raine paused. He actually appreciated that the judge cut right to the chase. So, he did too. "Because, Your Honor, she's innocent."

"Well, yes, of course," Judge Brenner scoffed. "Every criminal defendant is presumed innocent."

"No, not presumed," Raine clarified. "The jail is full of

guilty people who are presumed innocent. No, I'm talking about people who are innocent in fact. Actual innocence. Meredith Beauchamp is actually innocent."

Scarborough took the opportunity to add his own scoff, but Brenner raised a hand at him to be quiet.

"Go on," he directed Raine.

"Meredith did not murder Alexandra Pruitt," Raine asserted. "I know the prosecutor's summary of the facts known to date would seem to suggest otherwise. They say she snuck away to add poison to Alexandra's food. They say she did it to gain control of Alexandra's fortune. You know what I say? I say there's more to it than that. I say things aren't always as they seem. And I say, at trial, we will prove Meredith's innocence. But when we do that one thing will become crystal clear. If Meredith didn't murder Alexandra, then someone else did. Someone who will literally get away with murder if I'm not able to do my job to the best of my ability with the full assistance of my client, because the prosecutor certainly won't do it.

"This isn't just about justice for Meredith Beauchamp, Your Honor. It's about justice for Alexandra Pruitt. She deserves to have her real killer brought to justice. And Meredith deserves to be released from jail to await and work for that result. Thank you."

"May I respond?" Scarborough asked.

Judge Brenner frowned. "That's probably not necessary, counsel. Do you have anything new to add to your earlier argument or your summary of the allegations?"

Scarborough thought for a moment. "No, Your Honor."

Brenner nodded. "Then I'm ready to make my ruling."

Raine braced for the worst, even as he hoped for—well, not the best, but something better than the current situation.

Meredith wasn't getting released on her own recognizance, but maybe she could post a reduced bail.

"My earlier comments notwithstanding," Judge Brenner began, "I am mindful that my decision regarding bail is governed by Court Rule 3.2. I am further aware that Court Rule 3.2, by its own terms, presumes a defendant should be released on their own personal recognizance whenever possible, and the least restrictive conditions should be imposed to ensure the defendant returns to court and the community is safeguarded."

Maybe she is getting PR'd, Raine allowed himself to think.

"I am not releasing a murder defendant on their own recognizance," Brenner dashed Raine's short-lived spark of hope. "However, there comes a point when a bail is high enough. High enough that the promise of the return of the funds at the conclusion of the case is sufficient to secure presence at all future court dates. High enough to impress upon the defendant the seriousness of the allegations and the promise that any additional criminal activity will certainly result in a new bail amount that they would have no hope of posting. Any bail amount above that is simply punitive and, most importantly, contrary to the rule I am sworn to uphold."

Raine agreed with all of that. The only question was where the judge was going to land the bail plane.

"I do think three million dollars bail is excessive," Judge Brenner gave Raine half of what he wanted. "But I also think some significant bail is appropriate given the charges, the expected evidence, and the still existent risk of flight, if not re-offense. Accordingly, I am reducing bail in this case to one million dollars."

"One million dollars." Raine leaned in to ask Meredith under his breath. "Can you post that?"

"A million dollars?" She thought for a moment. "I think so. I mean, I'd have to sell some things, move some things around. It would take some time. A few days, maybe a week."

"Do it," Raine instructed, "and quick. We only have six weeks to find Alexandra's real killer, and I'm going to need all the help I can get."

11

"So, you didn't tell the Court about the eating disorder or the forged signature? Smart. Keep your powder dry. It wouldn't have helped anyway, and it would just give the prosecutor time to shore up those parts of the case. Better to spring it on him at trial when he doesn't have time to react."

Raine leaned onto his fist—his right fist; his left hand was still healing—and admired the woman across the restaurant table from him. Not only was Sawyer Mount the most beautiful woman in the place, not only did she have a sense of humor that could cut through glass, not only did she treat him well and seem to genuinely like him for himself—she was one hell of a lawyer. And a criminal defense lawyer at that. By choice. Go figure.

"I'm calling it a win," Raine declared. "I kept my powder dry, and I got my client out of jail. Well, almost. Soon. Probably."

"Must be nice to have enough assets to scare up a million cash." Sawyer smiled approvingly. Her red lipstick held a permanent gloss and set itself off from her black jacket and white lace top. Golden hoops dangled from her ears almost to the top of her shoulders, ending at the same level as her short blonde hair. Raine suspected she had just gotten it cut, but he hadn't thought to comment on it yet.

"I'm not sure it'll all be cash," Raine replied. "Or not all hers anyway. I think the plan is to put up some property for a loan or something."

"Or something?" Sawyer laughed. "Isn't your job to help your client with that sort of thing?"

Raine shrugged. "I'm more of an evidence and elements guy. Not bail money and liquidity."

"I know. I've seen your office," Sawyer teased him. "Not exactly high rent."

"I keep the lights on," Raine defended. "So far. This case will help."

"Rich client surcharge?" Sawyer grinned approvingly again.

Raine just smiled back. "So, enough about my case. What are you working on? Didn't you have a suppression motion on that robbery case?"

"Aw, you remembered." Sawyer lowered her lids at him. "Yes, actually, and you won't believe what happened—"

"Daniel Raine?" A man suddenly appeared at their table. He was young, early twenties, with shaggy hair, a few days' worth of stubble, and a messenger bag strapped across his chest. "Attorney Daniel Raine?"

Raine twisted his seat backward and braced his feet against the floor, squaring up to their unexpected guest but stopping short of standing up. "Who's asking?"

There were any number of people who might ask if he was 'Attorney Daniel Raine'. It could be an old client he didn't recognize, either still grateful for his services or still upset about how the case turned out. It could be a victim or witness or opposing party, again either happy or angry about how they were treated. It could be a colleague, although the man seemed a little young to have already graduated law school. Finally, it could be a potential new client. Raine needed to be ready to throw hands or throw a business card.

A quick glance to Sawyer revealed she was nonplussed. The man wasn't asking for her. She took a sip of her wine and waited for the scene to play out.

The man didn't respond. Instead, he started to reach into his messenger bag.

That was enough for Raine. That bag could hold any sort of weapon and Raine wasn't going to wait to see what it was. He swiftly sprang to his feet and grabbed the man's wrist. It felt surprisingly fragile in Raine's grip—like it would snap under the slightest pressure.

"Whoa! Dude!" the man yelled. "Let go! I'm just doing my job."

Raine did not let go. He leaned down and put his face inches away from the intruder's. "What's your job?"

"I'm a process server," the man answered. He was considerably smaller than Raine, both in height and breadth, but he didn't seem intimidated.

Raine appreciated that. And it served as confirmation of his claim—he'd probably experienced worse reactions in his line of work. He let go of the man's wrist and the man extracted a document from his bag which he handed to Raine.

"You've been served."

Raine looked down. Again, it could have been so many things. An old client suing him. An old victim suing him.

Another notice of another bar complaint. His entire professional life was about people being upset with other people; he couldn't always manage to stay out of everyone's crosshairs. But a scan of the document revealed no trace of his name. Meredith's on the other hand...

"Complaint for Damages," Raine read the caption of the pleading aloud. "Randall Newberry versus Meredith Beauchamp, *et alia*."

'*Et alia*' was Latin for 'and others'. Raine wondered who those others might be, but he at least knew the named defendant. "I represent Meredith Beauchamp," he confirmed, "but on a criminal matter. Not this."

The shaggy man shrugged. "I don't know, man. They pay me to deliver stuff, not to understand it. Good luck. Oh, and maybe look into an anger management class or something."

"Maybe don't interrupt people when they're having dinner and reach into a bag like you have a gun," Raine shot back.

The man pointed at him. "Yeah. That. You should maybe talk to somebody about that."

Raine threw his hands wide and looked to Sawyer for support. She shrugged.

"I think you did fine, Dan," she offered over her wine glass. "I definitely would have put money on him having a gun over having a complaint."

Raine turned back to the process server, but the man was already walking away and out of earshot. Raine gave up the argument about his alleged anger problem and looked down again at the complaint in his hands.

"So, who's suing who?" Sawyer asked. "And how are you involved exactly? You're not being sued, right?"

"Not yet," Raine answered as he sat down again. "Some

guy named Randall Newberry is suing my murder defendant."

"Wrongful death?" Sawyer ventured. "Is he like a relative of the victim or something?"

Raine took a few moments to review the document before answering. "No. He's a competitor of the victim. He's claiming he loaned her a bunch of money before her death, and she put up her companies as collateral. He's trying to block any transfer of the businesses without getting his money back."

"Sounds reasonable," Sawyer commented.

Raine wasn't so sure. "I've seen Alexandra's accounts. She didn't need a loan this large."

"Or maybe it looked like she didn't because she already had the money," Sawyer returned. "Are you sure you've seen all of her accounts? A lot of people keep two sets of books, you know."

Raine frowned. "Fraud?"

"Why not?" Sawyer shrugged. "We deal with people who literally kill other people. Is it that hard to imagine they might lie? Especially if it involves large amounts of money?"

"I've been lied to for a lot less," Raine admitted.

"Speaking of which, you look great tonight," Sawyer joked. "You're paying, right?"

12

_____

R aine was able to determine who the '*et alia*' were when he looked up the original complaint filed in the King County Superior Court's online portal.

Randall Newberry v. Meredith Beauchamp, Caroline Howard, Julia Kim, Fiona Mendoza, and Rebecca Sommers. Alphabetical order. Maybe Newberry had been in charge of getting the signatures on that partnership agreement Scarborough was going to mark as Exhibit A. Almost certainly not, however, since Newberry was trying to stop exactly the sort of transfer that partnership agreement would have effectuated, if it had been signed by all of the Fab Five. Which begged the question: why was he suing them all if only Meredith signed it?

The five named defendants might have some insight on that point, but Raine wasn't about to assemble all of them in one place. Not yet anyway, and not over this issue. Instead, he started with the two he had the closest connection to: his erstwhile companion, Rebecca Sommers, and his client on a different but undeniably related matter, Meredith

Beauchamp. Mercifully, they could have the meeting at Raine's office instead of another jail closet. Meredith had finally managed to post bail.

"Randall Newberry?" Sommers scowled at the complaint. "I hate that guy."

"He's the worst," Meredith agreed. She looked significantly better than she had while still in custody. Generally cleaner and better rested. Her clothes were also a marked improvement over the red jail scrubs.

"Who is he?" Raine asked.

A dull afternoon rain allowed only a dim light to struggle through the windows of Raine's conference room. Raine took a sip of coffee from his "World's Best Lawyer" coffee mug. The one his oldest son had given him for a Father's Day present years back. The son who barely talked to him since the divorce. Raine took another drink and shook the thoughts of ungrateful teenagers from his head. There was work to focus on.

"He's a slumlord," Meredith answered. "Probably the biggest one in Seattle."

"He owns most of the worst apartment complexes in the worst parts of town," Sommers explained. "Housing in Seattle is already so expensive. Even the most basic apartment is more than a lot of people can afford. He charges just a little less than that, but charges a bunch of upfront fees that he never refunds and does absolutely no upkeep unless the city forces him to."

"Which is almost never," Meredith added. "And even then, he hires the cheapest contractors to do the shoddiest work. You do not want to be unfortunate enough to live in one of his buildings."

"But he's rich?" Raine deduced.

"Oh yeah," Sommers confirmed. "Terrible human being, but smart businessman. If being completely amoral is smart."

Raine supposed it could be. It wasn't like he was defending Meredith for free.

"So, why would someone like that be involved with someone like Alexandra Pruitt?" he asked. "I thought she was all high-end condos and luxury estates."

"She was," Sommers agreed, "but she wasn't always, I'm sure."

"She never talked much about her early days," Meredith said. "Except that she worked hard to make it where she was."

"And she wanted to help us get there without having to work quite so hard," Sommers added.

"Or with people quite so terrible as Randall Newberry," Raine suspected. He reached for the complaint again and turned to page three. "He's alleging that shortly before Alexandra died he gave her a very sizeable loan to keep her business afloat while she planned some sort of reorganization."

"The partnership agreement," Sommers suggested.

Raine nodded. "He claims Alexandra put up a majority stake in her business as collateral for the loan. He said she came to him because she wanted it done quietly. That's why she didn't just go to a bank. Does any of that sound even remotely possible to either of you?"

Raine expected a pair of quick 'No!'s. Instead, Sommers and Meredith looked at each other, frowned, then turned back to him.

"Maybe." Sommers nodded.

"It's not completely out of the question," Meredith agreed.

"You don't get as rich as her without taking some chances," Sommers offered.

"And being willing to make the occasional deal with the devil," Meredith put in.

"Or a slumlord," Raine concluded.

Sommers suddenly snapped her fingers. "Randall! That folder on the thumb drive."

Raine remembered as well. "That must be where she kept the info on the loan."

"What thumb drive?" Meredith asked.

"Uh..." Sommers hesitated, looking at Raine.

"It's kind of a long story," Raine advised. He raised his bandaged hand. "Exciting, though."

"You're keeping secrets from me?" Meredith questioned.

"It looks like Alexandra was keeping secrets from everybody."

Sommers may have just been trying to change the subject, but she was right, and that was bad news. They say you should never meet your heroes. The corollary to that might be to never look too closely at your mentor's financials. But it didn't answer the larger question.

"But why is he suing you five?" Raine returned the conversation to Newberry's lawsuit. "His complaint just assumes that you all will be gaining control of the business. It doesn't say how that's supposed to happen."

"Well, it can't be the partnership agreement. I'm the only one who signed that," Meredith quipped with a grin.

Raine shook his head. "No jokes like that on the stand. Jurors don't always have good senses of humor. Judges never do."

"But she's right," Sommers jumped in. "It can't be the partnership agreement."

"Unless he thinks you all did sign it," Raine supposed.

"Which would suggest some sort of advance knowledge of Alexandra's plans," Sommers replied.

"And that's consistent with having secret financial arrangements with Alexandra," Meredith added. "Maybe he tried to collect the loan, and she told him what her plan was."

"That would be a reason to sue us," Sommers agreed.

"Or," Raine set down his mug, "it's a motive to murder Alexandra."

Sommers cocked her head at him. "How do you figure?"

Raine thought a bit more. "I suppose it depends on how many documents there were that might have moved Alexandra's assets out of Newberry's reach, and how far along they were to completion. It seems like Alexandra had several plans in motion at once."

Meredith nodded. "She always had a backup plan to her backup plan."

"That also explains why even on the night of her retirement dinner," Sommers added, "we still didn't know what her plans were."

"I don't think that thumb drive was complete," Raine ventured.

"I think you're right," Sommers conceded.

"What thumb drive?" Meredith repeated.

"We'll explain on the way," Raine answered, standing up.

"On the way to where?" Meredith asked, half standing herself as if to follow Raine to his feet, but unsure whether to do so.

"We need to talk with Alexandra's lawyer," Raine

answered. "The one who would have drafted all of the various documents we have, and maybe the ones that are missing."

"Like whatever was in the 'Randall' folder," Sommers said.

"And a will," Raine added. "If she had one, she had a lawyer draft it. And that lawyer would have kept a copy for his own records."

"Makes sense," Sommers agreed.

"The only problem is," Raine admitted, "I don't know who her lawyer is."

Sommers looked to Meredith, who nodded back.

"Duncan," Meredith said first.

"Duncan Chenoweth," Sommers expanded.

"Never heard of him," Raine said.

"Given that your practice area is going up against people who've made mistakes," Sommers observed, "I'd say that speaks very well of Mr. Chenoweth."

13

Duncan Chenoweth technically worked for one of Seattle's largest tax law firms. Practically, his association was minimal. He was 'of counsel'. Rather than a partner who held an ownership stake in the firm, or an associate who slaved away in the hopes of someday becoming partner, an attorney listed as 'of counsel' on a firm's letterhead was usually an older, established attorney who had their own separate stable of clients. The relationship allowed the firm the benefit of a knowledgeable attorney who might otherwise be competing for the same clients. And it allowed the 'of counsel' attorney access to the structural overhead advantages of a large firm while still maintaining control of their cases and client list.

It also meant that instead of having to front fifty hours a week of 'face time' at the firm's downtown skyscraper offices, they could work from their home office in Seattle's Sandpoint neighborhood.

His house had a view of the water. Of course.

"Are you sure this is the right place?" Sommers asked as they rolled to a stop in front of the house.

Architecturally, the frame was a classic Northwest craftsman, but the façade had been redone to look like an English cottage. Raine wasn't sure he liked it, but he supposed Chenoweth had earned more than enough money with clients like Alexandra Pruitt to do whatever he wanted with his home. He squinted slightly to confirm the house number.

"Yes, this is it," he assured them. "I looked him up on the bar website. His business address is the same as the firm's in the Columbia Tower downtown, but this is his home address for the Bar Association's Board of Governors elections."

"So, this is a guess?" Meredith questioned.

"An educated guess," Raine corrected. "A deduction, even. His year of admission to the bar is a year before I was born. This guy is at the end of his career. He's not fighting downtown traffic to impress partners twenty years younger than him."

Raine looked at his passengers, neither of whom seemed completely convinced.

"The traffic isn't great around here either," Meredith pointed out. "I know. I have to drive through here to get to my house in Matthews Beach."

"Fine." Raine opened his car door. "If he's not here, we can spend an hour driving downtown and searching for a parking space within five blocks of the Columbia Tower, just to have a receptionist tell us the seventy-year-old tax and trusts lawyer isn't there today."

Sommers followed his exit from the vehicle. "No need to get defensive, Dan. We're just asking questions."

Raine frowned. "I prefer asking the questions," he admitted. "But I also like being right, and I'm pretty sure I'm right."

They crossed the street and walked up the long walk to the covered front porch. Raine didn't observe any security cameras. Not even a video-equipped doorbell. It was a pretty nice neighborhood, he supposed, but not so nice as to be an obvious target, like those gated communities in Madison Park.

He gestured to the entrance. "Would you like to do the honors?" he asked Meredith.

"Oh, sure," she replied, then pushed the doorbell button.

A loud melody of electronic bells was clearly audible through the door. A little too audible, Raine thought.

He stepped forward and pushed the wooden front door with his index finger. The door swung open several inches. A stale scent escaped into their faces.

"Hello?" Raine called into the home. He didn't really expect an answer.

"Should we go in?" Sommers asked.

"I don't think so," Meredith answered, but Raine was already pushing the door the rest of the way open.

"Hello?" he repeated as he stepped inside. "Mr. Chenoweth?"

Inside, the home was luxurious and immaculate. Shiny wooden floors, walls filled with perfectly framed photos, ecru paint and dark wood accents. An original painting of the Seattle skyline over a massive fireplace. Beautifully restored antique armchairs. And not a sound.

"Are you sure about this, Dan?" Sommers asked. "Isn't this breaking and entering?"

"No such thing in Washington," Raine answered, scanning the house rather than looking at her as he spoke.

"Breaking and entering is an old-school term. Now it's just called burglary, and that requires an intent to commit a crime inside. We don't have that intent, so it's not burglary."

"So, it's not a crime to go into someone else's home?" Meredith questioned.

"Oh, it's totally a crime," Raine confirmed. "Criminal trespass in the first degree. But that's a misdemeanor, and there's a bunch of random exceptions and defenses. Necessity, duress, reasonable belief of license to enter."

"Which one are we doing?" Meredith asked.

Raine shrugged. "Depends on whether we get caught, and by whom. If the cops get here before we leave, lawyer up and let me do the talking."

"Or we could just leave," Sommers suggested.

Raine smiled. "Where's the fun in that?"

"I don't really want to go back to jail," Meredith put in.

"Me neither," Raine replied. "So, let's hurry. The old man is probably just in his back office and has his hearing aids out."

"What about the front door being open?" Sommers wondered.

"Didn't close it all the way after he got the mail?" Raine ventured.

Sommers crossed her arms. "If you really thought all that, we wouldn't be inside, would we?"

Raine had to smile at that. "Nope. Now, get behind me. They might still be here."

"Who?" Meredith squeaked.

Sommers put her finger to her lips and gently pushed Meredith behind her, then fell in behind Raine.

There was a single hallway from the front room that led toward the back of the house, a sharp bend to the right after just a few feet hiding what lay at its end. Raine guessed the home office was on the first floor, probably opposite the kitchen and near the guest bathroom. He also supposed they would pass a staircase that led to bedrooms and another bathroom upstairs. But they didn't pass the staircase. Because that's where they found Chenoweth's body, crumpled at the bottom of the hardwood landing.

Meredith screamed at the sight.

Neither Raine nor Sommers screamed. Sommers frowned. Raine leaned down to inspect the scene.

Chenoweth had come to rest on a square landing that was two steps up from the first floor, before the staircase turned ninety degrees and proceeded another dozen or so steps to the second floor. Every step was exposed hardwood. Not the sort of thing anyone would want to fall down, but especially dangerous for an elderly man. The body was in an awkward pile, with its back against the wall of the landing opposite the stairs to the upper floor, its arms and legs jutting out awkwardly, and its neck twisted at a very unnatural, and fatal, angle. A pool of blood was visible under the head, thick and already dried at the edges.

"Is he dead?" Meredith gasped.

"He is definitely dead," Raine answered. He reached out and gave a light tug at the arm at the top of the pile. It gave about as much resistance as he expected based on the state of the drying blood on the wood. "And he's been dead for a while."

"You can tell that from the rigor mortis?" Sommers asked.

"The lack of it actually," Raine answered. "Rigor sets in at about four hours as chemicals in the muscles drain away and leave them rigid. But after another six to eight hours, the muscles start to decompose themselves, making the body flexible again."

"That's super gross," Meredith said through the hands covering the lower half of her face.

"That's life." Raine shrugged. "Or death, I suppose. Either way, he's been dead for about ten or twelve hours."

Sommers looked at the fancy watch hanging from her wrist. "It's almost six. So, he died this morning?"

Raine nodded. Then realized something. He turned to Meredith. "What time did you get out?"

"Of jail?" she confirmed the question. "Last night. I posted the bail in the morning, but they didn't let me out until after dinner. Something about staffing shortages and shift changes."

"Yeah, that sounds right," Raine knew. He knew something else. "We need to get out of here. Now."

"Why?" Sommers asked. Then she gestured at the dead body. "I mean, apart from the obvious issue of trespassing inside a dead man's home. He died of natural causes. An old man fell down the stairs and broke his neck. It's tragic, and not very helpful for us, but it's not like it was a murder."

"That's just it." Raine pointed at the back of the dead man's bald skull, most but not all of it hidden against the wall. "All that blood is from a sharp-force wound to the back of his head. There's nothing on this staircase sharp enough to cause a wound that deep."

He looked to the top of the stairs. "He definitely fell down the stairs and broke his neck...after someone smashed him in the back of the head with something sharp. This was definitely a murder."

14

Raine sent Meredith home with strict instructions not to speak to anyone about their trip to the home of Duncan Chenoweth. He dispatched Sommers similarly, but without the nagging worry that she wouldn't follow his direction. Then he went back to his office to figure out what the hell to do next.

There were suddenly several priorities competing for his next course of action. On the one, and most dramatic, hand was the murder they stumbled upon. Should he call the police, or rely on someone at Chenoweth's law firm to notice he wasn't answering his phone or email? That could take days, although that injury to the back of his head was deep enough to have struck bone. A few days of decomposition wouldn't necessarily destroy evidence of the murder; not all of it anyway.

Perhaps more pressing, for his defense of Meredith, was getting his hands on the documents they had hoped to identify with Chenoweth's help. The thought of rifling through the dead man's office before leaving the house had flashed through Raine's mind, but it was immediately followed by the thought of being caught doing that and spending the rest of his life behind bars for aggravated murder one. "It's not what it looks like" wasn't going to work for that situation. And his earlier combat with Ernest Poplowski would be admissible at his trial for the murder of Duncan Chenoweth. *Modus operandi.* Classic admissibility. The jury would be out only as long as it took to write the word "guilty" on the verdict form.

Raine needed to know what Newberry was basing his claims on. It had stood to reason that, if there were any credence to those claims, then Alexandra's lawyer would know. And he probably did. He just couldn't tell them anymore. Dead lawyers tell no attorney-client confidences.

Unfortunately, that left the lawyer on the other end of the litigation. One Elisabeth Ungermann, the lawyer who had signed the complaint that had so rudely interrupted Raine's dinner with Sawyer. Raine hadn't heard of her either, but he had heard of her firm, although that was a bit of a wonder as well. It was one of the big firms that kept changing its name every time one of the named partners broke away to form their own firm and steal as many clients as they could on their way out the door. The latest iteration of their name was Ellis+JPG. "Ellis" was one of those names you ran across a lot if you were a lawyer in Seattle. Raine had no idea what the JPG stood for. Probably the last initials of the next three partners to bolt.

Raine's lack of familiarity with Elisabeth Ungermann personally was less a function of her not being the type of lawyer Raine might have locked horns with, and more a function of Raine's clients tending to have a lot less money than the clients who paid the overhead for Ellis+JPG's top-floor offices in Seattle's Two Union Square office tower. It wasn't the tallest building in town—it was the fourth tallest —but it was in the same complex as the Washington State Court of Appeals, so it had a certain cachet among the members of the bar.

Raine decided to take the 'don't call first' approach. He had his doubts about whether it would work, but she did think of him as one of her opposing lawyers, even if his focus on representing Meredith was the criminal case, not some lawsuit that didn't even seem to make sense. It would be normal for them to talk, even if not necessarily meet face to face. His concern was that a call would lead to, at best, a videoconference, but he really wanted to meet her in person. He wanted to size her up, and experience her reactions in three dimensions as he tested her knowledge of any secret agreements that might underpin Newberry's suit—and Meredith's innocence.

"Hello," Raine greeted the receptionist. He came alone this time. This was a lawyer-to-lawyer conversation. Sommers would have cramped his style, and put Ungermann on high alert. "My name is Daniel Raine. I'm the opposing lawyer on a case with Elisabeth Ungermann and I happened to be in the building. I don't suppose she might be available for a quick chat about our case?"

The receptionist was a woman whose age Raine couldn't quite figure out. Older than her twenties, younger than her fifties, maybe. She had the lanky physique and thin facial features of a long-distance runner. The sport was either keeping her young or aging her quickly. She hadn't been smiling when Raine began his introduction, but when he reached the word "lawyer" her expression lit up and her bony cheeks pulled her lips open into a toothy smile.

"I'll be happy to see if she's available," she said. "Which case is it?"

"Randall Newberry versus Meredith Beauchamp," Raine answered, "*et alia*. Ms. Ungermann represents Mr. Newberry."

The smile tightened, as if it wanted to get larger but wasn't permitted to do so. "Oh yes. I know that. Thank you. I'll message her."

Raine thanked the woman, then strolled over to the picture window with its view of Westlake Center, Pike Place Market, and Elliott Bay. He could see why some lawyers chose to stab each other in the backs for luxuries like fifty-story water views. He wondered how long Elisabeth Ungermann would last before she stole a client list and tried to replicate her success at a different office in a different skyscraper with basically the same view.

"Thank you, Mr. Newberry," Raine heard a woman's voice behind him. It wasn't the receptionist's scratchy athletic voice. It was more the voice of a lawyer bidding farewell to the exact client Raine wanted to talk about, and talk to.

Raine spun around to glimpse the man who had such a close relationship with Sommers's mentor that she would go to him when she had no one to turn to, even if he was a slumlord. Raine expected a physique and countenance to match his role in life. Squalid, gnarled, corrupted. A troll of a man who would gladly live under a bridge of others' misery. Raine's expectation was wrong. Very wrong.

Randall Newberry was a very tall, very distinguished, very handsome man in his late sixties, perhaps even early seventies. He was vibrant despite his years, with a strong spring in his step and a solid jaw atop a thick neck. A full head of salt-and-pepper hair was combed directly away from his face, with gray temples and a perfectly trimmed gray mustache. Pale eyes rested easily among the folds of skin that appeared as he smiled back at his attorney.

"No, thank you, Elisabeth. I will look forward to our next progress meeting. Give my regards to Arthur."

Arthur Ellis, Raine could guess. The only one important enough to have his full surname on the firm letterhead.

Raine wanted very much to cancel whatever appointment he was about to have with Elisabeth Ungermann and follow Newberry to the elevator to strike up a far more fruitful conversation. There were three problems with that. The first was that lawyers were prohibited by the Bar Association's Rules of Professional Conduct from knowingly speaking with a person who was represented by another lawyer. The second was that he had just admitted to the receptionist that he knew Newberry was represented by Ungermann. The third was that Ungermann was standing right there. It was only the combination of those three things, and the certainly of professional discipline they carried, that prevented Raine from jumping into the elevator and opening a conversation with something like, "Lovely day to exploit low-income renters, isn't it?"

"Mr. Raine, was it?" She stepped over to shake his hand. "I'm Elisabeth Ungermann."

Ungermann was in her early thirties, young for a lawyer. She was probably a decade away from stealing old clients and signing new leases. She might even stay, if Arthur was trusting her with big clients like Randall Newberry. She had straw-blonde hair pulled into a simple ponytail, with light makeup and a blazer and skirt that weren't a suit combination but matched nicely anyway. She seemed nice. Raine wasn't sure if that would help or hinder his mission.

"Yes, Dan Raine. Nice to meet you." He shook her hand, then decided to address the elephant that just left the room. He jerked a thumb toward the elevators. "Was that...?"

"Mr. Newberry?" Ungermann finished the sentence. "Yes, it was. Your timing is excellent. I already have the file on my desk. Follow me and let's see if we can't figure out a way to help each other."

Raine had to admit, he liked the sound of that. He didn't trust it, but he liked how it sounded.

Ungermann's office was actually rather small, and although it had the same floor-to-ceiling windows as the lobby, her view faced east, with a territorial view of Interstate 5 and the forest of medical office buildings on First Hill. The office of an associate, even one who might be on the partner track. She sat down behind her nondescript desk and invited Raine to sit opposite her in one of two upholstered guest chairs.

"So, what brings you to my office today, Mr. Raine?" Ungermann began.

"Call me Dan," he insisted, "and what brings me here is pretty straightforward. Your client is suing my client."

"That he is," Ungermann agreed with a grin. "His real beef is with Alexandra Pruitt, but she's dead, of course. So, the lawsuit falls onto your client and her associates, I'm afraid."

Raine leaned forward. "Yeah, let's talk about that. I'm a little unclear on your theory of liability here. None of the named defendants were parties to any loan your client might or might not have extended to Alexandra. Or am I missing something?"

"Well, actually, it might be me who's missing something," Ungermann admitted. "The loan agreement was oral only, for, well, reasons."

"That seems like a problem for you," Raine replied.

Ungermann shrugged. "A proof problem, maybe, but one that's easily overcome. Mr. Newberry will testify that there was a loan agreement, and Ms. Pruitt is in no position to rebut that."

"That's pretty dark." Raine frowned.

"It is," Ungermann admitted, "but then most of what we do is dark, isn't it? I mean, you're defending the woman who murdered Alexandra."

"She didn't murder her," Raine insisted. "Probably."

"Well, I don't know about that," Ungermann commented, "and I don't really care either. Except to the extent that it impacts my case."

"And what is that case again?" Raine pressed. "I still don't understand why you're suing the Fab Five."

Ungermann burst out laughing. "Do they really call themselves that?"

Raine sighed. "I guess so. I don't know. It doesn't matter. Why are you suing them?"

"Someone has to pay back the loan," Ungermann answered, "and they are her successors in interest."

Raine took a moment before uttering his next line in their verbal joust. He was there representing Meredith, in more ways than one apparently. But the criminal case had to take priority. If she had to pay back one-fifth of some ill-advised loan as part of some arrangement where she also received one-fifth of even some of Alexandra's assets, that didn't seem so bad. But if she were convicted of murder, she would die in prison, after a couple decades of misery. If

Ungermann had her hands on some superseding business agreement that would take precedence over the partially signed partnership, the prosecution's motive for the murder would evaporate.

"Prove it."

Ungermann smiled. "I like you, Dan Raine. Meredith made a good decision to hire you. How did that happen anyway? You and I haven't really crossed paths before. Are you mostly a criminal defense attorney? Maybe you're not the best person to represent her in a civil lawsuit. I mean, not that it's any of my business. Well, actually, I suppose that's exactly what it is: my business."

Raine didn't feel obligated to explain his relationship to his client, or his relationship to Sommers, who would probably be his client in the civil suit too if he couldn't figure out how to short-circuit it. But Ungermann did need to know that he wasn't in over his head. And he wasn't intimidated by Ungermann, her firm, or her client.

"I do a little bit of everything," Raine answered. "I defend people accused of crimes and I defend people who get sued by slumlords. I also sue people for malicious prosecution and defamation. And while my hourly rate might not be as high as that of the attorneys here at Ellis and 'jay-peg', I'm pretty good at getting attorney fee awards too."

Ungermann held her smile but it weakened slightly.

"So, if you have a document," he continued, "that would both support your claim in this civil case while simultaneously undercutting the prosecution's claims in the criminal case, then I would really love to have that, and sooner rather than later."

He leaned forward again. "We both know I'll get it eventually, but we also both know that civil discovery is plodding and slow. I can send over my interrogatories and demands for production, and demand to schedule the deposition of your client. You can object to all of that and refuse to provide whatever it is I really want in order to make me have to go to the judge and drive up costs."

Ungermann nodded along. He had convinced her he knew what he was doing. Now to convince her to not make him have to do it.

"And normally, I'd be fine with that," he continued. "More costs means more fees, and more fees means more money in my bank account, too. But I don't have the luxury of a long, protracted discovery battle. The criminal case is set for trial in just a few weeks. I need that agreement now. So, can we dispense with the posturing and get to the heart of the matter. Give me whatever it is that you think makes the Fab Five liable for Alexandra's loan and let me use that to keep an innocent woman from going to prison for the rest of her life for a murder she didn't commit."

Ungermann leaned back in her chair and tapped a finger on her lips. "What's in it for me? Why not let your client get convicted?"

"One less person you can collect from," Raine answered. "I can guarantee you she won't earn enough from making license plates to pay you back."

"Fair point." Ungermann nodded. "But not enough. I want something in return."

"What?"

"Switch sides," Ungermann said. "Admit that there was an agreement for this Fab Five to take over all of Alexandra's business, assets and liabilities, including the loan to Mr. Newberry. In exchange for that, Mr. Newberry would be willing to drop the case against Ms. Beauchamp and even add her as a plaintiff against the others."

Raine leaned back again as well. He raised one hand to his mouth and stroked his chin as he considered Ungermann's offer. Or rather, what the offer revealed.

"You don't have an actual written agreement, do you?" he realized. "No loan agreement and no agreement showing Alexandra transferred anything to any of the Fab Five."

Ungermann didn't reply instantly.

"What about a will?" Raine probed. "I'm hearing she didn't have a will, but if anyone can find one, it has to be a firm like this one, right? Have you not found that yet either?"

"We are in the process of confirming there is no will," Ungermann answered, "but we are not interested in the time and expense of litigating our claim through probate." She exhaled through her nose and her mouth tightened into a thin line. "Remember that tortuous discovery process you mentioned earlier? We intend to use that to find the documentation necessary to prove that Ms. Beauchamp and the others did in fact take possession of Ms. Pruitt's businesses prior to, or at the time of, her death."

Raine shook his head. "Damn it. I really thought you'd have something more concrete. This has been a complete waste of time."

"It doesn't have to be," Ungermann countered. "If Ms. Beauchamp were willing to agree that she and the others have to repay the loan, I think Mr. Newberry would be favorably inclined to testify at your trial that Ms. Pruitt told him that all five of them would receive equal shares of her business. That should be enough to at least cast doubt, reasonable doubt, on the prosecution's motive, don't you think?"

Raine just blinked at her. Notwithstanding his earlier

desire to violate the ethical rules and speak directly to Newberry, despite knowing he was represented, he hadn't actually done it. What Ungermann was proposing was something far worse.

"Suborning perjury?" He shook his head at her. "You want me to suborn perjury?"

Ungermann shrugged. "It's only suborning perjury if you know it isn't true. Do you really know what Ms. Pruitt might have said to Mr. Newberry? And more importantly, how are you going to get that sort of evidence any other way?"

"Exactly that. Any other way." Raine stood up. "Thank you for your time, Ms. Ungermann. I think we're done."

"Done for now, maybe." Ungermann smiled as she stood up as well. "But don't think I'm going to dismiss this lawsuit just because you don't want to play ball. There are others who will be more than happy to accept my offer."

Raine frowned and his brows knitted together. "Who?"

But he knew as soon as he asked.

15

"Caroline Howard," Raine repeated the name of the person they had come to see. "Is she available?"

The offices for Howard Premier Brokerage were on the fourth floor of a seven-story office building at the north end of the Seattle Waterfront. Not exactly top-floor skyscraper status, but there was a peekaboo view of Elliott Bay between the roofs of the Seattle Aquarium and the Edgewater Inn.

Sommers had come with Raine this time. She stepped forward to address the receptionist who was clearly reticent to allow them access to the boss. "I'm a friend."

The receptionist frowned. He was young, barely twenty, Raine guessed, with that haircut all the young men were wearing despite how it actually looked. He wore all black, but of different fabrics, indicating it was a directive, not a choice. "What's your name, ma'am?"

"Rebecca Sommers," she answered. "Tell her it's about the Newberry account. She'll know what that means."

The receptionist seemed dubious, but he finally reached

for his keyboard. "I'll see if Ms. Howard is available. Please have a seat. She might be a while."

Raine took that as a win. Or at least, not a loss. Not yet. Even if Caroline refused to see them, that would also be information. But he hoped to get more than just that sliver. He sat down next to Sommers and looked out the window. Gray waves reflected gray clouds, although there was a lighter spot in the sky where the sun probably was. At least it wasn't raining. Just then, anyway.

"Ms. Howard will see you now," the receptionist called out far sooner than Raine had expected. He wasn't sure he even expected the receptionist to say that at all. He wasn't sure what to say.

"Good." Sommers had no such problem. She stood up and strode forcefully toward the door to the interior of the office.

Raine had to hurry to keep up and the receptionist had to hurry even more to buzz it open before Sommers grasped the door handle.

"I'll show you the way," he offered.

Sommers threw a hand toward him. "No need," she declared. "I'm sure I can find her."

Raine hurried behind as the receptionist gave up the chase, and Sommers followed the narrow hallway past the row of small doors with their small offices to the end of the corridor and the large door with the enormous office. Within, wearing a dark business suit and irritated expression, sat Caroline Howard.

"This better be good, Rebecca," she snarled as they broke the plane of her office. "I'm a busy woman."

Sommers laughed. "Every office between the receptionist and here was empty, Caroline. If you're busy, it's because you're not making enough to pay anyone except minimum wage to some college kid."

"Andrew is in art school," Caroline corrected, "and it's an externship. I'm not even paying him. He pays the school, they give him class credit, and I get a free employee."

Sommers took a moment. "Are things really that bad?"

Her voice actually sounded like the friend she told the art school student she was. Raine supposed there had probably been a time when all five of them were friends, even if that time had long passed.

Caroline sighed. "Honestly, yes. They were." But then her face broke into a wide grin. "But not anymore. I have a new partner and a new venture. Things are finally about to turn around for Sweet Caroline."

Whatever warmth had been in Sommers's expression drained away. "What do you mean, Caroline? What did you do?"

"Oh, Rebecca." Caroline's smile broadened. "I thought you already knew. The Newberry account, right?"

Sommers shook her head. "Please tell me you didn't make a deal with the devil."

"Better the devil you know," Caroline responded. "Of course I made a deal. That's what we do. Make deals. You're no different from me, Rebecca. You're no better than me."

Sommers threw her hands up in exasperation.

Raine stepped into the breach. "What was the deal? Is he going to drop you from the complaint?"

"Yes," Caroline confirmed. "In exchange for a promise to pay back his loan when I gain control of Alexandra's assets."

Sommers's still agitated hands fell to her sides. "Gain control of Alexandra's assets? How the hell are you going to pull that off? The only one who signed the partnership agreement was Meredith."

"Well, actually—" Raine started to interrupt, but Sommers waved him off.

"Hush, Dan," she scolded. "You have no claim to Alexandra's assets, Caroline. No more than me or Julia or Fiona. If anyone, Ernest has the best claim."

"After Meredith," Raine tried to support Sommers's argument, even if he was going to tell the jury the exact opposite.

"Meredith's claim will evaporate as soon as she's convicted," Caroline scoffed. "And Alexandra never married Ernest. If she wanted him to get her business, she knew how to do that, and she didn't. Which only makes sense. He's no real estate broker. It makes much more sense to pass it on to someone who would know how to run it. Someone like me."

Sommers took a moment. "Are you claiming you had some sort of an agreement with Alexandra?"

"An oral agreement," Caroline clarified. "Yes."

"Oral agreement?" Sommers laughed. "You can't prove you had an oral agreement with her."

"Prove I didn't," Caroline challenged.

Sommers opened her mouth to respond, but had nothing. She looked to Raine.

He shrugged. "An oral contract is still a contract," he conceded. "It's just a lot harder to prove it existed. If Caroline says she had a contract with Alexandra and the court believes her, she could win."

"And destroy everything Alexandra built," Sommers spat, "to pay Newberry back for a loan that probably isn't any more real than the oral contract you made up."

Caroline shrugged and offered a lopsided smirk. "Beats

having Newberry take everything I've built to pay back a loan I didn't take out."

Sommers looked around her environs. "You haven't built much, Caroline."

"All the more reason to protect it, Rebecca," Caroline responded. "And I bet Julia and Fiona will see it the same way. Not all of us have a free lawyer we can lead around by the nose."

"Wow," was all Sommers managed to say.

Raine knew not to say anything. Not in reply anyway. "I think we're done here. Thanks for the information, Ms. Howard. Good luck with your devil. I'm sure that won't come back to bite you at all."

"We'll let ourselves out," Sommers added. "See you in court."

That seemed increasingly likely, Raine agreed to himself. He just wasn't sure for which case. And he was starting to think there might be more to come.

16

The next conversation had to be with Julia Kim. Raine needed to know whether she was going to throw in with Caroline or remain onside with Sommers and Meredith. And Fiona. That was the other reason Julia was next. Sommers wanted to put off talking with Fiona until it was absolutely necessary. That bought at least three days because Julia couldn't fit them into her schedule for two days. Caroline was a show up without a call, like the one to Ernest that went so well. But if they pulled that with Julia, there was a more than even chance that she wouldn't be there, but instead out closing a sale somewhere. Besides, there was no need. Julia was on their side. Hopefully.

Julia's office was on the top floor of an old ten-story brick building in Pioneer Square. No real view of the water, but a nice one of the Smith Tower and the southern end of the skyline. Raine expected she could probably pay her staff as well. The receptionist who greeted them was in her thirties in a coordinated outfit and pleasant expression, as if she enjoyed working there. Other actual employees were visible walking the hall behind her.

"Good morning," the receptionist greeted them. "You must be Ms. Sommers and Mr. Raine."

"We must be," Raine confirmed.

"We are." Sommers shot him a glare. "Is Ms. Kim available yet? We're a few minutes early."

"Let me check." The receptionist stood up and turned toward the interior of the office. "I'll be right back."

"I like her better than Andrew," Raine commented as the two of them stepped away from the welcome desk.

"Andrew seemed fine," Sommers replied. "It was Caroline that was terrible."

"Is Fiona still your least favorite after that?" Raine asked. "Or did Caroline take her crown?"

Sommers thought for a moment. "Still Fiona."

"Ms. Kim is ready," the receptionist called out to them upon her return. "Follow me."

The receptionist led them down a hallway of full and busy offices to the last one, whose door was closed. Raine wondered at that, since they were expected, and wondered even more as the receptionist opened the door revealing a completely dark interior. Completely dark save for a dim flicker of candlelight.

"Ms. Sommers and her friend are here to see you, Ms. Kim," the receptionist announced into the darkness.

"Oh good!" came a muffled reply. "Come in! Come in!"

Sommers entered first. Raine followed directly behind. It took a moment for Raine's eyes to adjust to the dimness, but after that moment he could make out a standard office desk and chair on the far side of the room, a wall of windows with room-darkening shades closed, and a massage table in the center of the room. Julia was lying face down, topless if not completely naked under a single sheet, with a large man pressing down on her oiled back.

"I hope you don't mind." Julia lifted her head slightly out of the face rest. "You said it was urgent and the only way I could fit you in was to double-book you with my weekly massage therapy."

"Uh, no, no problem," Sommers answered for the both of them. "I mean, it is kind of a sensitive topic…"

"Oh, don't worry about Paolo," Julia reassured. "Unless we're going to be speaking Portuguese, he's not going to understand much. Right, Paolo?"

"*Sim, senhora,*" Paolo replied.

Raine found the reply confusing. If he didn't understand English, how did he know to agree that he didn't understand English? But he supposed it wasn't that big of a deal. Paolo probably spent his workdays ignoring whatever conversations his clients had. He likely had no interest in Julia's finances beyond being paid. Sommers didn't seem bothered by the masseur's presence either.

"We'll get right to it, Julia," Sommers began. "Did you get served with Newberry's lawsuit yet?"

"Oh yes," Julia confirmed. "Some skinny guy with a beard interrupted a very nice dinner with my husband."

"*Modus operandi,*" Raine muttered. The guy probably enjoyed ruining people's dinners. At least he'd found a way to make his job more interesting, Raine supposed.

"Seems ridiculous," Julia continued. "Why would we have to pay back a loan Alexandra took out?"

"If she even did," Sommers added. "I don't trust Newberry as far as I can throw him."

"I don't either," Julia agreed, "but I'm not sure he's lying about this. Alexandra might well have gone to him for money. If she wanted to keep it quiet, I mean. It wouldn't have been the first time."

"What?" Sommers gasped. "What do you mean not the first time?"

Julia lifted her head slightly again to reply. "Remember that waterfront condo expansion she wanted to do in Madison Park? Two dozen units on a pier sticking into Lake Washington. She couldn't get any of the banks to fund it because it was too risky. And they were right. She could never get the permits approved. But she got seed money from Newberry. They go way back, apparently."

"I never knew that." Sommers frowned. "How did you know? Did she tell you or something?"

'Tell you and not me' was the subtext of Sommers's question.

"No, I found out accidentally," Julia assured her. "I was at her office, talking about something I don't even remember, when her assistant walked in and started talking about the deal without realizing I was there. I asked her if she was really doing a deal with Newberry."

"What did she say?" Sommers asked.

"Better the devil you know," Julia answered.

"I've heard that before," Raine commented. "Speaking of which, Caroline is striking a deal with the same devil. She's going to claim she had an oral agreement with Alexandra for the business and Newberry is going to drop her from the lawsuit. Then, if she wins, with his help, she'll pay him back from Alexandra's assets."

"Before running the rest of the business into the ground like she did to her own company," Julia finished. She shook her head as much as was possible in the face rest. "Alexandra deserves better than that for her legacy. She built that company from the ground up."

"That's why we're here," Sommers said.

"To make sure I didn't join Caroline?" Julia asked. "Don't worry. I don't need to lie to be successful. Well, not in a lawsuit anyway. I can't say I never embellish a little when needed. We're in sales after all. *Caveat emptor* and all that."

"Please turn over now, Ms. Kim," Paolo said in perfect English.

Raine became even more suspicious of Paolo's lack of comprehension but didn't have time to think much about it before Julia pushed herself up and turned over, pulling the sheet over herself again. She was definitely naked. He instinctively looked away even though she was covered up now.

"We need to get our hands on all of Alexandra's business records," Sommers mused. "Everything that would go to any transfer of assets. Sales agreements, partnership agreements, even her will."

"Especially her will," Raine put in. "If we can show that the partnership agreement Meredith allegedly signed is a fraud and also show that Caroline is an opportunist and a liar with no oral agreement, that would leave her will. Maybe Ernest gets everything."

Sommers and Julia both laughed.

"Ernest won't get everything," Sommers said. "He'll get enough to take care of him, but that's it."

Julia agreed. "Alexandra loved him, but she would never leave her business to him. She gave him an allowance, but even then, she monitored all of his purchases. He's handsome and loyal, but he's terrible with money. I think that was part of what she liked about him. He wasn't a threat to her success."

"So, we need the will and whatever else she might have prepared," Sommers confirmed.

Raine was about to suggest a visit to Alexandra's business office when Julia interjected.

"Well, don't go to her lawyer, Chenoweth or whatever his name was," she said calmly. Far calmer than Raine or Sommers would have been able to say, given their additional knowledge regarding that particular lawyer.

"Why?" Sommers managed to ask with a sideways glance at Raine.

Was? Raine noticed. But he didn't say anything aloud.

"Didn't you hear?" Julia opened her eyes and looked backward at her guests. "He's dead. Fell down the stairs or something. Poor guy."

Raine wasn't sure what to say. Sommers got an excuse not to reply. She looked down at her phone, which was suddenly lighting up. Raine looked at the number on the screen. He didn't recognize the number, but he did know the prefix.

"Take that," he told her. He jerked his head toward the hallway behind them.

Sommers hesitated, then excused herself and stepped out of the office.

"Thank you for your time, Ms. Kim," Raine ended their visit. They had confirmed Julia was on their side. That was the goal, and he didn't feel comfortable alone in the dark room with her and Paolo. Besides, he was pretty sure he was about to have something else to do.

"Anytime, Dan," Julia answered without opening her

eyes. "Keep me posted. And please close the door on your way out."

Raine did as he was asked and met Sommers in the hallway outside Julia's office. She was just hanging up the call. Her expression was one of complete disbelief.

"That was Meredith," she confirmed Raine's suspicion. "They just arrested her for the murder of Duncan Chenoweth."

17

R aine couldn't decide whether to hurry to the King County Jail or not to bother rushing because it was already too late. He just hoped Meredith had remembered his advice to lawyer up and let him do the talking.

They parked the car as near as they could, which was still several blocks away, and walked back to the lobby of the gray cement structure. Just like the times before, they exchanged their drivers' licenses for visitor badges and made their way up to attorney-client meeting cubicles. And just like last time, Meredith Beauchamp stepped into the opposite side of the partitioned room, dressed in red scrubs and facing a murder charge.

"I didn't say anything this time," she was eager to report, managing a nervous smile despite the circumstances.

"Good." Raine let himself exhale. "Did they say anything to you? Did they tell you why they arrested you? What evidence they had against you? Whatever they told you to try to make you talk, do you remember any of it?"

Meredith nodded. "My fingerprint. They said they found my fingerprint on Duncan's doorbell."

"Damn it," Raine hissed as he put his head in his hand. "I should have thought of that."

"Don't be too hard on yourself, Dan." Sommers put a hand on his shoulder. "That seems like a pretty weak basis for a murder case to me. How many murderers ring the doorbell first?"

That was a good point, Raine supposed. The more suspicious location for a fingerprint would be on the front door. Where he left his own print.

"They also looked at my phone and saw that I drove near the house that morning," Meredith added. "But I already told you that I drive by there on my way downtown from my own house."

"Did you tell them that?" Raine asked.

"I wanted to," Meredith answered, "but no. You said not to say anything."

"How did they get your phone?" Raine probed. "Did they have a warrant at the ready?"

"Warrant?" Meredith cocked her head. "No, they just asked me for it."

"And you gave it to them?" Sommers's incredulity matched Raine's.

"Apparently, I should have said don't give anything to the cops either," Raine said. "I thought that was implied."

"I'm sorry." Meredith choked back a sob. "I didn't know what to do. I don't want to be back in here. I can't do this again. I just can't!"

Raine took a moment before answering. One of his earliest mentors had taught him a phrase to use whenever a client needed to hear the hard truth and not just words of encouragement. The phrase was, 'I'm your lawyer, not your cheerleader.'

And the hard truth was, Meredith was not getting out of jail again any time soon. If ever. In Judge Brenner's eyes, the exact thing he had been afraid of had happened: he had lowered a murder defendant's bail, and the defendant murdered again. He was going to raise her bail on the old case to five million and he was going to set bail on the new case at a hundred-bazillion-gazillion. The only way she was getting out again was if a jury said, "Not guilty." Twice.

But cheerleader or no, he needed Meredith to maintain some modicum of hope. No, she wasn't getting out before the trial, or trials, but there was still a chance she would get out after that.

"I'm not going to lie to you, Meredith," he began. "This is not a good development. You know that already because you're back in jail. The judge is going to raise your bail and he's going to set an even higher bail on the new case. You need to get used to the idea that you're going to be in jail until the case is over."

"Wow." Sommers looked sideways at him. "Great pep talk, Dan."

"But," he raised a finger and didn't respond directly to Sommers, "there is some good news. A silver lining to this dark cloud of murder."

"What's that?" Meredith sniffed. Her eyes were welling but she was trying hard to keep herself together.

"We know you didn't kill Duncan," Raine answered, "and if the prosecution oversteps and tries hard to link these murders, then we might just be able to prove your innocence of Alexandra's murder by proving you didn't kill Duncan either."

"That seems..." Sommers put in, "risky."

"I didn't kill Duncan," Meredith insisted. "And I didn't kill Alexandra."

"I know." Raine tried to soothe her. "So, trust me at the arraignment tomorrow. It might look like I'm not fighting for you, but I will be. It just won't be the standard boxing match."

"What will it be?" Sommers asked.

"Judo," Raine answered. "We're going to use their own strength against them."

18

The problem with judo was that it required two combatants. When it was time for the arraignment on Meredith's newest murder charge, Raine's opponent stepped onto the mat and immediately called time out.

"A seventy-two-hour hold?" Raine looked at the single piece of paper Scarborough handed him when he entered Judge Brenner's courtroom. "You're not charging her?"

"Not today," Scarborough confirmed. "The investigation isn't complete. We're going to ask the judge to find probable cause for the charge and set bail, but then set the arraignment over two more days for us to make a final charging decision."

"Make the decision now," Raine challenged. "If you don't have enough to charge her now, you won't have any more in two days. She's not going to confess; I can tell you that."

Scarborough pursed his lips. "I assumed as much now that you're involved. And I don't need you to tell me how to do my job. The court rules allow us to proceed this way, and this is the way we're going to proceed."

"Fine." Raine shrugged. "So, we agree to release her and see if you file charges. I mean, no reason to impose more bail if you might not even charge her, right?"

Scarborough blinked at Raine several times. "That's not how the rules work. We can—"

"I know how the rules work, Kevin," Raine used his first name to bother him. "I'm talking about something larger than court rules. I'm talking about justice. We don't put people in jail while we decide whether they might be guilty."

Scarborough blinked again. "We do that all the time. The court rules—"

"Ugh." Raine cut off Scarborough with a raise of his hand. "Never mind. I'll tell it to the judge."

Scarborough nodded. "Good. I'll tell the bailiff we're ready."

Raine took his position at the bar and nodded to the guard. They knew which case he was there on. The guard opened the secure door to the holding cells and called for Meredith even as the bailiff called for the judge.

A few moments later everyone was assembled and the bailiff called out, "All rise! The King County Superior Court is in session, the Honorable Henry Brenner presiding!"

Brenner looked at his paper docket. "Are the parties ready on the matter of the State of Washington versus Meredith Beauchamp?" He paused and looked at the docket again. "There are two matters now?"

"Maybe," Raine spoke out of turn, his frustration at the situation getting the better of him momentarily.

Brenner frowned at him, then turned to Scarborough. "Are there new charges against Ms. Beauchamp?"

"Kevin Scarborough on behalf of the State of Washington, Your Honor," Scarborough started by making his appearance for the record. All very formal and proper. Then, to the judge's question. "The State is seeking a seventy-two-hour hold on Ms. Beauchamp while we consider filing additional charges."

"Additional charges related to the original charge?" Brenner gestured for Scarborough to hand forward the paperwork he was still holding at the ready.

"Not directly, Your Honor," Scarborough answered. He gave the paperwork to the bailiff, who passed it up to the judge; he also handed Raine his copies. The packet consisted of that one-page order for a seventy-two-hour hold, as well as a two-page declaration for determination of probable cause for the new charge, the murder of Duncan Chenoweth.

Judge Brenner frowned as he read the summary of the investigation so far. "This is troubling," he commented as he finished reading and looked up again. He looked to Raine. "Have you had a chance to review this, Mr. Raine?"

"I have, Your Honor," Raine answered, "just now. I have no objection to the State failing to file additional charges today. Ms. Beauchamp is more than ready to go home again. So, if we could just go ahead and release her on this new arrest and schedule a court date in two days, we will be happy to return to see whether the State has been able to scrape up more evidence than the apparently insufficient amount they currently possess."

The judge smiled down at Raine. "That's not how this works, Mr. Raine. You know that."

Raine did know that. That didn't mean he liked it. Or that he had to just accept it. "It should be how it works, Your

Honor. If the government wants to charge my client with a crime, then do it. If they can't, then let her go. It seems pretty simple to me, Your Honor. Let's not overthink it. Just because the court rules allow for a particular procedure doesn't mean it's the right procedure."

"I would disagree, Your Honor," Scarborough put in.

"Of course you would," Raine sneered.

"Enough!" Brenner bellowed. "Enough. Mr. Raine. This procedure is permitted under the court rules, and it is permitted for a reason. Sometimes a crime is so serious that a potential suspect cannot simply be allowed to walk out the door while the police gather the evidence necessary to charge the case."

"And sometimes, the police don't have the evidence and want to hold someone anyway." Raine wasn't about to be intimidated by a judge's raised voice. He could raise his too. "If they need a few more days, or a few more years, to find enough evidence to solve this murder, that's fine. Ms. Beauchamp is already out on a million dollars bail. She's not going anywhere."

"She's going to prison," Scarborough chimed in.

Brenner scowled at him. Raine actually appreciated seeing a little spark in his opponent. Although he detested the sentiment.

Raine pointed to his opponent. "Mr. Scarborough is getting ahead of himself, Your Honor. In more ways than one. I think we should all slow down and let the process work itself out. In the meantime, however, no one should lose their liberty. I propose setting a hearing in two days for everyone here to return. If Mr. Scarborough believes he has unsurfaced enough evidence to charge my client with the murder of Duncan Chenoweth, then he can file the complaint at that time, and we can discuss bail on both cases. If, as I suspect, he has not found enough evidence to file charges, then nothing has changed and nothing needs to be changed. We can all wish each other well and return to our preparations for the trial which is rapidly approaching."

It was an eminently reasonable position to propose. But he was the defense attorney, so he lost.

"We will schedule a hearing in two days' time, Mr. Raine," Judge Brenner said, "but I will not simply be releasing your client pending that hearing."

Raine was disappointed but in no way surprised. He looked to his client. Meredith looked devastated as she realized she had no hope of getting out of jail again before the trial.

"I have had a chance to review the State's declaration for determination of probable cause and I do find that there are facts sufficient to hold Ms. Beauchamp over for forty-eight more hours while the State finishes its investigation."

The judge looked directly at Raine. "Do you remember what I told you the last time we discussed bail for your client, Mr. Raine? Do you remember the one thing I was the most worried about if I set bail too low and your client posted it? Do you?"

Raine could only nod. "I do, Your Honor."

"What was it, Mr. Raine?" Brenner pressed. "What was I the most afraid might happen?"

"That Ms. Beauchamp might commit further offenses," Raine answered.

"Yes!" Judge Brenner slapped the bench. "And I would say that murder certainly qualifies as a new offense."

"I should point out, Your Honor," Raine responded, "that

even the prosecutor admits there is currently insufficient evidence to charge Ms. Beauchamp with that crime."

"Do you really think," Brenner asked him, "we're all going to be back here in two days for Mr. Scarborough to say, 'Never mind'?"

Raine did not think that. "I certainly hope so," he said.

"I think it unlikely," the judge scoffed. He sat upright in his chair and looked down at the prosecutor. "What is the State's recommendation regarding bail?"

"I would again recommend three million dollars, Your Honor," Scarborough answered. "On each case."

"Six million dollars?" Raine laughed darkly. "That's it? Not ten million? Twenty?"

"That's enough, Mr. Raine," Brenner growled. "If I had listened to Mr. Scarborough on the first case, perhaps there wouldn't even be a second case. I will follow the State's recommendation as to bail on the two cases."

"Did the Court wish to hear from the defense before making its decision?" Raine interjected. That was the usual procedure.

"I think I've heard quite enough from you today. Mr. Raine," Judge Brenner replied. "I know what your recommendation would have been, and I am rejecting it. I will see you in two days."

"But—" Raine tried.

"This matter is concluded," Judge Brenner declared. And that meant that it was.

Scarborough hurried to the exit, lest Raine continue to try to get Brenner to revisit his ruling.

The guard who had been standing motionless behind Meredith stepped forward and grabbed her shoulders to guide her back to the holding cells.

"So, that's it?" she whimpered. "I'm stuck in jail forever?"

"No," Raine answered. "I have two days to stop these charges from being filed and get you back out on your original bail."

"How will you do that?" Meredith pleaded as the guard pulled her away.

Raine didn't actually know, but he could hardly tell her that. He put on his most confident expression. "Trust me."

19

"The key to this case is whatever document Alexandra drafted to pass her business on to you five." Raine glared out his conference room window, hands clasped behind his back, eyes focused on nothing.

"You don't think it was that partnership agreement Meredith signed?" Sommers asked from her seat at the conference table. "Allegedly signed," she corrected.

Raine turned around. "I might," he admitted, "even though Meredith insisted she didn't sign it. That would make it a forgery, but she might also be lying to me. It wouldn't be the first time a client was afraid to tell me the truth if it made them guilty."

"So why don't you think that's the document?" Sommers asked.

"Because no one else does," Raine explained. "Elisabeth Ungermann doesn't think that's the real document. Whoever murdered Duncan Chenoweth definitely didn't think so. There's something else, and everyone is trying to find it."

"We need to find it first," Sommers said.

"Agreed," Raine replied. "But it isn't like we haven't tried. We have what the cops found. It wasn't on the files from Alexandra's personal computer. We tried to get it from Chenoweth, and I tried to get it from Ungermann. No luck anywhere."

"There's one more place we can try," Sommers said.

"Where?" Raine asked.

"Her real office," Sommers answered. "If it's still open."

Raine frowned. "Maybe we should have started there."

"No," Sommers consoled. "There would have been dozens of people there, all worried about whether they were going to lose their jobs. It was better to go where there were fewer people. And there will definitely be fewer people now. Anyone with any sense will have left for another job."

"You think so?" Raine questioned.

"Boss is murdered and the most likely people to take over are in jail and/or being sued?" Sommers posited. "Yeah, it's time for a new job. It's past time for anyone dependent on Alexandra Pruitt to move on."

ANYONE EXCEPT CAITLIN KENNEDY.

When Raine and Sommers arrived at the stand-alone building in Seattle's Beacon Hill neighborhood that served as the main offices for the Pruitt real estate empire, there was only one employee left, and she was packing up boxes.

"Caitlin?" Sommers called out as they walked through the door.

Caitlin was on the other side of the lobby with her back to the door. She turned around and clenched her fists when she saw them. "What are you doing here? Didn't you cause enough trouble at the condo?"

They had in fact caused quite a bit of trouble at the condo. Raine looked down at his hand. The cut was mostly healed but he still kept it covered with a light wrap of gauze.

"Sorry about that," he offered.

"This is different," Sommers assured. "Or at least no one is going to get into a knife fight this time. I hope. But we are here for the same reasons. We're trying to figure out what Alexandra's plan for her business was. It's the key to Meredith's defense."

"Maybe Meredith shouldn't be defended," Caitlin responded. "Maybe she's guilty. Maybe she should go to prison for the rest of her life for what she did."

"Maybe," Raine allowed, "but only if she did it."

"Tell her, Dan." Sommers pushed him forward. He took a few uncertain steps toward Caitlin while Sommers stayed back by the door.

"We need to find the documents necessary to prove she didn't do it," Raine continued, "and we think they might be here."

Caitlin laughed, a full, dark laugh. "Well, you're too late. There's nothing left here. Just the stuff no one else wanted. Need an empty stapler? What about a chipped coffee mug? I think there's some paper clips in the back, maybe a few rubber bands."

"What about the computers?" Raine ventured.

"Or paper files?" Sommers added. "Alexandra loved paper files."

"Gone and gone," Caitlin seemed almost happy to report. "The police took everything."

Raine raised a hand to his forehead. "Of course they did. When?"

"After Alexandra's lawyer was murdered," Caitlin answered. "I heard Meredith did that too. Great client you have there. You better win the case, or she might kill you too."

Raine frowned at Sommers, who returned the expression.

"Well, do you mind if we look around anyway?" Raine asked. "Maybe we'll find something helpful after all."

"You know what?" Caitlin stood up straight and pushed a fist onto her hip. "I do mind. I mind very much. You had no right to do what you did to Ernest, and you have no right to be here now. I just need to finish my work, and I can finally get on with my life. It's what Alexandra would have wanted."

Raine wasn't sure he could argue with that, or needed to. "We'll stay out of your way."

"Damn right you will," Caitlin answered. She suddenly seemed fiercer than her youth would have suggested. "The police have been here once. I won't hesitate to call them back. There's nothing more for you here. I just want you to leave me alone and let me finish what I set out to do."

There was no talking to her, Raine decided. "Fine. Thanks anyway. We'll show ourselves out."

"I should hope so," Caitlin huffed and she turned her attention back to the box she was packing. "Don't let the door hit you on the way out. Or do. I don't care. Just leave."

Sommers didn't seem ready to give up, but she acceded to Raine's decision to leave. Once they were outside, she questioned it. "You gave up pretty easily."

Raine shrugged. "That place has been cleaned out.

There's nothing of value in there. Especially if the police already took everything."

"I bet they didn't take everything," Sommers said, with a knowing smile.

"Thumb drive," Raine realized. "Do you think she did the same thing here?"

Sommers nodded. "I do. It may not have anything more than what was on the computers the cops took, but I'm sure they didn't find it. I bet Caitlin didn't either. But when the movers arrive and take the furniture away, it'll be gone forever."

Raine considered their options. "Whatever the police took, I'll get a copy of it, but they don't have to give it to me until after they file charges. That'll be too late."

"Looks like we have a date tonight." Sommers grinned. Then she held up a door key. "This was on the windowsill by the door. I grabbed it when you were arguing with Caitlin. It's not breaking and entering if you have a key."

Raine nodded. "It's not breaking, but it's still entering. But what's a little more trespassing among friends."

20

Raine considered the elements and defenses to burglary as they returned to Alexandra's business after midnight. How they entered wasn't really determinative. What mattered was knowing they weren't supposed to be there and whether they intended to commit a crime inside. Obviously, breaking out a back window and climbing in would suggest knowledge of unauthorized entry. Using a key helped, until the part about stealing it earlier in the day. Still, with no intent to commit a crime inside, it wasn't burglary. The crime inside would be theft—theft of the thumb drive—but Raine told himself it wasn't theft to take something no one even knew was there.

"You seem nervous," Sommers whispered as they snuck up to the back of the empty building, crouching to prevent being seen and doing their best to avoid the light from nearby streetlights. A light rain was beginning to fall.

"Just thinking about my bar license," Raine whispered back, wrinkling his nose against the rain.

"Think of all the clients beating down your door,"

Sommers suggested, "when you get Meredith acquitted of not one, but two murders."

Raine nodded. That would be a trick. And would definitely help business. Still, he was having doubts whether they were really going to find that definitive of a smoking gun—or smoking thumb drive.

"Second thoughts?" Sommers asked as they reached the back door.

"More like fifth or sixth thoughts," Raine answered. But if they were going to go inside, they should hurry before their shoes got wet and they squeaked with every step. "Let's just do this and hope for the best. The worst that happens is we don't find anything, or we do and it's worthless. Then I'll deal with whatever the cops found when they examined the computers. It'll probably be in the first dump of discovery I get at Meredith's new arraignment."

"That's the spirit." Sommers patted him on the shoulder. "Now, let's break and enter."

"It's not called—" Raine stopped himself when he realized Sommers was teasing him. He appreciated his partner's efforts to keep his mind off the possible negative results of their endeavor. "Right. Go on, then."

Sommers produced the key she had lifted from the office earlier that day.

Raine wondered whether Caitlin even noticed it was gone. Probably, but she seemed fairly upset, and not particularly organized just then. It was probably difficult work winding down the personal and professional operations of the woman you were the professional assistant to. He wondered what she would do next. It was tough luck to get a job like that only to lose it within a year because of someone else's criminal actions, even if that someone else wasn't Meredith. Probably.

The key worked and made only the slightest click as Sommers unlocked the door. She turned the knob slowly and quietly and pushed the door open the same way. They hurried inside and she closed the door behind them.

"Where's her office?" Raine asked.

Sommers took a moment. "I've been here before, but it's been a while. And it was daytime." She extracted one of the two small flashlights they brought from her pocket. She turned it on and pointed it straight down. Raine kept his turned off, for the time being anyway. "It will take me a minute to figure out how to get there in the dark."

Raine had no choice but to follow his literal partner in crime. He certainly had no idea where Alexandra's office was. He supposed maybe the upper floor of the two-story building. Maybe an open penthouse-like suite looking out at the city she had spent a lifetime buying and selling piece by piece. But he didn't know where the stairs were.

"This way," Sommers whispered. She found the stairway easily enough and led them up the winding staircase.

Raine felt some small pride at having guessed at least that much correctly. He hoped Sommers was equally correct about a thumb drive being taped to the bottom of the desk that might or might not still be there.

The upstairs was not a large penthouse, but rather a narrow hallway of doors, most of which were open to varying degrees. Raine turned on his flashlight to shine into each room in turn. The walls were bare and various papers and random office supplies littered the floors. About half of them still had furniture in them, buoying Raine's hope that

Alexandra's desk would be there to greet them when they reached her office at the end of the hall.

When they reached the final door, centered in the end of the hallway, Sommers paused. It was closed.

Raine's heart dropped. What if it was locked? The outdoor key, a copy of which every employee probably had, was unlikely to also open the boss's office.

"What's wrong?" he whispered. "It's not locked, is it?"

Sommers shook her head. "No. I just... I thought I heard something."

Raine turned to the darkness behind them and strained to hear any sound other than his own breathing.

Nothing.

"Just nerves," Sommers whispered after a moment. "This isn't how I would have wanted to treat Alexandra after her death."

"Don't think of it as how you're treating Alexandra," Raine counseled. "Think of it as how you're treating Meredith. This may be our last chance to figure out why Alexandra was killed, and that will lead us to who did it."

Sommers nodded, barely perceptible in the reflection of the flashlight off the floorboards. "Ready?"

Raine nodded, and Sommers reached for the doorknob.

It turned without any problem and Sommers pushed open the door to her dead mentor's office.

It held the same half-abandoned feel as the other offices on the floor, even if it was three times the size. The walls were bare, and the floor was mostly bare as well. No stray papers, although Raine suspected there were paperclips and staples wedged into the carpet. More importantly, however, Alexandra's desk was still there, positioned to take advantage of that view Raine had hypothesized.

"There's her desk," Sommers whispered, somewhat unnecessarily, and she hurried over to it.

Raine stepped in the general direction of the desk but hung back. There wouldn't be room for both of them under there anyway. He raised his beam and guided it across the room to glean some feel for the person his client was supposed to have murdered. Maybe there was something that could help him gain an insight that could turn the case in his favor.

Or maybe not.

"There's no thumb drive," Sommers reported in a hushed voice from under the desk.

Raine rushed over to her. "Are you sure? Maybe it's in a different place?"

"No, there's no thumb drive taped under the desk." Sommers crawled back out from under the desk. She held up a small brass key stuck to a length of black electrical tape. "But this was."

Sommers handed it to Raine. He shone his flashlight on it. It was small, too small for a door. More like a locker, a safety deposit box. He was about to offer his assessment, when the sound of a wet shoe squealing downstairs changed the subject.

"Someone else is here!" Sommers hissed, dropping into a crouch.

Raine shoved the key into his pocket and squatted down as well. He held a finger to his lips, then turned off his flashlight. Sommers nodded and turned off her light as well. The darkness rang in their ears.

Several questions raced through Raine's mind. The most obvious was, who was inside the building with them? The next most obvious was, why? Then came the more personal questions: Would the person find them? And if so, what would the person do? Raine became very aware that he hadn't brought any weapon short of the small flashlight in his hand. That was unlikely to be effective against pretty much any actual weapon their co-burglar might have brought.

In any event, the best result for them would be to remain undiscovered until whoever had joined them left again. That was a reasonable goal if the person had, like them, come with some intent to steal something within—perhaps it was a drug addict looking for copper wire to strip for pawn. The goal was considerably less attainable if the person had come not for copper wire, but for them. As if in support of the latter theory, the slow creak of careful footsteps on the stairs filled the silence.

There was enough ambient light from the streetlights to allow Raine and Sommers to see each other's faces. Raine pointed toward the desk and made a gesture he hoped communicated that they hide behind it. Sommers nodded in reply and lowered herself onto her hands and knees to crawl behind the desk. Raine gave her a moment, then followed behind, praying the floor didn't squeak like the stairs under their visitor's feet.

But of course it did. Only one squeak, but it was unmistakable. The creak of the weight of a grown man pressing down then releasing from a decades-old floorboard.

The only sound worse than the creak under Raine was the sudden cessation of the slow and steady creaks on the stairs.

They had been heard. Located. The desk would only delay their discovery. Flight was not going to work. Raine finished his otherwise silent journey behind the desk and prepared for the fight.

He didn't have to wait long. The slow creaks on the stairs turned into confident strides in the hallway and, almost before Raine could react, running across Alexandra's office to their hiding place. Raine steeled himself. There was a chance it was someone he didn't want to hit. Caitlin, perhaps, responding to a silent alarm they hadn't considered. Or a security guard doing the same. That addict who just wanted some copper wire. It was like one of those combat simulations with the figures that popped out of doorways and windows. Shoot the bad guys, don't shoot the civilians, split second to decide.

Raine jumped to his feet, ready to throw the first punch, unsure whether he should.

Man. Tall. All black clothing. Ski mask over face. Large flashlight in hand, a veritable club. Eyes wide, then narrowing. Inches away.

Not Caitlin, not a security guard. If it was an addict looking for valuables to pawn, he wasn't looking to leave Raine and Sommers to their own criminal activity. The arm with the flashlight started backward to wind up for a debilitating blow to Raine's head.

Raine didn't have time to throw that hard of a punch before the flashlight struck him first. So instead, he threw a fast jab into the man's stomach, knocking the breath out of him and momentarily staving off any swing of the flashlight as he stumbled backward and doubled over.

Raine knew to press his advantage. He stepped toward the man and drove a knee into his lowered head. He missed the nose, his knee glancing off the man's forehead. The pain to Raine's knee probably exceeded whatever the man experienced from the strike, but it sent him off balance again. Raine pushed off his other leg and tackled the man to the floor. There was less chance of getting brained with the flashlight if they were on the ground, especially if the man dropped it as they fell.

No such luck, however. Raine landed on top of the man, but he managed to keep his grip on the flashlight. He swung it and landed a weak blow to the back of Raine's head. It wasn't enough to endanger Raine's consciousness, but it still hurt. Raine reared up and delivered a punch to the side of the man's face. He'd aimed for the nose, but the man turned his head as the punch landed. Another bang of the flashlight to the back of Raine's head. Another punch to the side of the man's face, just under his eye.

Raine expected a third strike of the flashlight and tensed against it, but that only served to allow the man to push Raine off him. Raine fell onto his back and instinctively raised his hands to cover his face from the anticipated clubbing from the flashlight.

Instead, however, the man pushed himself to his feet and ran for the door.

"Don't let him get away!" Sommers yelled.

But Raine decided that was exactly what he was going to do. He reached up and touched the back of his head. He could feel the slickness of blood on his fingertips. He'd been fortunate not to have been injured further. And he'd gotten a few good licks in. He'd call it a win.

"Nah, I think we're good," Raine responded. "He's not coming back."

Sommers didn't argue. She had turned to look out the window. Raine could see that because her face was suddenly lit up by a red and blue strobe from the street.

"The police!" he exclaimed. "We need to get out of here."

"That wasn't a cop, was it?" Sommers asked even as Raine grabbed her wrist and pulled her toward the hallway and the stairs and exit beyond.

"That was definitely not a cop," Raine answered. "Now, come on. If you can see their lights, it's already too late."

Raine's warning proved prophetic. A glance through the lobby showed two parked patrol cars and the silhouettes of two patrol officers approaching the front door.

They had to go out the way they came. Raine led the way, but kept his grip on Sommers's arm lest they get separated. But when he threw open the back door, he not only let go of Sommers's arm, but he did so after shoving the key in her hand and flinging her out of sight into the darkest corner of the room.

"Dan Raine?" Detective Olivia Kahale said as he came face to face with the detective from the night of Alexandra's murder. He recognized her even with the hood of her raincoat over her head. "The attorney?"

"Guilty as charged," Raine quipped, although he immediately regretted it. He told himself it was the head injury that led to that most unfortunate choice of words.

"If you say so," Kahale laughed. "You're under arrest for burglary."

21

There were several reasons not to talk with the cops and only one good reason to do so. The reason to do it was the rare occasion when an honest explanation of your conduct is believed and exonerates you from suspicion. That was beyond rare. If you were already in the interrogation room, there was a reason, and the cops were unlikely to give up on that reason just because they might be wrong.

The other catch to that approach was that it really did need to be the truth. Lying to a cop about anything that might be material to a pending investigation was a crime in and of itself. If a cop walks up to you out of the blue and asks you your name, you can say, "Mickey Mouse," because it's not material to anything important. But if you're sitting in Interrogation Room B of the Seattle Police Department's main precinct, anything you say is material to something important. If you were going to lie, you needed to be sure you were going to get away with it.

Which led Raine to his conundrum. He had a reasonable

explanation as to why Detective Kahale found him inside his murder client's murder victim's business after midnight. It wasn't a true explanation, but it was reasonable. It could have been true. And it was supported by the physical evidence of the laceration on the back of his head.

He was out late at night, thinking about the case or whatever, when he decided to drive by the business offices of his client's alleged victim. He didn't know what he might find so late at night, but it was a mostly free country so he figured he'd go and see what he might see. But when he got there, he observed a masked figure sneaking into the building. Should he have stayed outside and called the police? Of course. But hindsight is twenty-twenty and he made the different decision to go in after the man and stop whatever nefarious misdeeds he had planned. Add something about being a man and being overconfident in his own strength and power to win any fight. Once inside, however, the true burglar surprised him and struck him in the back of the head with his giant flashlight, then escaped into the night. Someone else must have called the police and they arrived just as he was leaving the building to call the police himself.

It was a good story. The problem Raine had was that he had no idea how much information Kahale had that could rebut all or part of it. It was a lie, after all. Maybe the 911 caller reported seeing a man and a woman entering the building. Maybe the cops had been there long enough to see all three of them enter. Were there cameras somewhere? Had they also arrested the other man and not told him? Raine could have been in a prisoner's dilemma without even knowing it.

No, the wiser decision was to hang onto that story, get whatever information he could from his captor, and be prepared to explain himself later, when he could tailor the story to fit the evidence, and probably through a lawyer, whose assertions would be inoculated from any accusation of criminal false statement. He wondered whether Sawyer would take the case. Probably not.

The door to the interrogation room unlocked with a loud clank and Detective Kahale pushed it open. She seemed pleased to see him. Like a cat seeing a mouse, especially a mouse handcuffed to a steel chair bolted to the floor. It was going to be a battle of wills, of intellects, of two experts in their adjacent fields, each trying to get information from the other without divulging any of their own data. A hint of a smile curled into the corner of Raine's mouth at the thought of the impending struggle. Glory to the victor, and no glory without battle.

"It looks like we made a mistake." Kahale stepped around and uncuffed Raine. "You're free to go."

"What?" Raine practically protested. "Why?"

Kahale took a moment. "Do you want us to not release you?"

"Well, no, of course not," Raine answered. He stood up and rubbed the soreness off his wrists. "But, I mean, can I get an explanation or something?"

"Do you want an explanation of why I arrested you when I found you inside your client's victim's business in the middle of the night after the security guard from the company that patrols several of the businesses up there called 911 to report someone entering the building?" Kahale asked. "Do you really need an explanation for that?"

Raine thought for a moment. "No, I suppose not. I can see why you did what you did. So why are you letting me go now?"

"The description of the security guard doesn't match you," Kahale answered, "or Ms. Sommers."

Raine's eyebrows shot up despite himself.

"Yes, we know she was with you," Kahale answered the question on Raine's face despite his effort to hide it. "I left an officer behind to watch the building. She left about thirty minutes later. You should be grateful we did see her."

"Why?" Raine went ahead and asked.

"Because I trust her a lot more than I trust you," Kahale explained. "I don't know what you were doing in there, but I know there was a third person, a man dressed in all black and carrying a large flashlight. That cut on the back of your head tells me you ran into him too."

Raine neither confirmed nor denied the source of his injury.

"So, I'm releasing you from custody," Kahale continued. "But I'd still like to talk with you."

"Talk with me?" Raine repeated the proposal back, uncertain what it meant. "Like, not as a suspect?"

"Right," Kahale confirmed. "As a witness, maybe. Or better yet, as an advocate for your client."

"Meredith?" Raine questioned. He finally shook his head. "I don't understand. You want to talk with Meredith? You know I can't allow it. First rule of criminal defense is, don't talk to the cops."

"Not Meredith, you," Kahale answered. "And what if talking to the cops helps your client get her charges dropped?"

Raine freely allowed his eyebrows to rise that time. "I'm listening."

"Sit down," Kahale said. It was an invitation, not an order. He had been formally released from custody after all.

His hands were free. The door was open. He could just walk out.

He sat down.

Kahale joined him. "The prosecutor thinks your client murdered Duncan Chenoweth while she was out on bail."

Raine nodded. "I'm aware."

"I think he's wrong," Kahale continued, quite to Raine's surprise.

"I think so too," Raine replied carefully. He still didn't trust a cop, and the conversation was strange enough that he couldn't tell where it was going. "I'm currently trying to prevent those charges from being filed."

"Do you want to know why I think he's wrong?" Kahale asked.

Raine did. He said as much.

"Three reasons," Kahale explained. She held up her fingers to count them off. "First, their case is based on your client's fingerprint being on the doorbell. Second, even if I think she might have been capable of doing it, I don't think you are. And third, your fingerprint is on the front door too."

Raine closed his eyes and tipped his head back. It wasn't an admission *per se,* but it was the next best thing.

"We have your prints because this isn't the first time you've been detained by the police," Kahale added.

"I'm aware of that too." Raine lowered his head again. He wasn't sure what to say. No handcuffs and open door aside, he certainly felt like he was a suspect again. He'd even been upgraded from burglar to murderer.

"So, when that fingerprint comparison came back from the lab, I set it aside," Kahale said. "I'll have to turn it over eventually. But it doesn't make sense for a lawyer to murder a potential witness to his case. You guys do a lot of crazy stuff.

Alcohol abuse, drug addiction, taking payment in the form of sexual favors, stealing client funds. Do you remember that public defender who had sex with her in-custody client up in the jail? That was nuts. She didn't even lose her license, just got a suspension. And you guys have a noticeably high suicide rate. I've been out to more than one attorney's office with brains on the ceiling. But you know what I've never seen? I've never seen a lawyer murder a witness. Scare them off from testifying? Sure. Pay them off? Definitely. But murder. No, that's too far."

Raine winced at the recitation of his profession's apparently obvious foibles. "Thanks?"

"But if you were there with her," Kahale continued, "and you didn't kill him, then it stands to reason she didn't either. At least not while you were there. And if you thought she had done it, you wouldn't have broken into Alexandra Pruitt's office to try to find some evidence of her innocence."

Raine did his best not to react. "No comment."

Kahale motioned toward his head. "I think you got the punishment you deserved for that act of stupidity. But if we're going to be partners, I will want you to tell me eventually if you find anything."

"I don't think I can be partners with the lead detective on my client's murder case," Raine protested.

"Even if it means keeping her from being charged with another murder?" Kahale questioned.

Raine frowned. "Unfortunately, yes. Scarborough is going to call you as a witness in the trial. His main witness. You're going to tell the jury you arrested Meredith for the murder. I'm going to have to cross-examine you and try to make the jury believe you were wrong. I'd be compromised in my duties to my client in that case if I enter into some side agreement with you about a different case."

"A related case," Kahale pointed out.

"That's worse," Raine replied. "You see how that's worse, right?"

"I see that your client is about to be charged with a murder I don't think she committed," Kahale answered, "and I don't want that to happen."

Raine cocked his head at the detective. "Why not?"

Kahale took a moment, then frowned at him. "Really? You don't know why not?"

Raine shook his head. "I really don't."

"How about the truth?" Kahale threw her hands up. "I care about the truth."

"Oh." Raine nodded. "That hadn't actually occurred to me."

"I find that distressing." Kahale crossed her arms.

"Not as distressing as Meredith Beauchamp finds being held in custody at the King County Jail," Raine responded. "Can you skip ahead to the part where you offer me something useful?"

"I'm offering to let you go for burglary and insulate you from murder charges," Kahale replied. "If that's not enough, I can put the cuffs back on."

"I thought you cared about the truth," Raine challenged.

Kahale smiled. "Tell me why you were there. At Chenoweth's. What were you trying to accomplish? What did you think he was going to tell you?"

Raine narrowed his eyes at the detective across the metal table. "Why do you want to know that?"

"Because whoever did kill him ransacked his home office and took everything even remotely related to Alexandra

Pruitt," Kahale explained. "If I know why you went there, I might be able to guess what the real killer took, and why."

Raine took a long, deep breath. Deals with the devil never worked out. Well, maybe for that kid in Georgia with the violin. But not for anyone else. On the other hand, he suddenly had an ally on the other side. He had complained about being compromised at trial. What he didn't mention was that she would be compromised too.

"Let me think about it," Raine finally said. "This is an unusual proposal. I need time to consider all of the ramifications."

"I can respect that," Kahale allowed, "but you better hurry. That arraignment is only one day away now. And I can only sit on that fingerprint match for so long."

Raine stood up to leave. He didn't try to shake Kahale's hand. They weren't partners yet.

"One question," Raine said. "I need you to answer one question for me."

"What is it?"

"Did you catch the other guy who was in Alexandra's office tonight?"

Kahale hesitated. Then she shook her head. "No. He got away."

Raine nodded. It was what he expected, but he appreciated the confirmation. He headed for the door.

"Is that a good thing?" Kahale asked after him.

Raine stopped and thought for a moment. "No, probably not."

22

"Fiona?" Sommers asked.

"Fiona," Raine answered.

Sommers rolled her eyes practically out of the back of her head. "She's the last person I want to talk to."

It was the next morning, or rather later that same morning. Raine had gone home and stolen a few hours of sleep before reconnecting with Sommers at his office after breakfast—and another quick trip to urgent care where they glued the skin on the back of his head together.

"She's the last person we can talk to," Raine returned. "After her, there's no one left. If she can't give us any insight into what Alexandra's real plan was, Meredith is going to be charged with Duncan's murder tomorrow, and then she's going to get convicted of both of them at trial."

Sommers dropped her head sideways at Raine. "You're her lawyer. Aren't you supposed to stop that from happening?"

"That's what I'm trying to do," Raine answered. "That's why we have to talk to Fiona."

"Ugh, fine," Sommers relented. "But we're driving separately so I can leave early if I just can't bear it anymore."

Raine didn't argue, but he did wonder what could possibly be so bad about Fiona Mendoza.

FIONA WORKED out of her home, a two-story, four-bedroom house in the suburbs. Mercer Island, to be specific—a literal island in the middle of Lake Washington, halfway between Seattle to the west and Bellevue to the east. Mercer Island was the most expensive suburb, in part because of its insular exclusivity. The only ways on or off the island were bridges to Seattle and Bellevue, and those were part of Interstate 90, which passed over the northernmost part of the island.

Fiona's house was halfway to the southern tip of the island. The house itself was actually nothing special, maybe even starting to look a little dated, but it was in the right zip code, so it was probably worth more than the astronomical bail Judge Brenner was going to impose on Meredith the next day if the trip to Fiona's proved as fruitless as the rest of Raine's efforts to date.

Fiona was working in her front garden when Raine pulled into the driveway. Sommers parked on the street—for a fast getaway, Raine guessed. When Fiona saw Raine, she seemed confused, but when Sommers walked up the drive to join him, she recognized her fellow Fab Fiver.

"Rebecca! What a pleasant surprise," Fiona called out. She pulled off her gardening gloves and set them on a small table she had set up for her pruning tools and a glass of what appeared to be iced tea. She walked across her lawn to her guests. "To what do I owe this unexpected pleasure?"

"Oh yeah," Raine whispered to Sommers, "she's a monster."

"You don't understand," Sommers replied. "Do you like candy?"

Raine frowned at the whispered question. "I mean, I guess so. Some candy."

"Think of a candy you really like," Sommers said. "Your favorite candy."

"Okay," Raine said after a moment. Mounds. He really liked Mounds bars. Simple but delicious. Dark chocolate over coconut. And no one else seemed to like them, so he never had to share.

"Now imagine eating a hundred thousand pieces of that candy," Sommers said. "Two hundred thousand. A million. Do you think you'd still like that candy?"

"Probably not," Raine admitted.

"Exactly," Sommers concluded. Then she threw open her arms and stepped toward their host. "Fiona, how are you holding up?"

Raine looked at the expertly manicured yard, her stylish gardening outfit, and that refreshing glass of iced tea and thought that Fiona was holding up just fine.

"Oh, Rebecca, I'm doing my best," Fiona answered. "But enough about me. You and your lawyer friend are in the thick of it, aren't you? I can't believe Meredith murdered Alexandra."

"She didn't," Raine put in. "Probably."

"Oh, I know," Fiona defended. "That's what I mean. I can't believe it. I don't believe it. It just doesn't make sense. Poor Meredith. I'm sure she appreciates how much you two are doing for her."

Raine was starting to taste that third or fourth Mounds bar. It was time to move on from the pleasantries.

"We were hoping you might have a few minutes to talk with us, Fiona," he said. "There's a piece missing from the puzzle and we're hoping you might help us find it."

"Oh! Well, that sounds very important indeed." Fiona's hands flittered like two birds unsure where to land. "Please, follow me. We'll be more comfortable on the porch."

The "porch" was the entire back section of the house, with a screened-in outdoor seating area the width of the house and facing the water, visible through the trees and houses between there and the shore. Somehow, Fiona already had a small table set with glasses and a full pitcher of iced tea.

"Can I offer you something to drink?" she said as they sat down on the outdoor wicker furniture with its overstuffed cushions. "Iced tea?"

"Thank you, yes," Raine accepted.

Sommers declined with a wave of her hand. "No. Thank you, Fiona. Let's just get this over with, shall we? What do you know about whatever Alexandra had planned for her business and us?"

"You mean the plan she was going to announce that night at her retirement party?" Fiona asked as she poured a glass of iced tea.

"Yes, exactly," Raine encouraged.

"Oh, I know all about it," Fiona answered. She handed Raine the full glass.

"What?" Raine asked. "Seriously?"

"Seriously," Fiona assured.

"How?" Sommers challenged. "How do you know when none of the rest of us do?"

Fiona thought for a moment. "I asked."

Raine smiled at that, but Sommers slapped a hand to her forehead. "You asked? Of course you did. You just walked up to Alexandra before she was ready to make her announcement, because of course you couldn't wait like the rest of us, and asked her what her plan was. And to make you go away, she told you. That actually makes too much sense."

Raine looked at Sommers for a moment. She must have eaten a lot of Mounds bars over the years. For his part, Raine was happy for the information he was about to receive.

"So, what was the plan, Fiona?" he asked. "What did she tell you?"

"She told me that she wanted the five of us to take over her business," Fiona explained. "She said she wanted it to be five equal shares. She said she looked into just leaving it to us in her will, but her lawyer, Duncan, told her there would be significant negative tax implications if she did that. Instead, he recommended making all of us partners with her. That way, when she passed away, the business would already be ours, but with one less partner."

"A partnership agreement?" Raine shook his head. "Exactly what the prosecutors said."

"She even showed it to me," Fiona continued. "It was several pages long. I'm not quite sure how many, but obviously a complicated and important legal document. On the last page there was a spot for her signature at the top, and then five spaces for each of us to sign."

"Had anyone signed it yet when you saw it?" Raine had to ask.

"Oh, no. No one had signed it," Fiona recounted. "So, I guess her business will pass through her will after all, whatever that says. I think Duncan drafted that for her too. He was really good at that sort of thing. It's a shame what happened to him. I hope they catch whoever did it."

"They think Meredith did it," Sommers growled.

"They do?" Fiona's eyes widened. "Oh dear. I hope not. That would really be just too much."

Yeah, those Mounds bars were starting to make Raine sick. He set his untouched glass of iced tea down on the wicker coffee table they were seated around. "Thank you for your time, Fiona. You gave us the information we came for."

"I hope it was helpful," Fiona offered.

"Not at all," Sommers spat. "It was the least helpful information possible. Affirmatively bad, in fact."

"Oh." Fiona looked down for a moment as she considered Sommers's words. "But it is the truth."

"I know," Raine said. "That's the worst part."

23

I t had been two days since Scarborough asked Judge Brenner for forty-eight hours to make a charging decision. Those forty-eight hours passed, and Scarborough made his decision: one count of aggravated murder in the first degree. A murder committed during the course of, or in furtherance of, a burglary. Mandatory life in prison.

Raine accepted his copy of the criminal complaint that Scarborough handed to him upon walking into the courtroom. He skimmed it, confirmed his worst fears, then looked up again.

"Aggravated Murder One?" Raine scoffed. "That all you got?"

"No, actually." Scarborough reached into his folder and extracted a second pleading. He handed it to Raine.

"Motion to Join Cases for Trial," he read the caption aloud. "You want to try the Duncan Chenoweth murder case at the same time as the Alexandra Pruitt murder case?"

"Yes," Scarborough answered.

"To the same jury?" Raine continued.

"Yes."

"In just under four weeks from today?"

Scarborough thought for a moment, but then provided another, "Yes."

"Ah, but you hesitated." Raine wagged a finger at him. "Four weeks is not enough time to get ready for a murder trial."

"It is if the murderer already murdered someone else," Scarborough returned. "I will be ready."

Raine had his doubts, and he was glad for them. Scarborough's hubris in thinking he could be ready in that short a period of time could work to Meredith's benefit. Or Scarborough really could get ready that fast and it would be Raine who was underprepared trying to get ready to defend his client against not one but two murders.

"They aren't even really related," Raine protested.

"They are if your client committed them both," Scarborough replied. "Killing Mr. Chenoweth to destroy documents which were evidence of her culpability for her murder of Ms. Pruitt. That seems very related indeed."

Raine nodded along but decided not to argue anymore.

"All rise!" shouted the bailiff. "The King County Superior Court is now in session. The Honorable Henry Brenner presiding."

The judge took his seat above the litigants and looked down to see Raine and Scarborough closest to the bar. "You're back again," he observed. "Is that matter ready?"

"It is ready, Your Honor," Scarborough reported.

Raine nodded in agreement, then nodded again to the guard.

A few moments later, Meredith was escorted into the courtroom.

"I expected to see you before this hearing," she whispered.

"I've been busy," Raine replied, also under his breath, "trying to find some evidence to convince the prosecutor not to charge you with Duncan's murder."

"Did you?" Meredith asked. She seemed to want to be hopeful, but Raine wasn't giving off hopeful vibes.

"No," he admitted. "Kind of the opposite."

"What?" Meredith squeaked, a bit too loudly. The judge and the court staff looked at her. She lowered her voice again. "What does that mean?"

But Raine shook his head. "We can't talk here. Just hang on. You're about to get railroaded."

Meredith blinked at her lawyer, then her shoulders dropped, and she turned to face the judge.

"This is the matter of The State of Washington versus Meredith Beauchamp," Judge Brenner announced for the record. Then, he corrected himself. "Actually, these are the matters of the State of Washington versus Meredith Beauchamp. The newer matter is on for a return after a seventy-two-hour hold. The older matter is tracking and on for a bail hearing, depending on the State's decision regarding the newer case. Mr. Scarborough, how will the State be proceeding on the newer case?"

Scarborough handed the original of the complaint to the bailiff. "The State is filing one count of aggravated murder in the first degree against the defendant. We would ask the Court to conduct the arraignment, then address bail on both cases."

Judge Brenner looked to Raine. "Does that sound good to you, Mr. Raine?"

"Not really, Your Honor," Raine answered. "It definitely

does not sound good to me that my client is being charged with a second murder, and upon the flimsiest of theories, one entirely dependent on the State's ability to prove the first murder they have unjustly charged her with."

"I meant," the judge grumbled, "is that proposed order of events this morning acceptable to the defense. I know you don't want your client charged with murder. I also know there's nothing you can do to stop it. Finally, we both know that we will be proceeding exactly as Mr. Scarborough suggested. I was only trying to be polite. Lesson learned."

"Thank you for the clarification, Your Honor," Raine replied. "The defense is ready to proceed as proposed."

"Proceed with the arraignment then." Judge Brenner waved a hand at the lawyers to begin.

"The State of Washington," Scarborough stated formally for the record, "has filed one count of murder in the first degree with aggravating factors against Meredith Ann Beauchamp for the premeditated intentional murder of Duncan Chenoweth, during the course of, or in furtherance of, a burglary, contrary to RCW 9A.32.030 and RCW 10.95.020.

"We would ask the defense to acknowledge receipt of the complaint, waiver further formal reading of the charges, and enter a plea."

Brenner raised an eyebrow at Raine.

"The defense acknowledges receipt of the complaint," he stated as if reading from the script he'd memorized hundreds of arraignments ago, "waives further formal reading, and asks the Court to enter a plea of not guilty to the charge of murder in the first degree with aggravating circumstances."

"A plea of not guilty will be entered," Judge Brenner

declared. "I will now hear from the parties regarding conditions of release. Please address both this case and also whether bail should be adjusted on the older case in light of this new allegation of criminal behavior."

Whether. Raine suppressed a scoff. *More like, how much should it be increased.*

"Am I getting out today?" Meredith ventured in another whisper.

Raine shook his head but kept his eye on the judge. "Absolutely not."

"The State is once again recommending the Court set bail at three million dollars," Scarborough began the bail hearing. The prosecution always went first. "And we are recommending that amount on both cases, for a total of six million dollars. Had the Court followed our bail recommendation, then perhaps—"

"No," Judge Brenner interrupted him. "Watch your words, Mr. Scarborough. We are discussing what bail to set today, not what bail should have been set before. Is that understood?"

Scarborough's face made it clear that he did not fully understand why he couldn't just tell the truth, but he did understand that he should move along regardless. "Yes. Well, then. So, that is our bail recommendation. Six million total. Hopefully that will keep the defendant behind bars long enough to protect any further potential victims."

Brenner scowled at Scarborough again but didn't say anything. Instead, he swung his head heavily to Raine. "Does the defense wish to be heard?"

The normal procedure in any hearing would be for the defense to respond after the prosecution made their argument. Judge Brenner asking Raine if he even wished to be heard was code for, "It won't matter anyway." Still, Raine had a job to do.

"Yes, Your Honor," he began. "Thank you. The defense is going to ask the Court to set bail in the matter at one million dollars and keep the bail at the one million dollars that was already posted. You see, Your Honor—"

Judge Brenner slammed his gavel onto the bench. "Bail will be set at three million dollars on each case. The one million dollars previously posted will be exonerated and all new bail will need to be posted, if possible."

"If possible" was also code. It meant, "that's probably not going to be possible." Not only could Meredith not scrape up six million in cash, but there was no bonding company in town who would risk posting it for her when she was accused of getting out and then killing again. It was hard to sue a bonding company for wrongful death, but it wasn't impossible.

"I can't post that," Meredith whispered to Raine.

"I know," he answered. "And so do they. That's the point."

"Now, let us discuss future court dates," Brenner moved the hearing to its next and last issue. "The trial in the older matter is already scheduled. Do the parties wish to schedule the pretrial on the new case for before or after the trial on the older case?"

"Actually, Your Honor," Scarborough replied, "the State is going to ask that the matters be joined for trial, and on our currently scheduled trial date." He handed the original of his motion to join to the bailiff, who passed it up to the judge.

"Have you seen this, Mr. Raine?" Brenner asked.

"I have, Your Honor," Raine answered.

"Are you prepared to address it now?" the judge asked.

"I am not, Your Honor," Raine responded. "I need time to consider the request, whether to resist it, and if so, on what grounds."

Brenner frowned. "That trial date is fast approaching."

"I'm aware of that, Your Honor," Raine said, "but I didn't create this situation."

"I believe Ms. Beauchamp is the one who created the situation," Scarborough interjected.

"Enough," Brenner warned. "Fine. We will set the motion to join for a hearing. How much time do you need, Mr. Raine?"

"The court rules require five days' notice, not counting weekends, for any hearing, Your Honor," Raine reminded everyone. "And I do know how this Court likes to adhere to the court rules."

Brenner nodded even as he suppressed a sneer. "Fine. Five court days. One week. The parties will return in one week for a ruling on whether this new case will be joined for trial with the older case. That won't give the parties much time to prepare."

Raine nodded. He was counting on that.

24

The week between the arraignment and the motion to join was filled mostly with the mundane tasks that tended to pile up between court hearings. Returning calls and answering emails, usually to people who were already irritated that you didn't respond immediately and doubly so that it took another few days to get to them.

Laura, Raine's office assistant, made sure he was filled with coffee, Sawyer was too busy with her own cases to see him during the week, and it was his weekend with the boys so whatever calls or emails didn't get returned by 5:00 on Friday were going to wait until Monday morning. Maybe even Tuesday.

The weekend with the boys was nice. Raine's condo could feel a little small for three people, especially when his older son was in a teenage funk, so Raine had rented a place north of the city on the water to get away from everything for a bit. Jordan, the younger boy, loved the beach and the pool and the ice cream shop up the block. Jason, the older one, loved staring at his phone. Or maybe he didn't love it—he seemed as moody while interacting with the device as any other time—but it was what he did most of the trip anyway.

It was a mixed weekend, but Raine forced himself to leave work at the office, at least until he could get back to it. One of the bright spots of weekends with his kids was the pickup and drop-off when he had a chance to talk, however briefly, with his ex-wife. Natalie was still living in their old house, so when he stood on the porch and made small talk while the boys got ready, he could almost pretend it was the old days before the divorce he never wanted anyway.

That weekend, however, Nat was already out of town when Raine arrived to pick up the boys; Jason was more than old enough to watch over his little brother for a few hours. And when he dropped them off, they jumped out of the car and ran to the house before Raine could even unbuckle his seat belt. The boys rushed inside, Nat never stepped into view, and Raine drove away, alone.

He wasn't in a hurry to go back to his empty condo, which had seemed too small on Friday but would seem too big on Sunday. He took the long way home, stopped for gas even though the tank was still half full, and cruised up and down the waterfront until the light rain that had started when he was at the gas station turned into a hard enough rain that he couldn't see the ferries on Elliott Bay anymore.

By the time he finally got home and parked his car in the garage under his condo building, he was ready for a good night's sleep. He was definitely not ready for what happened next.

"Raine!" a man shouted.

He froze for a moment, then pushed his back against his car and scanned the shadows surrounding the parked cars and cement columns that filled the garage. In theory it could have been one of those happy former clients or a long-lost friend from high school. But he knew it wasn't. There was a tire iron in the trunk, he thought. Maybe. He wasn't really sure. Cars didn't get flat tires nearly as often as they used to. He had never needed to take out the jack and spare. His gun was upstairs.

"Who's there?" he called back.

"It doesn't matter who we are," came a different voice. "We know who you are."

The additional voice and the use of 'we' let Raine know he was outnumbered. Unarmed and outnumbered. Not a fight he was likely to win. Time to talk.

"What can I do for you, then?" he called out into the cavernous garage. Maybe if he kept them talking long enough another resident would come down to their car. But it was late, and a Sunday night. Anyone who could afford a condo there probably needed to get up early the next morning to do so. "You need a lawyer?"

"No, but you might need a doctor if you don't do exactly what we say."

That was reasonably direct. Raine tried to glean some information from the voices: an accent, a speech impediment, an unusual cadence. But there was nothing that stood out. He'd need to see them. He wasn't afraid of another trip to the doctor.

"Well, that's not very friendly," he called back. He moved slowly but smoothly toward the back of his car and pressed the 'trunk open' button on the key fob in his pocket. A loud electronic double-beep echoed in the garage.

"Don't move!" came the shouted instruction that preceded his visitors showing themselves, a necessary step to stopping Raine from getting into his trunk. They didn't know his gun was upstairs. They stepped out between two cars parked about halfway between Raine and the elevators.

He wasn't going to be able to make a run for it. That was the bad news. The good news was that there were only two of them and they weren't big. One on one, he could have taken either of them. That meant there was a chance he could take both of them if he got lucky, or one of them got scared. They wore ski masks over their faces; the same style of mask as the man at Alexandra's office. Raine suspected he had encountered one of the men before, at Alexandra's office. Raine had won that fight, but this time his opponent had a friend, and one of those tire irons already in his hand.

"This is getting boring, boys," Raine taunted them. "I know you're never supposed to be the first one to make an offer, but I have no idea what we're negotiating, so you're going to have to make the first move."

"This ain't a negotiation," the man on the left said as they closed the distance between themselves and Raine. He was slightly taller than the other man, but a little slimmer. Still several inches shorter than Raine. But he also had that tire iron. "It's instructions. You do what you're told and no one needs to get hurt."

Raine put up a hand. "Stop!"

Stunned, both men did so, about twenty feet away still.

"Any closer and this is going to turn physical," Raine said. "It just will. We'll all be too close to each other. Someone will flinch or do something suddenly and everyone else will react. And what good is that if I haven't even heard what you want me to do? Maybe I'll agree. Maybe you want me to drink a fifth of whiskey and a gallon of ice cream and get a good night's rest tonight. I'd be willing to do that. Maybe we can find a win-win."

"You like talking, don't ya, Raine?" the man without an obvious weapon in his hand said. He was shorter but solid, with thick arms noticeable under his dark clothing. He seemed to be the provisional leader.

"I'm a lawyer," Raine defended. "Tell me what you want."

"Lose the Beauchamp case," the shorter man said.

Raine thought for a moment. "Which one?"

That surprised his accosters. "Uh. The murder case."

"Again," Raine replied, "which one? She's accused of killing a couple of different people now. I would have thought you'd have been briefed on that before heading out into the field. Or garage. Whatever."

"The one about Alexandra!" the other man shouted.

Now Raine was getting somewhere. These two cared about Alexandra Pruitt, and they were on a first-name basis with her.

"Oh, that one." Raine nodded. "Yeah, no. Sorry. She's not guilty. Probably."

"It doesn't matter if she's guilty," the shorter man responded. "It just matters that she gets convicted."

He bumped the other man, and they started walking toward Raine again.

Raine noted that they were approaching more slowly, though, so that was something. He just needed them a little closer.

"Why is that?" he kept the conversation going. "I mean, if you have information that's she actually guilty, then as her attorney, I'm ethically bound to completely ignore it."

"Okay, that's it, smartass." The man with the tire iron quickened his gait, but the other man grabbed his arm to pull him back. That was the other good news. They didn't want to hurt him if they didn't have to.

"Why?" Raine threw at them. "If you want me to betray my client, tell me why."

"Because we'll break your legs if you don't," was the answer.

That general argument seemed obvious from the circumstances. It suggested no alternative method of persuasion. But it also didn't tell him who was behind his visitors. Because someone was obviously behind them. They weren't smart enough to be the ones in charge. The question was whether the person in charge thought they were smart enough to explain the reasons behind their assignment.

"I need more than that," Raine insisted. The men had stopped about ten feet from him. A little too far still. He took a step toward them. "How much do I get paid?"

"Paid?" the shorter man called out. "You wanna get paid?"

"Of course," Raine answered, as casually as he could muster over his racing heart. "I'm going to lose business if I lose a murder case. I need that loss to be offset. Plus a premium."

"How much of a premium?" the taller man asked.

But the other man slapped him in the arm. "He didn't send us to pay this guy, he sent us here to scare him."

"Just scare me?" Raine noted. He also noted their handler was a 'he'. "So, you're not actually prepared to hurt me?"

He was about to find out. He thought he knew the answer, his question notwithstanding. Raine lunged at the man with the tire iron. It was the only weapon they had, and he needed it. Unfortunately, the best way to get close enough to grab it was to have it come crashing down on him.

The taller man, obviously caught off guard by Raine's

sudden move and reacting on instinct, swung the tire iron at Raine. Luckily, he swung it sideways, at Raine's body, not at his head.

Raine raised his left arm and let the metal rod smash into his ribs, sending shock waves of pain radiating across his entire torso. But then he clamped his arm back down to his left side and twisted away from his attacker. The man's grip wasn't tight enough to offset the opposing torque caused by Raine's rotation and the tire iron slipped from his grasp. Raine had just enough time to seize the bar with his right hand before the two men, both unarmed now, jumped on him and tackled him to the cold, hard pavement.

Raine was still outnumbered but they were the ones who were unarmed. They clawed at the tire iron, but Raine managed to pull it away and land a glancing blow against the head of one of the men. He couldn't tell which one, since their comparative heights were neither discernable nor relevant. The man who was hit loosened his grip and raised a hand to his head. Raine used the opportunity to strike him again, aiming for the head, but striking him in the side of the neck. That wasn't going to break any bones, but it hurt. The man fell off Raine and rolled into a ball to focus on the pain in his head and neck.

That left Raine one-on-one with the other man. Raine was neither outnumbered nor unarmed. The man scurried off Raine and pulled himself into a defensive crouch.

"Should we start from the top?" Raine stood up and slapped the tire iron into his opposite palm. The wound from Ernest's knife was mostly healed but it was still sensitive. Raine suppressed a wince. "Who sent you?"

The man raised his hands at Raine. "Look, man. We weren't going to hurt you. Honest. We were just supposed to scare you. You need to lose that case. It's really important that she doesn't get Alexandra's businesses."

Raine thought for a second. "The partnership agreement she signed? That's real?"

Before the man could answer, the elevator door finally chimed and off stepped an entire family: a man, a woman, a stroller, and two other small children. The woman took one look at the altercation across the garage and let out a scream that sliced through the air and echoed off every surface.

It was loud enough to disorient Raine and give his attackers a chance to escape. The injured man pushed himself to his feet and scrambled after his compatriot, who was already halfway up the exit ramp. Raine considered giving chase, but he decided to count himself lucky he hadn't suffered a worse injury than some sore ribs. But he held onto the tire iron as he walked briskly toward the elevator.

The family scurried out of his way, the children behind the mother, and she behind her husband, all of their eyes wide and glued to him.

He pressed the elevator call button and thankfully the car hadn't left. The doors opened with a ding.

Raine offered the family a nod. He instinctively raised the tire iron as well, as if saluting with it. "Lovely evening, isn't it?"

They didn't reply, but that was just as well. Raine wasn't looking for any more human interaction that night. He had a big hearing in the morning. And the more he considered it, probably a couple of fractured ribs.

25

Urgent care didn't open until after the hearing was scheduled to start. Raine didn't feel like going to the emergency room and getting no sleep while he sat alone in a room and waited for the staff to have a break between gunshot wounds and heart attacks. He searched up the treatments for fractured ribs and it turned out there weren't any anyway. Maybe a tight wrap to help reduce pain by reducing movement, but mostly he would just have to wait for them to heal while he consumed bottle after bottle of over-the-counter pain relievers.

So, when he showed up for the hearing on Scarborough's motion to consolidate cases for trial, the pain in his ribs was so distracting that he almost didn't notice the unexpected group of spectators in the back of the courtroom.

Observers were a relative rarity in courthouses, despite the standard rows of seats in each courtroom. Usually, the only people who came to watch a case were family of either the defendant or the victim. Occasionally, there was a case that was high profile enough to attract larger crowds and even the media. But even on those cases, people came to the trial, not preliminary hearings. Raine had wondered if Alexandra's fortune might entice a few people in the industry to stop by for a half day here and there during the trial, but he never expected to see anyone prior to opening statements.

It took a moment to recognize them, but after he did, he was no longer surprised they were present. It wasn't celebrity or even morbid curiosity. It was business.

"Ms. Ungermann." Raine walked over to greet his other opposing counsel and her client. "Mr. Newberry."

"Mr. Raine." Ungermann flashed a cobralike smile. "Big hearing today, huh?"

"I suppose." Raine wanted to come across as unbothered. "My job is to win either way."

"Oh, bravo." She offered a polite little clap. "But seriously, it must be more difficult to defend a client against two murders than just one. I mean, after a while, the jury will think she's probably just the kind of person who commits murders."

"That's the main argument against it," Raine replied. "Half of the evidence rules are keeping out prior bad acts lest a jury decide a case based on lazy assumptions rather than actual evidence. Speaking of lazy, are you still planning on letting the prosecutor do your dirty work when it comes to Meredith?"

"We certainly don't want to stand in the way of the government obtaining justice for Alexandra's murder," Ungermann responded, still smiling. "And if that makes it impossible for Meredith to collect any portion of Alexandra's estate, well, then yes, that would be less work for me, I suppose."

Raine noted Ungermann's use of the word 'estate' for the first time, rather than 'businesses'. Had she finally located a copy of Alexandra's will? And was Meredith one of the beneficiaries? But he didn't get the time to probe the issue.

"All rise!" the bailiff bellowed. "The King County Superior Court is now in session, the Honorable Henry Brenner presiding!"

"That's my cue," Raine said. "Enjoy the show."

"We will, Mr. Raine," Ungermann replied. She didn't wish him luck.

The judge was the same, but the courtroom was different. When Brenner handled the daily calendars of in-custody arraignments and in-custody guilty pleas, he did it in the secure courtroom on the twelfth floor where the guard could securely transport dozens of inmates for their court hearings. But that courtroom was used by whatever judge was presiding over those calendars on a given day, and that assignment rotated among the judges, largely because it was terrible.

When not in Courtroom 1201, Judge Brenner had a regular courtroom on the seventh floor of the courthouse. One without bulletproof glass separating the judge's bench from the gallery benches. One with full-sized tables for the attorneys and a box for a jury.

When the trial started in a few short weeks, whether one or both cases, it would be in Brenner's usual courtroom. Meredith would be brought specially from the jail by a detail of two guards. For the trial, she would be dressed in street clothes, and the guards would sit casually near the exits, lest the jury realize she was in custody and draw the reasonable inference therefrom that the judge thought she was dangerous. But for just a motion hearing, she was still brought by two guards, but she was in her red jail scrubs, and the guards hovered within lunging distance of her at all times.

The guards had been standing with Meredith in a hallway that ran along one side of the courtroom. Upon the bailiff's call, they opened the door and brought her to the defense table. Raine made his way to sit next to his client even as the guards took off her handcuffs. Scarborough was already at the prosecution table, fully ignoring Raine and his client. That was fine by Raine.

"Are the parties ready," Judge Brenner asked, "on the matters of *The State of Washington versus Meredith Ann Beauchamp?*"

"The State is ready, Your Honor," Scarborough answered. He had been standing from the bailiff's call until that response. He finally sat down again.

Raine looked to his client. He was standing, but she had missed the "All rise!" and was pushed into her chair by the guards anyway. "Ready?"

Meredith shrugged. "I'm not even sure what's going on today. I'm ready to go home. Anything else, I'm probably not ready for it."

Raine supposed that was a fair answer. He looked up to the judge. "The defense is ready, Your Honor."

Raine sat down next to his client and Brenner began the hearing.

"This is the State's motion to consolidate the two cases against the defendant into a single trial," the judge started. "So, I will hear first from Mr. Scarborough."

Scarborough stood up again. He hadn't unbuttoned his suit coat when he sat down, so he didn't need to rebutton it upon standing. He clasped his hands in front of himself, as if unsure what else to do with them.

"A motion to consolidate cases for trial," Scarborough began, "is governed by Criminal Court Rule 4.3.1. That rule states that cases should be joined for trial if they were or could have been joined into a single complaint under Criminal Rule 4.3. In turn, Criminal Rule 4.3 states..."

Raine knew he should be paying attention to his opponent's argument, but he already knew how to read the rulebook. He glanced around the courtroom. Brenner seemed obligatorily engaged, but in no way enthralled. The bailiff and court reporter were busy doing their jobs; the court reporter paying close attention, the bailiff paying none. Meredith seemed shell shocked, incapable of any expression other than disbelief and fading hope. Behind him were Ungermann and Newberry. Ungermann saw him looking and waved. Raine turned quickly back to face the front, but not so fast that he missed the door to the hallway crack open. He turned back and saw another spectator enter the courtroom: Detective Kahale. She and Raine locked eyes for a moment before she broke it off. She didn't wave.

Raine turned back to his immediate task, forcing himself to listen to Scarborough.

"...the next factor is cross-admissibility of the evidence. While it might seem that much of the evidence in each case might be inadmissible in the other case, if one takes a more historical and expansive reading of Evidence Rule 404..."

Scarborough could quote rules and five-factor tests all morning—and he probably would—but Raine knew Brenner was going to make a decision based on what he felt was the right thing to do. There was always some rule or factor he could hang his decision on. In fact, the more rules and factors and elements and tests, the easier it would be for him to find a basis to justify what was basically just an emotional decision like everyone else made a hundred times each day.

Raine recalled reading about a medical patient from the turn of the previous century who suffered a non-fatal brain injury. It severed the decision-making portion of his brain from where the emotions were stored. The doctors thought he would become the perfect decision-maker, unburdened by troublesome, distracting emotion. It turned out to be exactly the opposite. He couldn't make any decisions.

Humans have feelings for a reason, and one of the biggest reasons is to decide what to do. It's only after the decision is made based on emotion that objective reasons are painted onto the decision to make it seem somehow more legitimate. As if crossing a field of wildflowers because it was the shortest distance was somehow better than crossing it because it was beautiful.

Which was to say that there was very little chance Brenner was going to join two different murder trials into a single case, to be tried to a single jury, with less than a month to prepare. It just wasn't fair to the defendant, let alone Raine. It was hard enough to work long hours every night; Brenner didn't even know about his ribs. The only way Brenner would consolidate the cases for trial was if Raine didn't object—the 'judo' strategy Raine had previously considered: agree to Scarborough's request and then try to use it against him.

But it wasn't judo. It was a murder trial. It was Meredith's life. The rest of her life, maybe in prison. For a murder, or murders, she didn't commit. Definitely.

He didn't believe she had committed the murders. There was too much else going on. If she were guilty, there wouldn't be a lawyer, a slumlord, and a detective sitting behind him. And he wouldn't be favoring the cracked ribs under his suit coat.

It wasn't judo. It was justice.

"...and so, for all of those reasons, Your Honor, the State respectfully requests the Court grant its motion to consolidate these matters for trial. Thank you."

Scarborough sat down and Judge Brenner turned to the defense table.

"Your response, Mr. Raine, whenever you're ready," the judge invited.

Raine nodded to himself as he came to a decision. Another glance around the courtroom. Client, prosecutor, lawyer, slumlord, detective, guards and bailiff and court reporter. And him. All eyes on him. All of Meredith's hopes on him.

Not judo. Justice.

He looked up at Judge Brenner.

"Justice delayed is justice denied," he said. "No objection to consolidation, Your Honor."

Brenner's eyebrows shot so far up, Raine thought they might fly off his head. "Are you certain, Mr. Raine? There are many factors to consider when making this decision. I am willing to hear you out before putting you, and your client, in this position."

Raine had considered several factors as well. They were all sitting behind him.

"I'm certain, Your Honor," Raine confirmed. "Now, if we could adjourn, I would be very grateful. I have a lot of work to do."

He sat down again while Brenner tried to find the words to declare the hearing over.

"Why did you do that?" Meredith practically pleaded. "I can't beat two murder charges."

"Maybe not," Raine replied, "but I can."

"How?"

That, Raine knew, was a very good question. He didn't have an actual answer just yet. Not one made up of words. It was a feeling. But he trusted it. He would add the reasons later. "Hard work and good decisions. The usual."

Meredith shook her head. "You're not very convincing right now. I hope you do better at the trial."

"I will," Raine assured. "Now, leave it to me. I have a plan. We don't have to prove you didn't do it."

Meredith frowned. "We don't?"

"No," Raine explained. "The State has to prove the charge beyond a reasonable doubt. We don't have to prove anything."

Meredith thought for a few moments. "But wouldn't it be better if we did prove I didn't do it?"

"It would," Raine admitted, "but that might be hard to do, given the circumstantial evidence against you. So, we'll do the next best thing."

"What's that?"

"We don't have to prove you didn't do it," Raine repeated. "We just have to prove someone else might have done it."

"But who?" Meredith threw her hand wide.

Raine frowned. "I don't know yet."

Meredith didn't say anything in response. She just shook her head and seemed almost relieved when the guards stepped up and ended their conversation. After she was handcuffed again, she looked back at her lawyer. "I don't know if I trust you, Mr. Raine. But I trust Rebecca and she trusts you. I guess that will have to be enough."

The guards led her away then and Raine took a moment to assess the courtroom again. Brenner was long gone from the bench, along with his bailiff and court reporter. Scarborough was still packing up his briefcase, fiddling with the rules book to make sure it fit in at a perfect ninety-degree angle. Kahale had slipped out. Ungermann and Newberry hovered near the doors in the back, as if waiting for him. Raine gathered his own things and walked toward the exit.

"Interesting strategy," Ungermann said when Raine approached. "Do you always capitulate in the face of a rules-based argument?"

"I always make the best decision for my client," Raine answered, "even when others might mistake it for capitulation."

Ungermann seemed ready to fire back some additional smarmy comment when the door to the hallway opened and a man in a black suit and chauffeur's hat stepped in.

"The car is ready, Mr. Newberry," he announced. "We can get to Fall City before noon if we leave now." Then he realized there were other people standing there.

And Raine realized the man had a large, long bruise on the side of his neck. They met eyes and Raine could see the panic in the man's eyes. But Raine knew better than to say anything. Not right then anyway. Not yet.

"Well, then, you'd better get going, Mr. Newberry." Raine gestured toward the hallway. "I'm sure your driver wouldn't want to get caught in the garage."

26

T he next three weeks flew by even faster than Raine feared. He didn't have much time. Which meant neither did Kahale.

"Tell her attorney Daniel Raine is here to see her," Raine directed the officer at the front desk of the downtown Seattle Police precinct Kahale worked out of. "She'll know what it's about."

Generally, Raine thought to himself. The specifics were still up in the air. But there were backs to be scratched and he was ready to set up a schedule.

"Detective Kahale will be out in a moment," the officer informed him after a few moments of messaging the detective. He gestured toward the minimalist waiting area. There were no chairs. They weren't about to encourage anyone to stay any longer than necessary to finish whatever business they had. Serve and protect, not sit and relax.

A door on the side of the lobby opened and Kahale stepped out. She was dressed casually, with her black hair in a ponytail and a University of Hawaii hoodie. Raine felt like he was interrupting her Saturday. "Raine. You wanted to talk to me?"

"I'd like to continue our last conversation," he said. "I have a proposal."

Kahale frowned at that. "Okay. I'm always open to a good idea. Let's see if you can manage that."

She led him into the back of the precinct where the detectives worked. About half of the desks were occupied with cops working on cases. Most were dressed as casually as Kahale, although a couple were dressed a bit nicer, as if they might be about to meet with members of the public, and one of them was in a full suit, as if they might be getting ready to testify in court. Kahale's office was a small affair, internal with no windows, and a view back out toward those half-filled desks. There was enough room for Kahale and one guest—at that moment, Raine.

"So, what's your proposal?" Kahale got right to it. "Or is your proposal to accept my proposal? Do you have the document I want?"

"No," Raine admitted. "But I think I know who does. Randall Newberry."

Kahale stared at him for several seconds. "Who's that?"

Raine shook his head at her. "Aren't you supposed to be a detective? He's an old friend of Alexandra Pruitt's. In fact, he's suing my client, along with my investigator and three other women, to recoup a bad loan he made to Alexandra shortly before she died."

"Before she was murdered," Kahale corrected.

"To-may-toe, to-mah-toe," Raine replied. "His lawyer wants the same documents you do."

Kahale shrugged. "Sounds like your area of expertise.

Lawyers and courts and documents. Why are you talking to me?"

"Dealing with his lawyer is my area of expertise," Raine allowed, "but Newberry himself is far more up your alley."

"Oh yeah?" Kahale half smiled. "Why?"

"For one thing, he's a piece of crap," Raine answered. "A slumlord. I'm sure he's breaking a dozen ordinances on every building he owns."

"I'm a major crimes detective," Kahale reminded Raine, "not a code enforcement officer."

"Assault with a deadly weapon is a major crime, right?" Raine returned. "Well, he sent two masked goons to assault me with a tire iron unless I agreed to throw the case and let Meredith get convicted."

Kahale leaned forward. "Really? Did they actually assault you with the tire iron? Or just sort of menace you with it? Cause menacing is not a major crime."

"They started with menacing," Raine recounted. "Then moved to extortion, and finally assault. I have the fractured ribs to prove it."

"Ribs?" Kahale winced. "Those hurt. And there's nothing the doctors can do really."

"So I've learned," Raine replied. "But you should see the other guy."

Kahale grinned weakly. "Right. Good one."

"No, seriously," Raine said. "You should see the other guy. I did. I got the tire iron away from them and managed to hit one of them in the neck."

"The neck?" Kahale questioned.

Raine shrugged. "I was aiming for the head, but I had two of them trying to pin me to the ground, so my aim was a little off."

"Ah," Kahale allowed.

"But it was hard enough to leave a mark," Raine continued, "and the next morning, who did I see with a bruise on his neck the exact size and shape of the tire iron?"

"Who?"

"Newberry's driver," Raine finally told her. "He sent them to threaten me into intentionally losing the case. Then the next day in court, his lawyer mentioned Alexandra's estate instead of her businesses."

Kahale frowned at the overabundance of new information. "Estate means a will. No one has found a will."

"Exactly." Raine pointed at her. "So, arrest that driver for assaulting me and turn him into a snitch against Newberry."

Kahale hesitated then burst out laughing. "That would never work."

"Why not?"

"First of all, they were wearing masks," Kahale answered. "That bruise is good evidence, but it's not enough. We'd need him to confess, and why would he do that? He's got a rich boss who will just pay him to keep his mouth shut."

"I'm telling you," Raine insisted, "that guy is the chink in the armor of this case. The thin edge of the wedge. The tip of the arrow. Some other saying that's similar. It's worth a try."

Kahale crossed her arms and leaned back in her chair, thinking.

"You wanted the documents stolen by whoever killed Duncan Chenoweth," Raine reminded her. "I'm giving you someone who might know and probable cause to arrest him. Take that and do something with it."

"And what do you want in return?" Kahale asked. "I already offered to keep your fingerprint on that door quiet. But I have the feeling you want more."

Raine leaned forward. "Here's what I want." He pointed at the detective. "It's simple. Should be easy, but then again, you are a cop."

Kahale leaned forward as well. Their faces were inches apart. "What is it, Raine?"

Raine smiled. "Tell the truth when you testify at Meredith's trial."

Kahale took a moment then leaned back again. She laughed. "Is that all?"

Raine didn't laugh. "It's everything."

27

Sawyer stepped out of the bathroom wearing nothing but a towel on her head. She seemed oblivious to her nakedness, and her beauty.

Raine smiled at his girlfriend from his spot on the bed, sitting up and leaning against a pillow. The delivery food had arrived while she was in the shower. He was already eating some kung pao chicken and felt remarkably at peace for a lawyer with a double murder trial starting the following Monday. It helped that he had someone to talk to about it. Someone who enjoyed talking shop.

Sawyer sat down on the bed next to him and opened the box of pot stickers. "So, what's your theme?" she asked as she tore open a package of chopsticks.

"Right, my theme." Raine nodded. Every course on trial advocacy said you had to have a theme. A 'case theory'. "I think I'm going with, 'She didn't do it'."

"A little thin," Sawyer assessed. She took a bite of pot sticker. "I feel like that's implied by the fact that she didn't plead guilty."

"I suppose so," Raine agreed. "What about, 'Someone else did it'?"

Sawyer finished the pot sticker then pulled the towel off her head and wrapped it around her body. "Again, implied by the assertion that she didn't do it. Unless you think the jury might buy a double suicide claim?"

"Double accident maybe," Raine replied, "but no. I'm not going to win the case claiming the victims weren't murdered. I need to convince the jury someone else did it."

"Who?" Sawyer asked.

"I just told you," Raine pointed his chopsticks at her. "Someone else."

"Yeah, but which someone?" Sawyer pressed. "Who's your prime suspect?"

Raine smiled and shook his head. "No, see, that's the beauty of it. They're all prime suspects."

"Don't you want to pick someone and point the jury toward them?" Sawyer argued.

"I thought about that," Raine answered. "That's the obvious thing. The expected thing. And honestly, I would do that if there were really one person the evidence pointed to. But there isn't. So, it's everybody. Everybody is a suspect."

Sawyer extracted some chicken from the box Raine was holding and chewed her bite thoughtfully. "That's risky."

"Maybe," Raine allowed.

"But sometimes you have to take risks in trial," Sawyer acknowledged.

"Exactly." Raine smiled. "I don't have to prove Meredith didn't do it. The burden of proof is on them to prove she did it. I just need to create enough reasonable doubt to get to an acquittal. I don't have to convince the jury that one other suspect probably did it if I can convince them that all of the other suspects might have done it."

28

T he first day of trial was its own event. There was no chance that they would possibly get to anything substantive like opening statements, let alone witness testimony. That was doubly so when it was really two trials in one, Frankensteined together into a lumbering husk of unevenly related police reports, autopsy findings, scene photographs, and the like.

Scarborough may have bitten off more than he could chew, and Raine was happy to not help him in the least. Judge Brenner on the other hand had a personal interest in getting the trial off the ground and flying smoothly. The less organized everything was, the longer it would take, and the longer he would be stuck presiding over a messy trial he had been counting on Raine to keep him from suffering through.

Raine wasn't going to be obstructionist—not yet anyway. He was simply going to represent his client's interests to the best of his ability. Even if, as was evident by her expression when she sat down next to him that morning, his client wasn't convinced he was doing that.

The guards removed her handcuffs and retreated to their strategically placed chairs, one by each exit. The only other way out of the courtroom was through the judge's chambers, and Meredith was unlikely to climb over the bar and bench before being tackled by the guards. She was clearly not happy, even though she had traded the jail scrubs for a very nice business suit Sommers fetched for her from her home.

"You still think it's a good idea to tell the jury I'm charged with two murders?" she challenged. "I feel like you could have fought against this."

"We are about to start the trial," Raine replied. "The next few days we will be dealing with preliminary matters like scheduling, simple evidentiary motions, and picking a jury. Once that is over, the prosecutor and I will give our opening statements and then they will start calling witnesses. It's going to be very important when we get to that stage that you trust not just my decisions, but my judgment, because things are going to be happening too fast for me to consult you on every argument and objection. You said you trusted Rebecca and she trusted me and that would be enough. Is it still enough?"

"I'd like more," Meredith told him.

"What do you need?" Raine asked. The judge would be out any minute, but his client needed that minute. Raine hoped it would be sufficient.

"Tell me why," Meredith asked. "Treat me like a partner in this. I'm an accomplished professional. Maybe not in the legal field, but in a field that requires a lot of smarts and a lot of people skills. You lawyers seem pretty smart, but your people skills can be severely lacking. Treat me like I have skin in the game because at the end of the day, I'm really the only one who does. No matter what the jury says, everyone

else in this room goes home at the end of the trial. I might
not."

Raine could hardly argue with anything Meredith said.
And he respected that she spoke up. And then that minute
was over.

"All rise! The King County Superior Court is now in
session, the Honorable Henry Brenner presiding."

Raine held up his index finger to Meredith. "Hold that
thought," he whispered.

She rolled her eyes and sighed as loudly as Raine had
ever heard someone sigh.

The judge bade everyone to, "Please be seated."

Raine and Meredith complied, as did Scarborough.
There had been no one in the back of the courtroom that
morning. Kahale wasn't allowed because she was going to be
a witness. Ungermann and Newberry were either waiting for
a more interesting portion of the trial, or Raine coming face
to face with Tire Iron Timmy had spooked them from
coming around again, at least on days Newberry needed to
be driven to Fall City.

Judge Brenner posed the obligatory question to the
lawyers of whether they were ready—they were—then
moved into those preliminary matters Raine had warned
Meredith about. Scheduling was the simplest. That only
took an hour or so.

Those preliminary evidence motions took longer. Two
full days of argument. Meredith's statements to the cops
when she was arrested for Alexandra's murder would be
admissible in the State's case-in-chief. The medical examiner would be permitted to give an opinion that the death
was homicide by cyanide poison but could not give an
opinion as to whether Meredith could have been the one

who did it. Witnesses who weren't currently testifying had to remain in the hallway until it was their turn to testify so they didn't hear other witnesses' testimony. Meredith's fingerprint on Chenoweth's doorbell was admissible. Raine's fingerprint on Chenoweth's door was apparently still buried in some overlooked supplemental report because Scarborough never brought it up.

Once the evidentiary disagreements were resolved, it was time to pick a jury. A single murder case could easily take months to try; a double murder case would take even longer. That meant a lot of potential jurors who were willing to do two weeks of jury duty like the summons said being unable to sit on a months-long trial, usually for financial reasons. In order to seat twelve jurors, Judge Brenner called for a panel of one hundred potential jurors. They were going to lose a lot of them for hardship, so they needed to have a lot left over.

It was the following Monday before the jury was selected and the final twelve were put in the jury box and sworn in by the judge.

Once that was accomplished, the judge read them some preliminary instructions about not talking about the case, even with each other, until they had heard all of the evidence and it was time to deliberate. Then, once that was done, it was finally time to start the trial in earnest.

Judge Brenner leaned forward and addressed the jury. "Members of the jury, please give your attention to Mr. Scarborough, who will deliver the opening statement on behalf of the plaintiff, the State of Washington."

29

S carborough stood up with a crisp, "Thank you, Your Honor."

He walked out from behind the prosecution table and took a spot in front of the jury box. It was about a step farther away than Raine was going to stand, but he supposed the jurors weren't going to mind a lawyer being slightly farther away from them.

"Murder!" Scarborough jabbed a finger into the air.

It wasn't a very smooth movement. Raine wasn't sure which was more jarring, the gesture or shouting the word 'murder'.

"Murder!" Scarborough shouted again. He jabbed his other hand into the air. "A murder and another murder! Two murders. The defendant committed two murders."

Raine assessed the jurors' reactions to Scarborough's presentation. It wasn't quite theatrics because theater required a certain level of talent. Scarborough was just taking advantage of standard trial procedure to force everyone to listen to him, no matter how awkward it was.

"The defendant is charged with two counts of murder in the first degree," he continued in a far more subdued tone. His usual courtroom voice. It was as if the shouts of 'Murder!' were his attempt at what the trial lawyers called an 'attention grabber', but he simply grafted it at the front of what was otherwise going to be the usual middling opening statement of a government lawyer.

"The first count of murder relates to victim Alexandra Pruitt," Scarborough continued. There was now an unnaturally complete absence of any bodily movement. He spoke as if reading from a form he had, of course, taken the time to memorize. "The second count of murder relates to Victim Duncan Chenoweth. Duncan Chenoweth was Alexandra Pruitt's lawyer. Their murders are connected. They are connected by being close in time. They are connected by having the same motive. And they are connected by being committed by the same person. That person is the defendant, Meredith Ann Beauchamp."

Raine looked over at the jurors again to gauge how they were reacting to Scarborough. At least some of them seemed offput, but they all wanted to know why they were there, why Meredith was charged with murder, what happened. They were mostly leaning forward, but not too far.

"Why did she murder them? How did she murder them? When did she murder them?" Scarborough posed the rhetorical questions rather than just provide the information that answered them.

It was a style, Raine supposed. He set his pen down and decided to just experience his opponent's style. It wasn't like he was going to say anything Raine didn't already know.

"She murdered them for money," Scarborough answered his first question, although in a very conclusory manner.

"She administered poison to Alexandra Pruitt, and she inflicted sharp-force trauma to the posterior of Duncan Chenoweth's skull. She committed these murders only weeks apart."

Raine allowed himself to hope Scarborough might actually sit down at that point. He had, barely, provided the facts he intended to prove at trial. That was the purpose of opening statement. Officially, anyway. It was also an opportunity to interact with the jury, tell them a compelling story, and hope to win some of them over to like you, maybe even trust you. Scarborough didn't seem like he was terribly capable of pursuing those secondary purposes.

Raine looked over to Meredith to see how she was holding up. But she didn't seem to share Raine's enjoyment at Scarborough's opening. She wasn't a lawyer. She didn't know a good, engaging opening from a dry, boring one. She was a murder defendant. She was nervous. Scared even. Raine turned his attention back to Scarborough.

"The first murder," Scarborough began his discussion of Alexandra's murder.

He said it like it was a chapter heading, a verbal tag, rather than a sentence. It wasn't Raine's style, but maybe the jury appreciated the road map. He decided he should stop being dismissive of Scarborough's opening. Style aside, this was the prosecution's theory of the case, and they had evidence to back it up. Some evidence. Not enough evidence, in Raine's estimation, but it would ultimately be the jury who decided that.

"Alexandra Pruitt's retirement party," Scarborough continued the list of noun phrases. "Alexandra Pruitt was a very successful real estate professional. She had a very large business empire. She wasn't married and had no children. She decided to pass her business to five other women she had mentored over the years. The defendant was one of those five women.

"Ms. Pruitt drafted a partnership agreement for all of them to sign. Ms. Pruitt signed first. After that, only the defendant signed, because after she signed, the defendant murdered Ms. Pruitt. She was hoping to take all of Ms. Pruitt's businesses because she was the only partner at the time of Ms. Pruitt's death. But you can't do that if you're the murderer, so she will not be receiving any of Ms. Pruitt's businesses."

Raine took another glance at his client. In part, he wanted to see how she was holding up. In another part, he wanted to see how she reacted to this portion of the story. She hadn't told Raine about the partnership until after the arraignment and they were first arguing bail. He still wasn't satisfied with her explanation—'that's my signature but I didn't sign it'—but he was stuck with it, at least until the full truth managed to make itself known. But Meredith's expression was stoic, and unchanged.

"Security video shows the defendant removing Ms. Pruitt's bowl of soup from the kitchen," Scarborough continued. "She took it into the bathroom where there were no cameras. She added the cyanide, then she returned the soup to the refrigerator. Shortly after that, Ms. Pruitt took the soup out from the refrigerator, ate from it, and died almost instantly from cyanide poisoning."

He raised that one arm up awkwardly again, although he refrained from yelling anything. "That is one murder." He lowered his hand and gave the jury their next chapter heading. "The second murder. Duncan Chenoweth. Alexandra Pruitt's tax and estate lawyer. He was elderly. He was struck in the back of the head by something sharp and then fell down a flight of hard, wooden stairs. He died there. It was his home, but also his office. The defendant's fingerprint was recovered from the doorbell. That means she was the last person to come to Mr. Chenoweth's home before he died. Anyone who came afterward would have smeared the defendant's fingerprint off. That's how we know she was the last person to see him alive. And she was the last person to see him alive because she was the one who killed him."

Scarborough finally took a break to sip some water from the cup on the prosecution table. He hurried back to his spot in front of the jury and continued his story. "The defendant then searched Mr. Chenoweth's office for any documents that might be a challenge to her partnership agreement. She found, removed, and destroyed those documents. That's burglary, so the murder of Duncan Chenoweth is murder in the first degree with the aggravating circumstances that it was committed during the course of, or in furtherance of, a burglary."

Scarborough stopped talking and looked down at his hands. He counted off his fingers as he muttered to himself. He looked up again. "That's it, ladies and gentlemen. The defendant is guilty of both charges. Thank you for your attention."

Judge Brenner watched Scarborough walk quickly back to his seat, then spoke to the jurors again. "Members of the jury, please give your attention to Mr. Raine, who will deliver the opening statement on behalf of the defendant. Meredith Beauchamp."

It was showtime. Raine stood up, buttoned his suit coat, and offered the same, "Thank you, Your Honor."

He, too, came out from behind his counsel table, walked toward the jury box, and stopped on a particular spot in front of the center of the box and that one step closer than Scarborough had stood. The only significant difference between Raine's setup for his opening statement and Scarborough's was that Raine wasn't about to scream and shove his hands in the air.

"Alexandra Pruitt was murdered on the night of her retirement party," Raine began, a seeming admission from the defense attorney. "And a few weeks later, her lawyer, Duncan Chenoweth, died after being struck in the back of the head and falling down a flight of wooden stairs."

He paused and glanced back at Scarborough. "All of that is one hundred percent true." Then he looked at Meredith. "And Meredith Beauchamp didn't do any of it."

Meredith smiled weakly at the sound of someone defending her publicly.

"But," Raine turned back to the jurors, his expression deadly serious, "that means someone else did. Your job in this trial will be to figure out who."

"Objection!" Scarborough stood up. "That is most certainly not the jury's role in this trial. They are to determine whether the defendant is guilty or innocent. They are not a group of amateur detectives on an investigation adventure."

"Any response, Mr. Raine?" Judge Brenner gave him a chance before sustaining the objection.

"Yes, Your Honor," Raine replied. "Ms. Beauchamp did not commit these murders. That is our official legal position, and I believe I am permitted to advocate for that. Now, if you assume for a moment that Ms. Beauchamp did not commit the murders, then that must mean someone else did. When the jury says, 'not guilty', twice, at the end of this trial, it will only stand to reason that they may have uncovered who really committed these murders."

Brenner narrowed his eyes at Raine. "I'm going to sustain the objection. You told the jurors their job is to discover who really committed these murders. That is not their job. Their job is to determine whether the State has proved beyond a reasonable doubt that the defendant committed the murders."

"Thank you, Your Honor." Raine nodded. "I will rephrase."

He took a moment then said the same thing a different way. "When you hear the evidence in this case, you will conclude Meredith did not commit either of these murders, and you will do that because you will realize that someone else did."

Several of the jurors frowned at his verbal pretzel efforts to say what he said before but in a way that would survive an objection. He didn't like how he'd built the sentence either. And he didn't want to lose the jury.

"So, let's go ahead and look at the other suspects who might have murdered Alexandra Pruitt," he suggested enthusiastically, "because remember, it was a party. That place was packed. It could have been anyone."

The frowning jurors softened their expressions. Several of them leaned forward. He had them again. Good.

"Let's start with Alexandra's long-time boyfriend, but not husband, Ernest Poplowski," Raine began the list. "He was there that night. There were also five successful business-women whom Alexandra had mentored. They called themselves the Fab Five. Meredith was certainly one of them, but there were four others: Caroline Howard, Julia Kim, Fiona Mendoza, and Rebecca Sommers."

Raine suddenly realized he might end up including his own part-time investigator as a suspect. He didn't like that, but he could hardly change it to the Fab Four without being exposed later. He just wouldn't play her up as much as the rest. And he certainly wasn't going to include himself as a suspect.

"Julia's husband was there," he continued. "Caroline had a date that evening as well. And let's not forget the catering staff. How many people is that? At least a dozen. Meredith was only one of a dozen or more possible suspects. The only reason she was arrested was because Alexandra's security video showed her removing something from the refrigerator, taking it into the bathroom, then returning it."

He raised his hands slightly, "Now, I'll admit that might look suspicious, but there is actually a perfectly innocent explanation, an explanation Meredith herself will tell you when it's finally her turn to testify."

He looked softly at his client. "Meredith has struggled with eating disorders on and off her entire life. Without getting into the specific term for it right now, Meredith will tell you that she snuck some potatoes into the bathroom, chewed them up so she could taste them, then spit them into the toilet. It's private, it's not something she likes to talk about, and it's something she hid from everyone. But it's also not murder. A bowl of potatoes looks a lot like a bowl of soup from a camera in the corner of the ceiling. The police made a mistake. That's okay. That happens. But," he did finally a jab a finger into the air, not nearly as large as Scarborough's gesture, and directed toward the jury box, "don't you make the same mistake."

Raine lowered his pointing finger and used it to count off suspects on his other hand. "Ernest Poplowski. Despite years of faithful and dutiful relationship, Alexandra didn't want to marry Ernest because she had significantly more money than him. Was he jealous? Did he want to stop Alexandra from giving her fortune away to her mentees instead of him?

"Caroline Howard. Caroline was never as successful as the other Fab Five. Did she harbor resentment? Was she afraid she might be left out of whatever plan Alexandra was going to announce that night?

"Julia Kim. Julia seemed like a successful professional, but the rumor was that she and her husband were living well beyond their means. Designer dresses and massages at the office. Did she become desperate and ask Alexandra for help? Did Alexandra say no, enraging Julia?

"Fiona Mendoza. Fiona wasn't well liked among the other Fab Five. Did she blame Alexandra for not protecting her more? Did she lash out in a moment of weakness? Not everyone kills for money; some people just snap. Is that what happened?

Raine hesitated at the next name, but not for too long. He was a professional.

"Rebecca Sommers. The last member of the Fab Five. Yeah, it probably wasn't her. Not everyone who was there had a motive.

"And then let's not forget about the catering staff," he suggested. "Alexandra could be a harsh task master. Did she push one of the caterers too far? Or was it all maybe an accident and the caterers mixed up the bowls in the refrigerator?

Maybe the poison was supposed to be added to the potatoes. Maybe Meredith was the real target."

"Objection again, Your Honor." Scarborough stood up again. But he didn't have a legal basis. "Ms. Beauchamp is the defendant," he sputtered, "not a target."

"I'm just telling the jury what I think the evidence will show, Your Honor," Raine defended. "That's what opening statement is for."

Judge Brenner sighed but said, "I'll overrule the objection. But maybe move things along, Mr. Raine. This is starting to sound like a list of everyone Ms. Pruitt knew, not a statement of expected evidence in this case."

"Understood, Your Honor," Raine answered.

He turned his attention back to the jury. "Now, let's talk about the murder of Duncan Chenoweth. This is sort of the opposite of Alexandra's murder. Then, there were so many people in her condo that it's impossible to pick just one person to accuse with any actual certainty. But for Duncan's murder, there are no suspects at all. He was an elderly man, living alone, still practicing law out of his home office. Whoever did it stole some very important documents. Documents about Alexandra's businesses and estate. So, that circles us back to all of the same suspects we just discussed."

He wanted to skip over it, but he had to address that fingerprint, even if he didn't have a good explanation. Sometimes it's best to leave the audience curious, wanting more. "As for Meredith's fingerprint being found on Duncan's doorbell, well, you'll hear the explanation for that as well when Meredith testifies, but for now I want to point out something else."

He spread his arms wide. "We were able to identify a dozen other suspects just from one event at Alexandra's condo, but what about all of the other people who knew Alexandra and may have had a reason to want to harm her? There's too many to list now, but imagine some competitor from her past who feels entitled to her money and employs a team of henchmen who prowl through parking garages with tire irons in their hands."

Several jurors narrowed their eyes or cocked their heads at him.

"Let's see how the evidence comes out, is all I'm saying," Raine offered. "And when it does, you will see that there are at least ten other people who had greater means, and motive, than Meredith to murder either Alexandra Pruitt or Duncan Chenoweth."

He gestured up toward the bench. "The judge is right. Your job is not to determine who murdered Alexandra Pruitt or Duncan Chenoweth. In fact, I think it's very likely that at the end of this trial, you won't know which of the many suspects I listed today committed these murders, let alone someone we don't even know about. But while you might not know who did it, you'll know what you need to do. The State has to prove beyond a reasonable doubt that Meredith Beauchamp did in fact commit these murders. And if you think it's even reasonably possible that it was any of these other people, then that's reasonable doubt. That's an acquittal. That's a verdict of 'not guilty.' And at the end of this trial, after you've heard all of the evidence and considered all of the suspects, I will ask you to return verdicts of not guilty to both counts of murder. Thank you."

Raine returned directly to his seat and sat down next to Meredith. "What did you think?" he whispered to her.

"Honestly?" Meredith whispered back. "Not bad. Now I'm curious about who really did it. If the jurors are too—"

"Then we're halfway there," Raine agreed. Now he just had to accuse a dozen people in open court of a murder they also didn't commit. Probably.

I wonder who's first, he asked himself.

"You may call your first witness, Mr. Scarborough," Judge Brenner directed.

Scarborough stood up. "The State calls Ernest Poplowski to the stand."

30

E rnest Poplowski walked into the courtroom looking considerably more in control of his faculties than the last time Raine had seen him. Raine wondered whether Ernest would even remember the previous event. He seemed very detached from reality at the time. His memories might have been taking root in some very shallow soil.

That morning he was dressed in a navy blue suit and striped tie, not an uncinched robe, and his hair was neatly coiffed, not a scraggly nest atop his head. He made his way to the front of the courtroom and raised his right hand.

"Do you swear or affirm to tell the truth, the whole truth, and nothing but the truth?" Judge Brenner asked him.

"I do," Ernest confirmed.

"Please be seated in the witness stand," the judge directed. Then, to the prosecutor, "Whenever you're ready, Mr. Scarborough."

Scarborough had stood up to announce his first witness and hadn't sat down again while Ernest appeared and made his way to the witness stand. Once Ernest was seated, Scarborough moved from his counsel table to stand at the end of the jury box farthest from the witness stand. By standing next to the jury box, Scarborough forced the witness to face the jurors as he gave his responses to the prosecutor's questions. By standing at the far end of the box, Scarborough could make sure the witness was speaking loudly enough for even the farthest juror to hear.

"Please state your full name for the record," Scarborough began.

"Ernest Dean Poplowski."

"What city do you live in, Mr. Poplowski?"

"Seattle."

He hadn't moved from the condo, Raine knew. Not yet. That mortgage wasn't going to pay itself, though.

"How old are you?" Scarborough continued.

"I am sixty-seven years old."

"What is your occupation?"

Poplowski hesitated. "I'm retired."

Scarborough had his questions printed out and attached to a clipboard. He was checking off the information as Poplowski provided it, but his nose was pointed directly at the sheet, rather than at the witness. He was going to miss the nonverbal communication that was a core aspect of live testimony. The jurors wouldn't, however, and Raine made sure to keep his eyes trained on Ernest as they moved into the more substantive questions.

"Did you know a person named Alexandra Pruitt?"

Ernest opened his mouth to answer, but only managed a squeak. He looked away and even from his spot at the defense table, Raine could see tears welling in Ernest's eyes.

Scarborough looked up from his clipboard but didn't say

anything. He just waited for the answer, the tip of his pen hovering over the paper.

Finally, Ernest gathered himself sufficiently to answer, with a crack in his voice, "Yes."

"How did you know Ms. Pruitt?" Scarborough asked almost before Ernest had finished his one-word answer.

"She was my common-law wife," Ernest reported.

That was the first time Raine had heard anyone describe their relationship that way. Most people thought a common-law marriage was when a couple lived together for a long time. But legally speaking, it meant two people who declared to each other that they were married but never had the marriage approved or recorded by a government or church agency. Only a handful of states even recognize a true common-law marriage, and in the ones that do, a common-law married couple who wants to split up need to go through formal divorce proceedings just like anyone else. But they also inherit like any other spouse and Raine suspected that might be Ernest's motivation for his new characterization of his relationship with Alexandra. Too bad for him. Washington was not one of the states that recognized common-law marriage.

Duncan Chenoweth could have told Ernest that, Raine thought. And maybe he did. Maybe that's why Ernest lost his temper and pushed Chenoweth down the stairs to his death.

Raine smiled lightly to himself. He didn't think any of that was very likely, but he didn't need it to be likely, just reasonable. As in reasonable doubt. Something to put into his closing argument perhaps.

"How long were you and Ms. Pruitt romantically involved?" Scarborough continued his questioning.

"Nineteen years," Ernest answered with obvious pride in

his voice. His brain was thinking of happier times and his voice didn't crack. That wasn't going to last. It was a murder case, after all.

"Did you have any children together?" was Scarborough's next question.

Raine wondered how much more biographical data Scarborough was going to illicit before he got to the actual night of the murder.

"Uh, no," Ernest answered, some sadness creeping back into his voice. "By the time we met, we were both too old to start a family."

"Okay, let's talk about the night of Ms. Pruitt's murder," Scarborough announced. He did look up to say it, but he didn't seem particularly interested in Ernest's response; he just didn't have a question to check off at that exact moment because of the theme switch.

Raine definitely watched Ernest's reaction to the words 'Ms. Pruitt's murder'. The jurors did too. His eyes widened, then drooped. His face blanched but his neck blotched. His shoulders fell. If he'd murdered Alexandra, he was one hell of an actor.

"Uh, okay," Ernest agreed quietly.

Scarborough dropped his face back to his clipboard. "What was happening that night at your residence?"

"It was a little get-together for some friends, mostly friends of Alexandra's," Ernest answered.

"A party?" Scarborough gave him the word he wanted him to use. "A retirement party?"

Raine could have objected that Scarborough was leading the witness, but no one was going to contest it was Alexandra's retirement party.

"I wouldn't really call it that."

Except Ernest.

Scarborough looked up from his prepared questions, obviously surprised by the answer and unsure what to do next.

Raine leaned toward his client to whisper, "It was a retirement party, right?"

Meredith nodded. "Yeah, that was the only reason all five of us were there. We don't really hang out together anymore."

"You wouldn't call it a retirement party?" Scarborough repeated back. "Why not?"

Ernest smiled. "Because Alexandra was never going to retire. She loved her work. She found herself in her work. If she ever really retired, she would have shriveled up and died, I think. That's why she was doing what she was doing with her business. Not retiring from it, but bringing more people on so she could slow down a little without worrying that everything she had built would just crumble away."

"Did she tell you what her plan was?" Scarborough was finally off script.

Raine was glad for it, actually. He was stuck in the courtroom for the entire trial with Scarborough. He didn't want his opponent to do a fantastic job, but he didn't want him to be boring the entire time either.

Ernest leaned forward and raised a tentative finger. "Not exactly," he admitted. "Alexandra was pretty private about her business stuff. She made sure the bills were paid and I never wanted for anything, but I couldn't tell you how much anything in the house cost, for example. No, the entire point of the evening was that she hadn't told anyone and was going to announce it to everyone, including me, all at once."

"But she never got a chance to do that, did she?" Scarborough pointed out.

"No." Ernest's expression dropped again. "No, she didn't."

"Let's talk about that then," Scarborough moved back to his outline. "Where did you discover her body?"

Ernest took a moment to gather himself before responding. "Um, she was in the kitchen."

"On the floor, correct?" Scarborough plowed ahead.

"Uh, yeah. Yes. The kitchen."

Scarborough lowered his clipboard and walked across the 'well'—the empty area between the judge's bench, the lawyers' tables, the jury box, and the witness stand—and picked up a pile of photographs, blown up onto glossy 8.5" x 11" sheets. "I'm going to show you a series of photos from the crime scene, and I would like you to identify and describe what is depicted in each photograph."

He started toward the witness stand, but Ernest put his hands up.

"Are those pictures of Alexandra after she died?" he asked.

Scarborough thought for a moment. "Yes. I just said that."

"Then no." Ernest shook his head and waved Scarborough away. "I don't want to see those."

Scarborough looked down at the photos in his hand. "But you just testified that you found her on the floor. These are just photographs of what you've already seen, so the jury can see too."

Ernest shook his head even harder. He crossed his arms and turned away from Scarborough. "I won't do it."

Another pause from Scarborough as he tried to figure

out how to proceed. "You have to. You're a witness. You are under subpoena. You answer the questions put to you."

"I'll answer any question you ask," Ernest half-shouted back, "but I will not look at those photographs."

Raine was enjoying watching Scarborough squirm, but he also had a chance to score points with the jurors, all of whom must have been sympathetic with Ernest by that point. He stood up, "Your Honor, I have no objection to the admission of the photographs. I've seen them. They're accurate. Let's admit them and give them directly to the jury. Mr. Poplowski doesn't need to relive that night any more than he already has."

"Are you making a motion to admit the photographs, Mr. Raine?" Judge Brenner asked.

"Sure," Raine replied, then he sat down.

"Mr. Scarborough," Brenner asked him next, "any objection?"

"Well, no. I guess not," Scarborough answered. "But I had a lot of questions for this witness about what's in the photographs."

"I imagine the photographs speak strongly for themselves," the judge counseled. "Perhaps you could move on to your next topic."

Scarborough frowned and reengaged with his clipboard. He flipped to the next page, then the next page, then to the one after that. "I don't think I have any other questions for Mr. Poplowski, Your Honor."

Raine considered that. Relationship, finances, Alexandra's secret plan, found her dead. Yes, that seemed like a full direct examination, especially if everything after 'found her dead' was excluded.

Scarborough sat down and Judge Brenner looked to the defense table. "Any cross-examination, Mr. Raine?"

Raine stood up again. "Yes, Your Honor. Thank you."

He stepped out from behind the defense table and walked about halfway to the witness stand. He didn't stand next to the jury box like Scarborough because this was cross-examination. Cross-examination was about confrontation. For direct examination of a friendly witness, the jurors want to see and hear what the witness says to them. On cross-examination, the jurors want to see the lawyer challenging the witness. Hiding behind the jury box would communicate fear.

Raine had a bigger challenge than where to stand. His plan was to show the jury that any one of the prosecution's witnesses could have committed the murder—except Sommers. In order to do that, he would need to attack each of the witnesses, and that could become a problem. Jurors could appreciate an aggressive defense attorney doing their job, but no one liked a jerk. One or two or even three aggressive and accusatory cross-examinations would be bearable, even entertaining. Ten of them and the jury would turn off. It was always easier to defer to the judgment of the prosecutor and assume they wouldn't have charged someone who wasn't guilty. Annoying the jury wasn't a winning defense strategy. He would need to be efficient. Quick, interesting, effective. Polite and professional. Then sit down.

"You said you were retired," he began, "but you haven't worked a day in twenty years, have you?"

Maybe a little aggressive. The jury would want to see some strength too. That was part of being interesting.

"What? No," Ernest stammered. "I mean, yes. Yes, I worked. I just... I retired early."

"Because Alexandra was rich," Raine said. "You just needed to look pretty and say, 'Yes, ma'am', isn't that right?"

"That is not right, sir." Ernest pulled himself up.

"You're calling yourself 'common-law husband' now." Raine made air quotes with his fingers when he said, 'common-law husband'. "That's because a real husband would inherit from her death, but you don't stand to inherit anything, do you? You're broke now."

"As far as anyone can tell, Alexandra never wrote a will," Ernest answered. "So, no, I don't know if I will inherit since I wasn't her real husband, as you say. But we loved each other and lived as husband and wife for almost twenty years. I don't care about the money, but I did care about Alexandra. Deeply. I will never stop missing her."

A heartfelt, sympathetic answer. The jury would like that. Raine needed to land a blow and sit down.

"Have you seen a lawyer about whether you could inherit something, anything," Raine asked, "since there's no will and you were sort of her husband?"

Ernest hesitated.

"You have," Raine deduced. "I don't suppose it was Elisabeth Ungermann of the law firm Ellis-plus-JPG, was it?"

"Wouldn't anything I said to a lawyer be protected by attorney-client privilege?" Ernest deflected.

Raine smiled. "If you want it to be. But I think we all know what that means." He looked up at the judge. "No further questions, Your Honor." He returned to his seat.

"That wasn't very nice," Meredith whispered to him.

"Do you want me to be nice," Raine whispered back, "or do you want to win the case?"

Meredith didn't answer, which was an answer in itself.

She wouldn't take much solace from her cell in Walla Walla that her lawyer had been nice during the trial.

"Mr. Scarborough," Judge Brenner called down to him. "Any redirect-examination based on Mr. Raine's questions?"

"Based on those questions?" Scarborough considered. That was the rule; redirect was limited to the topics raised on the cross-examination. "No, Your Honor."

That meant Ernest was done testifying.

"May this witness be excused?" Brenner asked the lawyers. 'Excused' meant they couldn't be called as a witness again in the trial. That would also allow them to sit in on the testimony of any remaining witnesses.

"Yes, Your Honor," Scarborough answered.

But Raine wanted to keep his powder dry in case he needed to call Ernest in his own case-in-chief. Trials, once begun, had lives of their own. They could go off the rails quickly. He might need Ernest to disprove some random fact some witness raised ten witnesses later. Plus, he didn't want the common-law widower sitting through the rest of the trial. That would generate too much sympathy for the prosecution.

"No, Your Honor," Raine said. "We would ask that this witness remain subject to recall."

Judge Brenner nodded and turned to Ernest. "Mr. Poplowski, you are finished testifying today but you are subject to being recalled as a witness. As a result, you may not sit in on the proceedings or listen to any other witnesses until you are finally excused. Do you understand?"

"Yes, Your Honor." Ernest nodded. "And that's fine. I couldn't sit and listen to what happened to my Alexandra anyway. It would break my heart all over again."

Ernest stood up and walked toward the exit, and Brenner invited Scarborough to call his next witness.

Despite his attacks, Raine didn't think there was anyone in the courtroom who actually thought Ernest was the murderer. That was okay with Raine. Ernest wasn't his prime suspect anyway.

"The State calls Caroline Howard to the stand."

31

If there was any prosecution witness who actually murdered Alexandra, Raine's money was on Caroline. Jealous, entitled, desperate.

When the police first showed up that night, Raine thought Caroline was the one most likely to be led away in handcuffs. But that was before Meredith made the mistake of talking to the cops, and before the cops watched the surveillance video. Caroline wasn't on the video tampering with Alexandra's food, but then again, Scarborough had only shared the part that made Meredith look guilty. Had Caroline arrived before the other guests? Had she handed a dish to one of the caterers to put in the refrigerator? Was there some other slanderous question Raine could pose in front of the jury to cast doubt on Caroline? Probably. It was time to find out.

"Do you swear to tell the truth, the whole truth, and nothing but the truth?" Brenner asked Caroline as she stood before the bench with her right hand raised.

"Absolutely," Caroline answered dramatically.

It was going to be easy to cast suspicion on her, Raine told himself. She was going to love the spotlight, despite herself. She took her seat on the witness stand and Raine leaned forward, intent to focus on every word that fell out of Caroline's mouth. But just as Scarborough picked up his clipboard and headed for the corner of the jury box, the courtroom door opened again and Raine couldn't help but turn to see who had just walked in.

Elisabeth Ungermann.

Raine nodded to her. She nodded back, with a confident smile. He really didn't like her. But he liked that she had come to watch Caroline's testimony. It confirmed to Raine that Caroline had switched sides. Another reason to distrust the least successful of the Fab Five.

"Please state your full name for the record." Scarborough began his examination.

"Caroline Michelle Howard," she seemed pleased to report.

"What city do you live in?"

"Seattle." More self-satisfaction. Living in the city and not the suburbs was a point of pride for most Seattleites.

"How old are you?" Scarborough continued through his 'name, rank, and serial number' questions. He was standing next to the jurors and looking down at his clipboard again.

Caroline laughed nervously. "Really? I mean, you never ask a woman her age, right?"

Scarborough blinked at her. "Do you want me to repeat the question?"

Caroline frowned. "Forty-two. I'm forty-two."

"How are you employed?"

The confidence returned to her expression. "I own my

own real estate business. Howard Premier Brokerage. Our main office is just off the waterfront. We specialize in—"

"Thank you," Scarborough cut off the rest of Caroline's answer. "Did you know Alexandra Pruitt?"

"Yes," Caroline answered. She sat up a little straighter in the witness chair. "Absolutely."

"How did you know her?" The next question on the script. He must have cut and pasted for each witness, Raine supposed.

"Alexandra was a colleague in the real estate industry," Caroline answered. "But more than that, she was a mentor and a friend. I miss her every day."

Raine stole a glance at the jurors to see if any of them had any visible reactions to Caroline so far. Most sat stone-faced, but a couple of them were already frowning. That was good. He'd minimized his accusations against Ernest. They weren't even accusations, just suggestions. Shade, as the kids would say. Maybe. He wasn't sure he was using that right. But it didn't matter. Scarborough was talking again.

"Were you present at Ms. Pruitt's residence the night she was murdered?"

Caroline's mouth tightened into a thin-lipped grimace. "Yes. Yes, I was there that terrible night."

Another glance at the jurors. Another couple of them frowning. So far, so good.

"Why were you there?" Scarborough followed up.

"I beg your pardon?" Caroline replied. "I just said she was my friend and mentor. Why wouldn't I have been invited?"

Scarborough looked up from his clipboard and blinked at his witness. "Of course," he gave her. "I mean, what was the purpose of the gathering?"

"Oh!" Caroline laughed lightly and nodded to the jurors. "Yes, that. It was supposedly Alexandra's retirement party, but I don't think she ever had any intention of actually retiring. I thought it was going to be more of a 'next stage in my illustrious career' party."

"Were there any announcements expected at this next stage in her career party?" Scarborough followed up.

Caroline nodded. "Yes. Well, I mean that was why we all went. I don't think anything less than that would have gotten all of us in the same room together. Alexandra may have liked all of us, but that didn't mean we all liked each other. We were competitors after all."

"Who is 'we'?" Scarborough asked.

"Oh, we called ourselves The Fab Five," Caroline answered. "Alexandra's five favorites. Five women she picked out to mentor and help succeed. We owe our careers to Alexandra."

How's that going for you? Raine wanted to ask. But he'd have to wait his turn.

"Who are these five women?" Scarborough asked. "And was the defendant, Meredith Beauchamp, one of them?"

Caroline nodded and braved the slightest glance at Meredith, sitting at the defendant's table and locked in to every word of her testimony.

"Yes." Caroline turned back to Scarborough. "It was me, Meredith, and three other women: Julia Kim, Rebecca Sommers, and Fiona Mendoza."

"Were all five of you there that night?"

"Oh yes," Caroline asked. "As I said, Alexandra's retirement was about the only thing that would bring us all together. Especially since we all expected some big announcement about our futures."

"Did you have any idea what the announcement might be?" Scarborough asked.

Raine probably could have objected, saying, 'Calls for speculation', but he was curious too.

Caroline took a moment. She turned slightly to one side and displayed a full-lipped smirk. "Well, yes, that was a significant topic of speculation that evening. Alexandra liked her surprises, and she liked an audience. I thought maybe she was going to establish a foundation in our names or something like that. Something big and charitable. A legacy, you know."

"Okay," Scarborough replied without committing to whether he did, in fact, know. "Is that what she announced?"

"She never announced anything," Caroline answered. "Meredith murdered her before she could."

Now it was time to object. Raine stood up. "Objection, Your Honor. That response was rank speculation. It also invades the province of the jury. Only the jury can decide who murdered Alexandra Pruitt, and it certainly wasn't Ms. Beauchamp."

"All right, all right." Judge Brenner raised a palm toward Raine. "Enough with the speaking objections. You could have stopped at 'calls for speculation'. I will sustain the objection. If you want this witness to state who murdered the victim, you will need to lay foundation that the witness has personal knowledge of that fact."

Scarborough wouldn't be able to establish personal knowledge because Caroline didn't have it.

"I will ask you not to speculate, Ms. Howard," Scarborough said. "Are you personally aware of any plans Ms. Pruitt might have been ready to announce regarding her business holdings?"

Caroline thought for a moment, then let it rip. "Here's what I do know. I know Alexandra promised each of us a big announcement. I know she promised it would be worth it for us to come. I also know that there was some sort of partnership agreement that had been drafted up for all of us to sign. And I know only Meredith and Alexandra signed it before Alexandra died. So, I know that if Meredith gets away with it, she's going to take control of everything Alexandra built and the rest of us will be left out in the cold. That sure sounds like a motive to me."

Raine pursed his lips. That was not helpful. He was going to enjoy his cross-examination.

"Do you really think Ms. Beauchamp would have been capable of murdering your shared mentor, Ms. Pruitt?" Scarborough asked.

Raine could have objected again, for basically the same reason. It allowed Caroline to offer her opinion as to Meredith's guilt. But he wanted to hear what she had to say, and why. And it would have been an ineffective objection anyway. If the judge had sustained it, and Caroline had been prohibited from answering it because of the defense attorney's objection, each and every juror would have known the answer would have been a resounding, 'Yes'. He couldn't challenge an answer that wasn't actually spoken. It was better to let her speak and hope she gave him enough rope to hang her.

Caroline took several moments before answering. Finally, she looked down and shook her head. "I do. I don't want to, but I do. I do think she's capable of it."

"Why?"

Caroline nodded. "Let me tell you a story about the last time all five of us were together. We were at Alexandra's cabin in Preston, up near the Snoqualmie Pass. Alexandra had set up some sort of elaborate scavenger hunt. The winner would find a bag filled with ten thousand dollars in cash, but the clues were impossible and none of us could figure it out. At one point, after we'd been trying to solve it for several hours already, Meredith said, 'This is so humiliating. She's making us run around like a bunch of trained monkeys. Why can't she just die already and leave everything to us? It's not like she has any family anyway.'"

Raine leaned over toward his client, but didn't look directly at her, lest a juror or two glance their way to gauge her reaction to Caroline's testimony and see them huddling over it.

"Did you really say that?" Raine whispered without looking at her.

Meredith sighed. "Yes. But I didn't really mean it. We never did find that stupid money."

Scarborough nodded and checked his script. "Did you personally see anyone administer poison to Ms. Pruitt's food?"

Caroline shook her head. "No."

"And did you interact with Ms. Pruitt's corpse at any time after the murder was discovered?"

Caroline wrinkled her nose. "No, definitely not."

"And finally," Scarborough wrapped up his examination, "did the defendant ever make any statements to you about Ms. Pruitt's death?"

"No," Meredith whispered to Raine.

"Why yes," Caroline answered after a moment, a broad smile unfurling across her face.

"What?" Scarborough asked. "What did she say?"

"After the police arrived, and we were forced to sit in that condominium the entire night," Caroline recounted. "At one point I found myself sitting next to Meredith and she said, 'I'm glad I signed that agreement in time.'"

"I never said that!" Meredith grabbed Raine's sleeve.

He removed her hand and held up a finger to tell her to wait a minute. He needed to listen to Caroline and Scarborough.

"I didn't understand what she meant then," Caroline continued. "And I was too tired to ask. But now I understand."

Scarborough nodded, seemingly in gratitude. "Thank you, Ms. Howard. No further questions."

It was Raine's turn. He had some damage to control. Bleeding to staunch, really. He needed to do that first. Then he could accuse her of being the real murderer, and gladly.

"Let's pick up right where you left off, Ms. Howard," he said as he stepped out from behind the defense table. "You claim that Ms. Beauchamp, what, wished Ms. Pruitt was dead, I guess? Just because she made the scavenger hunt clues a little too difficult? Doesn't that seem a bit farfetched, Ms. Howard?"

Caroline shrugged. "I don't know if it's farfetched. It's what she said."

"How long ago was this?" Raine asked. Maybe it was too distant in time to be truly relevant.

"Oh, a few years," Caroline admitted. "Maybe three? Four? I'm not sure. It was recent enough that it made sense to say something about Alexandra retiring. But it was long enough ago to be at the cabin. She used to host a lot of things out of that cabin. But then she just sort of stopped. Like she didn't want anyone to go there anymore."

Raine frowned at the answer. It wasn't helpful. Not obviously so, anyway. But he was struck mostly by the fact that he had never heard of this cabin before. It was a new lead. And he was stuck there in court, asking questions of someone who was going to lie to him anyway. He sighed to himself. Might as well get it over with.

"Your business is failing, isn't it?"

"You have no money and no employees, except for a work-study student you don't pay, correct?"

"You resented Alexandra for not supporting you enough, even if you needed more than the rest of The Fab Five, didn't you?"

"You were humiliated by your failure when everyone else was succeeding, isn't that right?"

"You were Alexandra's biggest disappointment, weren't you?"

"If she was going to leave her fortune and her business to only some of The Fab Five, you would have been the first one to be left out, isn't that right?"

"You were afraid she was going to humiliate you in front of everyone by giving her business to everyone except you, isn't that true?"

"You couldn't have lived with that humiliation, could you?"

"You would have done anything to prevent that, wouldn't you?"

"So you brought cyanide with you, snuck it into Alexandra's soup, and framed Meredith, isn't that true, Ms. Howard?"

"You murdered Alexandra Pruitt, didn't you?"

Of course, Caroline answered "No" to every one of Raine's questions. He expected that. Murderers don't confess on the stand, despite what you might see on television. But it didn't matter. Raine hadn't asked the questions for her to provide answers. He asked them for the jury to hear the questions. If it planted reasonable doubt in the mind of even one juror, it was a success.

Raine wanted to get out of there as soon as he could. There was a cabin to break into, after all. But a glance at the gallery reminded him he had one more area of inquiry he couldn't ignore.

"You got sued, didn't you?" he asked. "Because of a rather large loan that Ms. Pruitt made to an old friend of hers, a friend who seems to think you're going to end up with at least part of Ms. Pruitt's business holding when this is all over."

"Objection." Scarborough stood up again. "That's a compound question, and it calls for speculation by this witness as to what someone else thinks about the victim's finances."

Brenner nodded. "Sustained. On both grounds. Rephrase, Mr. Raine."

Raine stepped closer to the witness stand. An intentionally aggressive move. "You're being sued, right?"

Caroline took a moment, then a smile unfurled from the corners of the mouth. "No. I am not being sued."

Raine narrowed his eyes at his subject. He had rephrased his question and in doing so changed the tense of his verb.

"You did get sued, though, right?" he insisted. "By a man named Randall Newberry."

"We all got sued," Caroline answered. "All five of us, including Meredith, by the way. But the case against me has been dropped."

"Because you agreed to help Newberry," Raine accused. "You have a financial interest in keeping him happy. And nothing would make him and his lawyer happier than Meredith being convicted of Alexandra's murder."

"Is there a question in there somewhere?" Caroline sneered at him.

"Maybe not," Raine admitted, "but the truth is in there somewhere."

He shook his head at Caroline like a parent disappointed with a child who insists on lying despite the broken cookie jar at their feet. He turned and walked toward his counsel table. "No further questions, Your Honor."

"Any redirect-examination, Mr. Scarborough?" Judge Brenner invited.

Scarborough stood up. He seemed a bit perplexed by Raine's line of questions/accusations. "Did you murder Alexandra Pruitt, Ms. Howard?"

"No!" Caroline almost yelled. "Of course not."

Scarborough nodded. "No further questions."

"Anything based on that, Mr. Raine?" Brenner asked out of obligation.

There was nothing more Raine could ask and keep it limited to Scarborough's one redirect question. They could get into a tennis match of 'Did not/Did too!' but he knew the jury would really hate that.

"No, Your Honor," he said.

"May this witness be excused?" Brenner tried again.

But Raine didn't know what he and Sommers might find at that cabin. "No, Your Honor. The defense would ask the witness remain subject to recall."

"Are you going to ask that for every witness, Mr. Raine?" the judge asked.

Raine thought for a moment, then nodded. "Most likely, Your Honor."

Brenner sighed then instructed Caroline that she was free to go but she might have to come back.

Raine looked at the clock. They had spent the better part of the day in session. There was time to start another witness, but it was late enough in the afternoon that adjourning for the day wasn't completely unreasonable.

"Mr. Scarborough—" Brenner started, but Raine interrupted.

"Could we adjourn early today, Your Honor?" he asked. "I have some things I need to do in preparation of the next witness."

Judge Brenner turned to Scarborough. "Have you informed Mr. Raine who your next witness will be?"

Scarborough shook his head. "No, Your Honor."

"All the more reason I need time to prepare," Raine tried. Then, he repeated his request formally. "The defense would request we adjourn for the day."

Judge Brenner thought for a moment, then shrugged. "All right then. The attorneys need time to prepare for the next witness. Court will be adjourned until tomorrow morning at nine o'clock." He brought his gavel down on the bench.

They were done for the day. Everyone began filing out of the courtroom. Ungermann was the first one out the door.

"Why are we ending early?" Meredith asked. She had a few moments before she was taken back to her cell. The guards wouldn't approach her until the last of the jurors had filed into the jury room and the door closed behind them.

"Field trip," Raine answered.

"Field trip?" Meredith questioned.

"Yep." Raine nodded but offered no further explanation. "I'll bring you back a souvenir."

32

"Alexandra's cabin?" Sommers reacted when she finally answered Raine's call and he told her the plan. "I'd forgotten all about that place. The last time I was there, she had us do some impossible scavenger hunt."

"Yeah, I heard about that," Raine replied. "Do you remember where it is? Can you get us there?"

"I'm not sure," Sommer answered. "Maybe. Probably. When?"

"Tonight," Raine said.

"Are you serious?" Sommers asked. "I have plans tonight."

"Cancel them," Raine told her. "We're in trial now. Everything else can wait."

"You haven't seen the man I have plans with tonight," Sommers protested.

Raine sighed. "Raincheck him. If he's worth it, he's worth waiting for. This is important."

"How important?" Sommers questioned.

"Your friend going to prison for the rest of her life important," Raine answered.

Sommers paused for several seconds before replying. "Okay. Fine. I'll reschedule. You owe me."

"Meredith owes you," Raine said. "I'm just her lawyer."

"And I'm her friend," Sommers sighed. "I can be at your office in thirty minutes. I need to change. I can't wear this dress to a cabin in the mountains."

Raine picked her up thirty minutes later. The sun wasn't setting quite yet, but the shadows were getting longer. He followed the surface streets to the entrance for Interstate-90, eastbound. Only 3,000 miles to Boston, but they were going to stop well short of that. Fall City was less than 25 miles from Seattle, about halfway to Snoqualmie Pass, the closest, busiest, and easiest way over the Cascade Mountains. Sommers had dressed as if she were going to traverse the peaks on foot. She looked like she had stepped out of a camping equipment catalog.

"You know it's only the foothills, right?" Raine asked her as he merged onto the freeway. "We aren't actually going to be roasting s'mores with bears or anything."

She looked at his outfit; he was still in his suit. "We're not going to be selling the bears insurance either."

"Fair enough," he admitted. "How long has it been since you were at this cabin? Is there at least a gravel road? These shoes aren't trail rated."

"It's been a while," Sommers answered. "Honestly, I thought she'd sold it. It used to be this place we went to a lot. At least once every summer she hosted a getaway. Not just the Fab Five, but everyone who was important that year. But as we all kept growing apart, not everyone made it every year, and eventually they stopped. I haven't been out there in years."

Raine nodded at that, wondering what they might find when they finally reached the cabin. He leaned forward and hovered a finger over the radio. "A little music for the ride?"

Sommers smiled. "I doubt we like the same music."

"I like lots of different kinds of music," Raine defended.

"Exactly." Sommers laughed. "Let's just enjoy the scenery."

Raine shrugged, but acquiesced. They emerged from the tunnel under Seattle's Beacon Hill onto the first of two floating bridges connecting Seattle to Mercer Island, Fiona's hometown, and Mercer Island to Bellevue, the unofficial capital of the suburbs, with a budding skyline of its own, like Seattle's little brother.

After Bellevue came Issaquah, a former farm community that had turned into tracts of single-family homes and sprawling condo complexes, for the families who wanted more space than Seattle could offer but who couldn't quite afford Bellevue. The end of Issaquah was marked by the twin landmarks of a local chocolate factory that looked like a Swiss chalet and a giant sign in the shape of a root beer barrel. After that, the freeway tipped upwards and began to curve back and forth as they entered the foothills and began the climb toward the pass to the eastern half of the state.

"Look," Raine pointed out the window. "A waterfall."

It was less a waterfall than a few thin streams of water spilling down the rock face exposed from blasting a path for the interstate. The water had stained the exposed rock a pleasant orange color, an effect only enhanced by the rays of the lowering sun.

"Maybe we should go to Snoqualmie Falls when we

finish at the cabin," he thought aloud. "They light them up
at night. It's pretty breathtaking."

Sommers shrugged. "Let's see what we find at the cabin.
I'm not sure I'll be in the mood for anything afterward. This
is a business trip, not pleasure."

Raine looked over at his passenger. The entire case was
just business to him. He could forget it was more than that
for Sommers. Alexandra had been a friend. And another
friend was accused of murdering her. Even if Meredith
hadn't done it, that just meant a different friend, or colleague
at least, had. Sommers was so good at being 'on' all the time,
Raine found himself surprised when she turned it off long
enough to reveal a little bit of her actual feelings.

"Or maybe just a drink," Raine suggested. "I bet there's a
pretty good dive bar up here somewhere."

"Now you're talking," Sommers answered. "And speaking
of talking, let's not anymore until we get there."

Raine could do that.

It only took another ten minutes to reach the exit for
Preston, then five more along the aptly named Preston-Fall
City Road until they reached the outskirts of the town. A
sign welcomed them and announced the latest population
count: a whopping 2,032 residents. There were more people
than that in Seattle's Columbia Tower on a weekday. But the
cabin wasn't in the town proper.

"That road up there." Sommers pointed through the
windshield. "Turn right."

Raine did as instructed and turned the car onto a gravel
road with no name, or at least no street sign. The surface was
fairly even, and his city car didn't struggle much to drive into
the woods on the narrowing road. The sun was getting lower
though, and the increasing tree cover made it difficult to see

the road as well as Raine would have liked. There were definitely no streetlights.

"Yeah, I remember this drive." Sommers perked up a bit. "There's going to be a fork in the road up ahead. Stay to the right. To the left is private property and a lot of 'No Trespassing' signs. You don't want to get caught trespassing up here. People police their own properties, usually with a rifle."

"Get caught?" Raine grabbed onto that part of Sommers's advice.

She smiled. "There's a hell of a swimming hole not too far from here. You just have to know when to go." She looked up, out the car window. "Too bad it's cloudy. Nothing like a moonlight swim."

Raine suddenly wished he had met Sommers years earlier. Maybe he could have been invited to one of Alexandra's mountain getaways, instead of meeting her the same night she was murdered.

"Here." Sommers pointed out the windshield again. "Stay to the right."

Raine turned the car to follow the gravel road to the right. The road was becoming less smooth, and they bounced a little as they made their way forward.

"How much farther?" he asked.

"Not much," Sommers answered. "There's going to be a break in the tree cover and an apple orchard on the other side of the river. After that, we're almost there. You'll probably want to turn your headlights on soon. The cabin is surrounded by trees. It gets pitch black at night."

Raine reached down and turned on his headlights. When they reached the clearing, he could see the orchard and its rows of apple trees. He could also see the intermittent raindrops that splattered onto his windshield and danced in his headlight beams.

The trees enveloped the road again and Raine squinted ahead to make out the turns as they approached their destination. He didn't see any other buildings, but he didn't know if that was because there weren't any or because they were hidden in the trees and the dusk.

"There." Sommers pointed again. "That driveway on the left. That's it."

Raine slowed and turned onto the dirt path that Sommers had called a driveway. It seemed fairly well packed down, but if there were any potholes, Raine knew he would feel them before he saw them. He inched forward, the tall grass on either side of the drive brushing audibly against his car.

"It definitely feels abandoned," he commented.

"Yeah," Sommers agreed. "Caroline has always been full of crap. It's why her business never took off. You have to be able to trust someone to make a deal with them."

Alexandra's cabin appeared in Raine's headlights, and the roadway widened just enough to create a parking area to one side of the structure. Raine was surprised to find the structure to be rather small, and worthy of the name 'cabin'. He had expected a full-size house, and a large one at that, with stonework facades in several places, and enough space for every guest at her business parties to spend the night in their own room. Instead, it was a modest affair, with probably two bedrooms. There was moss on the roof and weeds growing up the sides of the front porch. The front screen door was discolored with rust.

Raine brought his vehicle to a stop and killed the engine. The only sound was rain hitting the trees above them.

"We might need flashlights soon," Raine observed. The sun wasn't down quite yet, but the dim light of dusk wasn't going to last much longer, especially among the trees, and the cabin looked like it had had its electricity cut off months ago.

He popped the trunk to fetch a pair of flashlights. He handed Sommers the heavier metal one and kept the lighter plastic one for himself. He wasn't expecting any trouble that far out, but he wanted Sommers to have the larger weapon, in case he was wrong.

They made their way to the cabin and climbed the three wooden steps onto the small, covered porch over the front door.

The rusted screen door swung open with a creak and Raine tried the door handle. "Locked." Hardly surprising. He squinted at the keyhole, wondering if the key they found in Alexandra's office was the key to the cabin, but the lock looked significantly too large for that small key.

"Hold on," Sommers said. She stepped to the far side of the porch and stood on the wooden railing. Raine was afraid the wood might be rotten and collapse under her weight, but she seemed confident in her own safety as she twisted herself to reach up into the rafters of the porch. A few moments later she pulled her hand out of the darkness.

"Ta da!" She had a key in her hand. "This is where Alexandra hid the spare key. Anyone who mattered knew."

"Even Caroline?" Raine suggested.

"Definitely," Sommers confirmed. "If anyone has been out here in the last few months, I bet it was her. It certainly wasn't Alexandra. She would have cleaned the place up at least a little."

That seemed consistent with what little Raine had

observed the two times he'd been to Alexandra's condo, even
if the second visit had been cut short.

Sommers jumped down for the railing and shoved the
key in the lock. A moment later the door was open, and a
moment after that they were inside.

A quick check of the light switch near the door
confirmed the electricity had been turned off. Sommers
turned on her flashlight. Raine followed suit and shone it
around the front room of the cabin. Wooden furniture with
upholstered cushions sat unused in the center of the room,
emanating a sweet smell of slowly rotting fabric. In fact, a
dank, musty smell filled the entire space, the result of a wet
climate, too many trees, and not enough human activity.

"So, what exactly are we looking for?" Sommers asked,
her own beam crisscrossing the room.

"Anything that might help Meredith," Raine answered.
"A will? One that leaves everything to anyone other than
Meredith. Something to show she didn't really have the
motive Scarborough is claiming."

"I'd love to find something that explained Alexandra's
connection to Newberry," Sommers replied. "I don't know if
that will help Meredith, but it would sure help me. I don't
understand why Alexandra would do business with a man
like that."

Raine recalled Newberry's henchman-slash-driver
mentioning a drive to Fall City. "Did Newberry have a cabin
up here too?"

Sommers stopped and turned to look at Raine, her face
only half lit by the flashlights. "I don't know. Why?"

"He came up here the other day," Raine explained. "I
mean, not this cabin. But Fall City. The guy I hit with the tire
iron drove him here."

Sommers took a beat. "You need to catch me up on some things."

Raine smiled. "Nothing to worry about. My ribs are healing up fine."

"Okay." Sommers didn't inquire further. "Well. It sure doesn't look like he came here. It doesn't look like anyone has been here for a while. There's dust on everything."

It was a greenish, sticky dust too. Resin from the evergreens surrounding them. There were no dishes out or anything that suggested a hurried departure of the last occupants. But the cabin wasn't in perfect order either. Random papers and items dotted the surfaces. It looked as if someone expected to return soon enough but then just didn't.

"Let's check the bedrooms," Raine suggested.

There were three total, one more than his original estimate. They had a similar musty smell, but one that added the scent of molding blankets. The first room had the least in it. Raine surmised it was the guest room. A double bed took up most of the floor space. A small nightstand was jammed into the far corner between the bed and the wall. A quick check confirmed nothing in or on the nightstand. The bed was similarly uninteresting, with two pillows and extra blankets folded and stacked at the foot.

Raine nodded toward the hallway, and they exited the room. The sun was essentially set by then. Whatever orange streaks might have been visible by the tourists on the Seattle waterfront watching the sunset over Puget Sound and the Olympic Mountains beyond were completely blocked by the forest surrounding the cabin. The floorboards creaked as Raine and Sommers made their way to the next bedroom.

"I can't believe so many of us used to spend the night here," Sommers recalled. "It seems so small now, but it just seemed so natural back then. This was the one place Alexandra seemed to actually be able to relax. To really be herself. She never let her guard down all the way, but it was lowest when she was here."

"Was she from here?" Raine ventured.

Sommers paused. "You know, I'm not sure. I don't know exactly where she's from. She never talked about growing up, or even her early career. It was always like she appeared in downtown Seattle, fully formed and rich. A force of nature."

"Like Athena from Zeus's head," Raine observed.

"Sure," Sommers agreed with a bemused smile. "Anyway, this place really seemed to be her happy place. I'm surprised to see she abandoned it."

They had reached the next room. It was also a small bedroom, with two twin beds inches apart. There wasn't room for a nightstand.

"Nothing in here either," Raine observed. "This may end up being a dead end."

"I'm sure you'll come up with some way to spin it in front of the jury," Sommers joked. "Meredith hadn't been to Alexandra's cabin for months, maybe even years. She couldn't be the murderer."

"That's kind of a *non sequitur*," Raine pointed out.

"Yeah, throw in some Latin too," Sommers teased. "You'll win those jurors over in no time."

"Let's try the last room," Raine changed the subject. "That's probably Alexandra's room. If there's anything useful, it'll be in there."

The last room definitely appeared to be the one Alexandra used as a bedroom. It had a twin bed and two nightstands, as well as a freestanding wardrobe. The bed wasn't made up as well as the others. Rather than tucked-in sheets and a smooth-top blanket, the covers had been pulled loosely up to the pillows, which were askew, at least compared to the perfectly centered ones in the previous rooms. Again, it appeared the last time Alexandra left the cabin, she had plans to return, and then just didn't. Either that or Goldilocks had stopped by.

Raine opened the wardrobe as Sommers checked the nightstands. The wardrobe wasn't completely full but there were a dozen or so items of clothing on the hangers. On the bottom were several pairs of different types of shoes. One of each major category. Sneakers, heels, boots, and slippers. In the far corner, tucked behind the skirts of a couple of longer dresses was a wooden box. Raine pulled it out and turned to open it up on the bed. When he did so, he found Sommers standing over a pile of envelopes she had dropped atop the bed, presumably from the open drawer of the nightstand nearest the window.

"What are those?" he asked.

"Empty envelopes," Sommers answered. "The letters that were in them are gone."

"That's weird," Raine remarked. He picked up several of the envelopes. There must have been at least twenty of them, all different shapes, sizes, and colors—and all of them empty. "Who saves the envelopes and throws away the letters?"

"Makes you wonder what was in the letters," Sommers said. "The postmarks are all from Seattle."

"Are they all from the same person?" Raine asked.

"I think so." Sommers pointed at the ones in Raine's hand. "Look at the handwriting."

Raine set down the box and picked up several of the

envelopes. Sure enough, the handwriting was the same on all of them. A neat, blocky print. "They're all addressed to 'G. Pruitt'. And there's no return address."

Sommers nodded. "I noticed that too."

"Who's G. Pruitt?" Raine asked. "Was Alexandra not her first name or something?"

Sommers shook her head. "No, Alexandra was her legal name. Think about that partnership agreement Meredith allegedly signed. I have no idea who G. Pruitt could be."

Raine didn't have any idea either. Then he remembered the box. Again, he wondered if maybe the key from Alexandra's office went to the box, but there was no lock. He flipped the clasp open and lifted the lid. Sommers shone her flashlight inside.

The box held three things. A small blanket or towel, its pink and blue lines almost completely faded away. A corroded golden ring with a tiny pink stone. And a cut-off medical bracelet bearing the name 'Pruitt, Alexandra' and a date over forty years earlier.

"What is this stuff?" Sommers asked.

"Whatever it is," Raine knew, "it was important to her."

Sommers picked up the ring. "This isn't even gold. She could have afforded a million of these now, literally."

Raine examined the medical bracelet. "St. Joseph Hospital. I've never heard of it. Is that in Seattle?"

"It used to be," the commercial real estate agent answered. "Up on First Hill. They tore it down decades ago to build a parking garage."

"So, that's a dead end," Raine opined. "Somebody gave her a cheap ring while she was in the hospital, and it was important enough to her to keep in this box for literally the rest of her life."

He thought for a moment. "G. Pruitt. Could that have been a secret husband?"

Sommers shrugged. "I don't think so. I think Pruitt was her maiden name. But like I said, she never talked about her early life. And I don't know why the letters would be mailed here."

"Unless she was hiding a secret husband up in the woods," Raine suggested.

But Sommers shook her head. "No. She was devoted to Ernest. She never married him, but she loved him."

"Maybe she never married him because she was already married," Raine suggested.

Sommers shook her head again. "Save your wild conspiracy theories for the courtroom, Dan."

Raine smiled. He might just do that, if he could figure out how he could make it help Meredith. "Do you think Caroline came out here and discovered whatever secret Alexandra was hiding?"

"I wouldn't put it past her," Sommers answered. "But Alexandra would never put up with being blackmailed. If Caroline made the mistake of thinking she could force Alexandra to give her money for her failing business, Alexandra would have destroyed her."

"Like cut her out of any partnership agreement?" Raine suggested. "And announce it in front of everyone at a retirement party to humiliate her?"

"And then Caroline found out what her plan was," Sommers continued.

"And killed her before she could reveal her blackmail and cut her off from any financial reward," Raine concluded. He nodded. "It's not a bad theory."

"It might even be true," Sommers commented.

"An added bonus." He looked down at the items on the bed and frowned.

Sommers looked at his expression. "What's wrong?"

"If I'm going to do that," Raine answered, "we're going to need to take these things. I feel bad about that."

Sommers looked at the envelopes and box as well. "Me too. Whatever this was, it was private. And it was important."

Raine waited a moment, then started gathering up the evidence. "We'll use it to catch her real killer."

"Is that enough justification?" Sommers wondered.

"It will have to be," Raine answered. "Now let's get out of here and find that dive bar. We've earned a drink."

33

Court started up again the next morning with Julia Kim on the stand and Raine uncertain about his way forward. He had told the jury he was going to go after every witness to show anyone could have committed the murder. He needed to follow through with that, if only because the jury was expecting it, and you should always try to give the jury what they want.

On the other hand, the stash of artifacts at Alexandra's cabin suggested a different path entirely. The problem was that he couldn't quite make out the path through the fog of the rest of the case. But the best way out was usually through, so he had little choice but to move forward as Scarborough continued to build his case against Meredith.

"Please state your full name for the record," Scarborough began as he had with the previous witnesses, and from his same spot next to the jury box.

"Julia Kim," she answered. She was wearing a dark suit with pearls and her hair loose on her shoulders.

"What city do you live in?" Scarborough asked next.

"Seattle." She was no suburbanite.

"How old are you?" Scarborough continued.

"Forty-five," she answered without hesitation or any apparent unease.

"What is your occupation?" The next question on the clipboard.

"I am a real estate broker and small business owner," Julia answered. "I own my own brokerage."

"Did you know Alexandra Pruitt?"

"I knew her very well."

"How did you know her?"

Julia took a moment to nod to herself. "When I started out, Alexandra was the person we all wanted to be. I got up the nerve to say hello to her at one of those professional conferences you have to go to if you want to move up in the field. She looked me up and down then asked me if I had time for a cup of coffee. As if I would say no. She could have had my whole day, my whole week.

"She bought me a latte and started asking me questions. Where was I from, where did I want to go, how was I going to get there. All of the things I was asking myself already. She listened intently to my answers. I could tell she was assessing me, judging me. I guess I passed. She gave me her business card and told me to call her after the conference. I did and the course of my life changed. She took me under her wing and taught me everything I needed to know to succeed."

Raine nodded along with the answer. It was what everyone else had said about Alexandra, except maybe for Caroline. Another reason to maybe focus his attacks on her. After that introduction, the jury wasn't likely to think Julia would have done Alexandra some harm. It wasn't going to get easier with Fiona. And Sommers was a whole different problem.

"Were you present at Ms. Pruitt's home the night she died?" Scarborough continued.

Julia nodded. Her usually bright expression dimmed ever so slightly. "Yes."

"Did you speak to her before her death?" Scarborough followed up.

"A little bit," Julia answered. "Here and there. Nothing too deep. She was really busy, rushing back and forth and attending to the catering staff, and the other guests, and Ernest, of course. Always Ernest." There was a warm smile on Julia's face when she mentioned Alexandra's attention to her boyfriend. It wasn't a complaint. "I mostly made small talk with my husband and the other guests."

"Did Alexandra mention anything about the announcement she was planning on making?" Scarborough followed up. "Any details as to what she might have had planned."

Julia shook her head. "She told us she had a big announcement but she died before she could tell anyone. Or at least before she could tell the whole group of us."

"And how did it turn out?" As if Scarborough didn't know.

Raine glanced at his client. Meredith wasn't going to like what Julia was about to say.

"As I understand it," Julia answered, "everything goes to Meredith, except it can't go to Meredith if she's the one who killed Alexandra, in which case no one seems to know where it goes, but I am being sued by someone who thinks it might go at least in part to me, because apparently Alexandra never bothered to write a will."

"That is surprising," Scarborough agreed.

"It's confusing, is what it is," Julia replied. "I don't understand what happened. I would have happily signed that partnership agreement, but I never got the chance." She turned and looked at Meredith. "I wish I truly knew why."

"You feel like you don't know what happened?" Scarborough asked.

"I know what happened," Julia answered. "I just don't know why. And I don't know who to believe. Honestly, I have a lot of difficulty believing Meredith could have murdered Alexandra."

Thank you, Raine thought with a grin.

"But then again, someone did," Julia continued, "and it was someone who was there that night, someone Alexandra trusted. I wouldn't have thought any of them capable of it. But one of them was. So, maybe that one was Meredith."

And never mind. The grin disappeared.

"Did you ever speak with the defendant that night?" Scarborough followed up.

"Meredith? Yes, I'm sure I did," Julia answered. "I don't really recall any specifics. It must not have been about anything important. Just more small talk."

"But one of the topics of small talk was whatever announcement Alexandra was planning to make, is that correct?" Scarborough sought to clarify.

"Definitely," Julia confirmed.

"So, more likely than not," Scarborough put to her, "Meredith talked to you about the financial implications of that night on her and the rest of you. Would you agree with that?"

Julia thought for a moment. "I guess that seems right."

"Did she ever tell you that she had in fact already signed the partnership agreement?" Scarborough asked.

Julia looked again at Meredith, eyes narrowing. "No. No, she did not."

Suddenly, Raine didn't feel so bad about going after Julia after all. She seemed fine with going after Meredith.

"So, to summarize," Scarborough began to wrap up his line of questioning, "you spoke with the defendant on and off during the evening and although she had signed a partnership agreement, she never mentioned it to you, is that correct?"

"That is correct," Julie agreed.

"And when Alexandra was murdered," he continued, "that prevented anyone else from joining the partnership agreement, is that correct?"

"Again, correct," Julia confirmed.

Scarborough finally looked up from his clipboard. "Can you account for the defendant's whereabouts at the time the poison was added to Alexandra's food?"

Julia shook her head. "No. I have no idea where she was when that happened. She wasn't with me or the other guests. I would have remembered that."

"Thank you, Ms. Kim." Scarborough tucked his clipboard under his arm. "No further questions."

Judge Brenner looked down to Raine even as Raine was already standing up. "Any cross-examination, counsel?"

"Oh yes, Your Honor," Raine answered.

He marched out from behind his table and directly toward the witness stand. He didn't need a clipboard, and his preferred spot wasn't on the other side of the courtroom. It was one step too close to the witness. Then he stepped back from the abyss. No one likes a jerk. He could make his point, let it sink in, then sit down.

"Good morning, Ms. Kim," he began.

"Good morning, Mr. Raine," she returned. "Good to see you again."

"You too," Raine returned the pleasantry, then set to work. "You obviously had great affection and admiration for Alexandra Pruitt, didn't you?"

"Absolutely," Julia agreed.

"But, that being said," he continued, "the financial benefits of sharing in her business would have been substantial, would they not?"

Julia took a moment. "I suppose so," she admitted.

"You own your business, is that correct?" Raine asked, knowing full well it was correct. She had just said as much.

"Yes," Julia answered. "I own a real estate brokerage."

"Real estate," Raine repeated. "That can be a boom-and-bust business sometimes, can't it?"

Julia shrugged. "I suppose. It depends on what type of real estate you deal in."

"But also macroeconomic factors you have no control over, right?" Raine suggested. "Interest rates, fluctuations in real income, things like that, right?"

"Sure," Julia agreed. "Sometimes you just have to weather the storms."

"And in lean times," Raine continued, "you might have to leverage your business a little bit, isn't that right?"

"Leverage," Julia repeated. "You mean loans?"

"Debt," Raine clarified. "I mean debt. You have taken on a not-insubstantial amount of debt to keep your business running, isn't that correct, Ms. Kim?"

It was a bit of a bluff. Raine didn't have the actual receipts—no bank statements or anything like that. But Sommers had told him that Julia had overleveraged her business, and as far as Raine was concerned, Sommers was the bank.

"We have some debt we are servicing, yes," Julia admitted. "But nothing out of the ordinary, and nothing we can't manage. My business is not in danger of failing."

"Oh, and I didn't mean to suggest it was." Raine threw his hands up innocently. "I'm not suggesting your brokerage will fail without an infusion of capital from Alexandra's business. No, no. I'm just saying, it would have been nice to pay off some of that debt, huh?"

Julia shifted in her seat. "It's always nice to pay off debt."

"And you and your husband were probably pretty excited to maybe get a piece of Alexandra's business that night, weren't you?" Raine asked. "I mean you got all dressed up and went to the party, right?"

"I would have gone regardless of the money," Julia replied coldly. "Alexandra was a friend. It was a celebration of her."

"And a payday for you," Raine insisted. "Maybe. But then, it didn't work out that way, did it?"

Julia shook her head. "It didn't work out any way at all. Alexandra was murdered."

"And before she was murdered," Raine pressed, "it looked like she was going to give everything to Meredith." Raine paused, then smiled slightly. "And nothing to you."

Julia sat there for a moment. "Is that a question?"

"Here's a question," Raine replied. "How did that make you feel?"

"I was distraught at the murder of my friend," Julia answered.

"And the lost opportunity to partake in that friend's

success," Raine added. "I'm not saying you wanted her dead. I'm just saying you would have liked that money. And you must have been very upset when you discovered you weren't getting it."

"Again," Julia sneered at him, "is that a question?"

Raine smiled back at her. "No, I don't think there's any question about that at all." He turned and walked back to his seat. "No further questions, Your Honor."

Brenner looked to the prosecution table. "Any redirect-examination, Mr. Scarborough?"

Scarborough thought for a moment, then turned to the witness stand without actually answering the judge's question. "Ms. Kim, did you murder Alexandra Pruitt?"

"No," Julie answered. "I most certainly did not."

"Thank you. Nothing else, Your Honor." Scarborough sat down again.

"Anything based on that, Mr. Raine?" Brenner invited.

Raine stood up and also called out his question from his spot behind his table. "Do you know who did? Really know?"

Julia thought for a moment. Then she shook her head. "No."

And that's how Julia's testimony ended. It wasn't a home run for Raine, but Scarborough didn't score either. Raine asked again for her to be subject to recall and Scarborough called his next witness.

"The State calls Fiona Mendoza to the stand."

Raine wasn't quite sure how he was going to play this particular hand. Fiona had been very kind when they spoke with her, and Sommers's biggest objection to the woman was that she was just too sweet for too long. A jury wouldn't have time to get sick of her over the course of one bout of testimony. If she remained sweet and above the fray, Raine would be willing to give her a pass. He wanted to get to the next set of witnesses anyway. After the civilian guests, Scarborough would be calling the cops, and Kahale in particular. She would be the bridge to the second murder investigation, and Raine was eager to cross that bridge with Kahale.

Fiona entered the courtroom almost meekly. She wore a floral dress under a linen coat, with a shoulder bag and comfortable shoes. Even dressed up in a courtroom, she looked like a gardener. It was easy to forget she was also a successful real estate professional.

Scarborough replaced the pages on his clipboard, walked over to the end of the jury box, and began his examination.

Fiona answered the same five opening questions the previous witnesses had all answered.

"My full name is Fiona Marie Mendoza."

"I live on Mercer Island."

"I'm forty-two years old."

"I'm a real estate agent."

"Yes, I knew Alexandra Pruitt."

And then the sixth question in Scarborough's standard litany. "How did you know Ms. Pruitt?"

Fiona smiled weakly, sadly. She nodded and looked down at the floor. Then she looked up and nodded again. "Alexandra Pruitt saved my life."

Oh boy, Raine thought. He was almost certainly not going after her on cross-examination. Although he'd thought the same thing about Julia and ended up going after her pretty hard after all. Still, everyone in the courtroom was hanging on her next words.

Except Scarborough, who seemed more confused than curious. "What do you mean? Literally? Like from drowning?"

"Drowning in a way," Fiona answered with that same sad smile. "I met her at a time when I could very well have been dragged under by life. I'd had some bad luck, and I'd made some bad decisions. Some of the luck was because of those decisions, and some of the decisions were because of that luck. My life could have gone downhill fast. Alexandra saw me and she put me on a road going up."

Raine had to admire the storytelling. He wanted to know what happened at least as much as the jurors. And none of it really had anything to do with who murdered Alexandra Pruitt.

"Can you be more specific?" Scarborough asked. "What exactly did Ms. Pruitt help you with?"

Fiona took a deep breath and let it out slowly, through pursed lips. "When I was young, before I knew what I wanted to do, before I really had a plan, I got pregnant."

Raine's eyebrows shot up. He hadn't expected that. He expected even less what came next.

"But I lost the baby," Fiona continued. "She was born with a chromosomal disorder. There was nothing to be done. She lived for five weeks and two days. I was with her every day. But when she died, a part of me died, too. And I just couldn't find a reason to live again."

There was no way Raine was going to go after her on cross. He might not even ask her any questions.

"I ran into Alexandra in line at a coffee shop downtown a few months after my little Rose died," Fiona continued. "I got in line behind her. She saw me and struck up a conversation. I didn't really want to talk to anyone, but there was something about her that made me want to connect with her. She offered to buy my coffee but only if I promised to sit with her while I drank it. I agreed and for the first time since I lost Rose, I felt some connection to the world again."

Scarborough was supposed to be asking questions and Raine could have objected to a witness providing a narrative answer. But Raine wasn't about to object, and Scarborough didn't seem to know what to ask. He fell back on the prosecutor's always useful stand-by question. "What happened next?"

"She made me promise to come back the same time the next day," Fiona explained, "so I did. I didn't have anything else to do. She told me she understood what I was going through, and I believed her. I wanted to believe her anyway. Then she offered me a job at her company. I didn't even know what she did, but she said it didn't matter. I should come to her office, and she would find something for me to do. So, I did it. She held me until I could walk again. And once I could walk, the only path I was going to travel was in her footsteps."

The courtroom was silent for several moments as everyone absorbed Fiona's story.

"I never knew that," Meredith whispered to Raine. "Now I feel bad we weren't nicer to her."

Another reason not to cross-examine Fiona. Raine didn't want the jury to hear his client had been unkind to the most sympathetic witness of the trial.

Meanwhile, Scarborough just stood there, apparently unsure how to move forward. Eventually he gave up and just crashed to the end. "Were you at Ms. Pruitt's residence the night she died?"

"Yes, I was," Fiona confirmed.

"Did you see who did it?"

"No, I didn't," she answered.

"Did you do it?" Scarborough asked one question too many, trying to head off Raine's cross examination. Little did he know there wouldn't be any.

Fiona offered that sad smile again. "No, sir, I did not. Alexandra gave me a new life. I would have done anything to save hers."

Scarborough nodded. "No further questions, Your Honor."

He hurried to his seat as Judge Brenner looked to Raine, one judicial eyebrow raised. "Any cross-examination, Mr. Raine?" he practically dared.

Raine stood up. "No, Your Honor. No questions."

"May this witness be excused?" Brenner asked.

Raine wasn't going to play any games with Fiona. "Yes, Your Honor. She may be excused."

Judge Brenner thanked Fiona for her testimony and excused her from his courtroom. It was time for Scarborough to call his next witness. He had called Caroline, Julia, and Fiona, and he couldn't call Meredith because he was prohibited from calling a criminal defendant to the stand.

That left Sommers as the last of the Fab Five, but there was the not very small issue of Sommers being part of Raine's defense team. She had been privy to confidential attorney-client conversations. At a minimum, Scarborough couldn't be allowed to ask her about that. He could probably limit his questions to just whether she was there that night and whether she saw who did it.

Raine was not going to suggest she also could have been guilty. He stood up, ready to object to Sommers being called and to ask for the jury to be removed from the courtroom while they hashed out what very limited testimony Scarborough could try to illicit from the defense investigator.

But to Raine's surprise, and relief, Scarborough decided to deprive Raine of his argument and sidestep the problem entirely. Sommers was off the hook.

"The State calls Caitlin Kennedy to the stand."

34

Caitlin entered the courtroom and glanced around. She wore a suit that looked like she had bought the previous night on clearance, and they didn't have her size so she had to buy one size too big. Raine half expected to see the price tag still hanging from her sleeve when she walked up to the judge to be sworn in. She raised her right hand, price tag free, and swore to tell the truth, the whole truth, and nothing but the truth.

She took her seat in the witness stand and pushed her glasses back up her nose.

Scarborough took his position by the jurors and placed his pen next to the first question on his clipboard. "Please state your full name for the record."

"Caitlin Nicole Kennedy," she answered.

"What city do you live in?"

"Pres—," Caitlin started. "I mean, Seattle now."

"How old are you?" Scarborough moved to his next question even as Raine lingered on the preceding answer.

"Twenty-two." She seemed even younger just then.

"What is your occupation?" Scarborough asked next.

"Uh, well, I guess I'm unemployed right now," Caitlin answered. "I was Alexandra Pruitt's personal assistant."

"Did you know Alexandra Pruitt?" Scarborough asked without even listening to the witness's previous answer. That was the danger of preparing a script for what should be the free-flowing give and take of a question-and-answer session.

"Uh, yes," Caitlin frowned at him. "I was Ms. Pruitt's personal assistant."

"Ah yes." Scarborough looked up long enough to nod a few times and then looked back down at his questions. "Let me see. Right, so that's how you knew her. Okay, yes. Were you present at Ms. Pruitt's residence on the night she was murdered?"

"Yes, I was," Caitlin answered. "It was Ms. Pruitt's retirement party. I was in charge of making sure it went off as planned. I was responsible for everything from the invitations to the decorations to the caterers."

"So, you were in charge?" Scarborough tried to summarize.

But Caitlin laughed. "Oh, no. Ms. Pruitt was in charge. She was always in charge. It was my job to execute her orders, but she was the one giving the orders."

"All right," Scarborough acknowledged the answer. "So, you must have been very busy that night; is that accurate?"

Caitlin nodded. "Yes, I was very busy. The guests were early. The caterers were late. And the decorations didn't meet Ms. Pruitt's expectations, so I had to order more."

"I see," Scarborough responded.

Before he could pose another question, Caitlin added, "Plus there was Ernest to deal with. Mr. Poplowski, I mean. I was always having to deal with Mr. Poplowski."

"Why is that?" Scarborough managed to follow up with a question not on his checklist.

Caitlin shrugged. "How do I explain? He was just sort of needy. I think he had some self-esteem issues when it came to his relationship with Ms. Pruitt. She was very successful and wealthy. He didn't really have a job. So, he just always needed a lot of reassurance about things. Especially when Ms. Pruitt's friends were around. He was struggling."

Scarborough nodded. "Okay. So, guests, caterers, decorations, Ms. Pruitt, Mr. Poplowski. You were very busy."

"Very," Caitlin agreed.

"Were you able to pay attention at all to what the guests were doing," Scarborough asked, "or were you too busy, say, keeping an eye on the caterers to do that?"

"Oh, I was definitely paying attention to the guests," Caitlin answered. "In fact, that was my primary responsibility. Decorations were the lowest priority. Getting dinner served on time was medium priority. Top priority were the guests."

"Why is that?" Scarborough asked.

"Because that's what Ms. Pruitt wanted," Caitlin answered. "She chose the people she was kind to, and these were the people she had chosen above all others. She wanted them taken care of."

"I barely saw her that night," Meredith whispered to Raine.

"I thought she was one of the caterers," Raine confided back.

"In fact," Scarborough followed up, "that was the entire point of the evening, correct? For Ms. Pruitt to announce what her plans were to take care of these five women she had mentored."

"Exactly." Caitlin nodded. "The night was all about them and Ms. Pruitt. And it was my job to make sure that happened."

"How did you do that exactly?"

"Well, there were two major things, really," Caitlin answered. "I was just supposed to make sure everyone seemed happy and had whatever drinks or food they wanted."

"That makes sense," Scarborough commented.

Caitlin nodded and continued. "The other major thing was to prepare for Ms. Pruitt's big announcement."

"You knew what the announcement was going to be?" Scarborough asked, making no effort to disguise the excitement in his voice.

"Of course," Caitlin answered. "I was Ms. Pruitt's personal assistant. It was my job to get everything signed, sealed, and delivered. Literally."

Raine turned slowly to Meredith, his brows lowered in a concerned scowl.

Meredith's expression matched his trepidation.

"What do you mean by that?" Scarborough asked. "You literally had things signed and sealed and delivered to Ms. Pruitt?"

"Well, I was supposed to," Caitlin said. "But I only got two signatures. Ms. Pruitt was one. She signed first."

"Who was the other person who signed?" Scarborough asked carefully, like he was trying not to drop a priceless vase.

Caitlin turned and pointed at the defense table. "Meredith Beauchamp."

The gasps from the jury box were audible.

"That's not true!" Meredith grabbed Raine's sleeve. "She's lying."

"Shh," Raine ordered her in a lowered voice. "You need to keep your composure."

"But she's lying!" Meredith whisper-shouted. "That never happened."

Scarborough crossed the well and picked up a several-page document with an exhibit sticker on the upper right corner of the first page. He stepped over to the witness stand and handed it to Caitlin. "I'm handing you what has previously been marked as Plaintiff's Exhibit 1. Is this the document Ms. Pruitt and the defendant signed that night?"

Caitlin took a very brief moment to review the document. "Yes. This is the partnership agreement I was supposed to get everyone's signature on."

"And whose signatures did you manage to get?" Scarborough asked again.

"Only Ms. Pruitt and Ms. Beauchamp's," Caitlin answered.

"Why didn't you get anyone else's signature?" Scarborough asked.

"Because," Caitlin explained, "after Ms. Beauchamp signed it, she murdered Ms. Pruitt so she could keep all of Ms. Pruitt's money to herself."

Raine pressed his eyes closed and pinched the bridge of his nose. It wasn't a poker face by any means, but it was earnest. He opened his eyes and glanced at the jury. Every one of them was staring at Meredith, and none of them looked happy. They had just been given the evidence they needed to believe the prosecutor like they wanted to. No one wanted to believe innocent people were charged with crimes. Caitlin had just taken that risk away.

Raine leaned in so he could whisper directly into his client's ear. "Is any of that true? You said it was your signature, but you didn't sign it. You never did explain that. If there's something you need to tell me, this is really your last chance. Did you sign it? Did you think the others would sign it next? I can work with that. It's not too late. But you have to tell me now."

It wouldn't have been the first time a client had lied to Raine, and it wouldn't be the last. It was part of the practice, and he had methods for dealing with it. But in that moment, Raine needed the complete and absolute truth from his client.

"I did not sign that," Meredith insisted. "She's lying."

Raine sighed. It was going to be hard to convince the jury that the only thing Caitlin was lying about was the one thing that proved her client guilty.

"How do you know the defendant was the one who poisoned Ms. Pruitt?" Scarborough took the partnership agreement back from Caitlin and set it among the other exhibits on the bar across the well.

"Two reasons," Caitlin answered. "The first is that she asked me a bunch of questions about who else had signed the agreement, who else was going to sign it, how much time she had before anyone else signed it. Looking back later, I understand now why she was asking."

"That's not true!" Meredith hissed at Raine. But he had to keep his attention on Caitlin.

"What was the other reason?" Scarborough followed up.

Caitlin frowned and looked down at the floor. "I saw her put the poison in Ms. Pruitt's soup."

"What?" Meredith made no effort to whisper. "That is a lie!"

Judge Brenner slammed his gavel onto the bench. "The defendant will remain silent during the witness's testimony. Mr. Raine, are you able to control your client?"

"Yes, Your Honor," Raine quickly assured the Court. He knew there were other ways to ensure Meredith's silence and all of them involved restraints that would prejudice the jury against her even more than Caitlin's testimony. If that were possible.

"You saw the defendant put the poison in Ms. Pruitt's soup?" Scarborough repeated. He seemed almost as surprised as Raine, although he obviously considered it a pleasant surprise.

"Well, again, I didn't realize it at the time," Caitlin answered, "but looking back now, I know what she was doing." She dropped her head into her hands. "If only I had realized what was happening then," she wailed through her fingers, "Ms. Pruitt might still be alive."

"What exactly did you see?" Scarborough pressed for details.

Caitlin lifted her head again. Her eyes were red-rimmed, and her cheeks were blotchy. "Right after she signed the agreement, she followed me into the kitchen. I had to deal with the caterers. Not only were they late, they were two workers short and had forgotten the charcuterie boards. Ms. Beauchamp started opening the refrigerators and asking what was inside. I was distracted and couldn't really engage fully in two conversations, so I just answered her quickly. And one of the things she asked about was Ms. Pruitt's tomato soup. She asked if we were all having tomato soup for dinner and I said no, it was Ms. Pruitt's and sometimes she'll eat a little soup before dinner so she doesn't overeat at the table. Especially on a busy day when she probably hadn't remembered to eat anything the entire day."

"None of that happened." Meredith grabbed Raine's sleeve again. "You have to believe me."

Raine was going to believe the security video. He tried to recall if they had watched far enough back to see Meredith in the kitchen with Caitlin. If that was on the recording, they were sunk. And listening to Caitlin, Raine felt confident it was on the recording.

"What happened next?" Scarborough asked. It was a powerfully useful question for a prosecutor encouraging a star witness to tell the story that will convict the defendant.

"I left the kitchen with the caterer to see what we could do to replace the charcuteries," Caitlin answered. "And Ms. Beauchamp stayed behind in the kitchen. Alone."

"When was the last time you saw Ms. Pruitt alive?" Scarborough asked. He was winding down. Caitlin had given him what he needed. He just needed to land the plane without breaking anything.

"Just like I said, she told me she was going to eat a quick bowl of soup before dinner," Caitlin recounted. "She told me to make sure no one came in while she was eating. She hated eating in front of other people. She was going to fill up on soup and then probably not eat any of the dinner she had catered."

"Did she say anything else to you before she went into the kitchen?" Scarborough asked.

"She asked me how many signatures I had gotten on the partnership agreement," Caitlin explained. "I told her just the one. She told me not to worry about it. That she would help me get the others after she finished her soup. She wanted everyone to sign before she made her big announcement."

"Wasn't the partnership agreement the big announcement?" Scarborough questioned.

"That was only part of it," Caitlin explained. "That was who was going to share the company. There was a bigger announcement. Something about a windfall from an investment she made with borrowed money. It was something I didn't know about, which surprised me, since I was her personal assistant. I thought I knew everything. But she said this was something she had done off the books."

No wonder Newberry had sued, Raine realized. He didn't just want his money back. He wanted whatever that windfall was. And they would have to take his word for it because that 'Randall' file folder was empty.

"Did you discover the body?" Scarborough continued.

Raine suppressed a wince. This wasn't going to help.

"No." Caitlin pointed at Raine. "Ms. Beauchamp's lawyer did."

Another collection of gasps from the jury box. "He and his investigator were in the kitchen when I came in and saw Ms. Pruitt dead on the floor. They told me to leave and they would call the police."

"Did you?" Scarborough asked. "Did they?"

"Yes," Caitlin answered. "And I guess so. The police arrived shortly after that. They kept us there all night and then eventually arrested Ms. Beauchamp."

"Based on what you told them?" Scarborough suggested.

Caitlin shook her head. "No. Based on the video. And the agreement only she signed. And what she told them. I guess they knew she was lying."

Scarborough nodded, obviously satisfied, happy even. "No further questions, Your Honor."

Judge Brenner looked to Raine. "Cross-examination, counsel?"

Raine could hardly say no. He couldn't let that testimony go unchallenged. "Yes, Your Honor."

He stood up and looked at his client.

"She's lying," Meredith assured him.

One of them was, Raine knew.

He stepped out from behind the defense table. Cross-examination was probably the most difficult, and most enjoyable, part of trial work. If you were crossing a witness, that already meant they had been called by the other side and were aligned against you. Then, they always had their guards up, expecting you to try to trick them or at least twist their words. Finally, the better the witness did on direct-examination, the more the jury expected some sort of dramatic reveal on cross-examination. An outburst at least; a confession at best.

Caitlin had done very well for the prosecution. Raine wasn't sure he was going to be able to generate the dramatic moment the jury wanted. He was sure he wasn't going to get a confession. No one in that courtroom believed Caitlin Kennedy murdered her boss. Unless she did.

"Who showed the video to the police?" Raine began. "You or Ernest?"

Caitlin had turned her body slightly away from Raine as he approached the witness stand. She relaxed slightly at the relative banality of the question. "It was me."

One last question. Raine pointed at the woman who had slipped into the courtroom at some point during Caitlin's testimony. Elisabeth Ungermann. "Who's that woman seated in the last row?"

Caitlin followed Raine's finger with her eyes. Then she shrugged. "I'm sure I don't know. She looks like a lawyer."

Raine looked at Ungermann as well and surrendered a smile. "She does, doesn't she?"

He looked up at Judge Brenner. "No further questions, Your Honor."

"Any redirect-examination?" Brenner asked Scarborough as Raine walked back to his seat next to Meredith.

Scarborough answered, "No, Your Honor."

"May this witness be excused?" the judge inquired.

"By the State, yes, Your Honor," Scarborough answered.

Raine considered keeping her subject to recall just to mess with her; there was no way he would be recalling her to the witness stand. But if Caitlin was excused and allowed to sit in the gallery for the remainder of the trial, would she? And if she did, would she sit with someone? Would she sit with Ungermann? Or was Ungermann's appearance just a general interest in the progress of the trial and coincidental as to the timing during Caitlin's testimony?

"By the defense as well, Your Honor." Raine sat down next to Meredith. He wanted to say something encouraging, but nothing came to mind.

"That was bad, wasn't it?" she asked him.

He could only nod. "I'm not sure how it could get worse."

Scarborough stood up. "The State calls Detective Olivia Kahale to the stand."

35

Detective Kahale marched confidently into the courtroom. It wasn't the first time she had testified. She wore a blazer and pants, with her badge on one hip and her pistol on the other. She stopped in front of the judge to swear to tell the truth, the whole truth, and nothing but the truth, then took her seat on the witness stand and waited for the prosecutor to toss her softballs.

Scarborough insisted on asking the same first five questions, even though he had already announced to the jury that her occupation was police detective, and the only way she knew Alexandra Pruitt was after she was dead.

She was an engaging witness. A professional witness even. Police officers received training on how to testify effectively. One of the big lessons was to deliver your answers directly to the jurors. Scarborough's placement almost among them made that easy for the detective. In addition, she had a pleasant way about her that made the jurors want to hear what she had to say. And, unfortunately for Raine and Meredith, she had a lot to say.

Scarborough took her through the initial callout and report of a murder, to the arrival at the scene, to the interviewing of all the witnesses, the viewing of the video, and the arrest of Meredith Beauchamp. Then Scarborough segued to the second murder, that of Alexandra's lawyer, Duncan Chenoweth. Kahale explained the professional relationship between the two victims and the fact that all of Duncan's records regarding Alexandra had been taken during the burglary/murder. She also explained that Meredith became a suspect after they located her fingerprint on the doorbell.

The jurors probably wondered why Meredith had been allowed to walk around free after being charged with one murder, but since they were all pretending she wasn't being detained in the jail in lieu of six million dollars bond during the trial, there wasn't any good way to explain why she had been released just to murder again—allegedly.

The evidence on the second murder was thinner than the first, but Kahale stressed the fingerprint and its fragile location, meaning a lot of people touch a doorbell and only the most recent fingerprint will be collectable, having smeared away and supplanted any previous visitors' prints. That meant not only was Meredith there, but she was the last person there before he was murdered. Throw in a motive to cover up financial details of the first murder and suddenly you have a decent case against Meredith Beauchamp.

Scarborough finished his direct examination with the story of Meredith's second arrest and booking into the King County Jail. Kahale couldn't tell the jury that Meredith pled the Fifth during that arrest, but they could probably deduce from the fact that the detective was able to report all the things Meredith said after the first arrest.

Scarborough competently extracted all of the relevant information the detective had regarding the cases and sat down.

Raine stood up and hoped the detective still cared about the information she didn't have. He took a moment to glance at the gallery. It had begun to fill up during the course of the trial. Ungermann was back, with Newberry sitting next to her. No sign of Tire Iron Timmy. Caitlin sat directly in front of them. Fiona was there, but not Caroline or Julia since they were still excluded. Ernest was absent for the same reason; Raine felt a little bad about that, but decisions have to be made when they have to be made. Next to Fiona, but not too close, sat Sommers. Once it became clear that Scarborough wasn't going to call Sommers as a witness, she was free to observe as well. And Raine wanted her close. Things were about to get crazy.

"Detective," Raine began his cross-examination, "would you agree with me that these two murders appear to be related?"

Kahale nodded. "I believe I just testified to that."

"Right," Raine agreed. "And if I recall correctly, you said they were likely connected because Duncan Chenoweth was Alexandra Pruitt's lawyer, is that right?"

"Yes," Kahale agreed. "That's right." She seemed bemused by Raine's questions so far.

"In fact," Raine continued, "Mr. Chenoweth wasn't just any type of lawyer. He specialized in taxes and wills, isn't that right?"

"Yes, that's right," Kahale confirmed.

"So, it would stand to reason," Raine put to her, "that Mr. Chenoweth probably did Ms. Pruitt's taxes and drafted her will. Wouldn't you agree?"

Kahale took a moment. "Well, I don't think he actually prepared her tax returns every year. I'm sure she had a C.P.A. for that. But he certainly was the type of lawyer who could give advice on how to best reduce potential tax liability. As for a will, we were never able to locate a will drafted by or for Ms. Pruitt."

"You never found Ms. Pruitt's will?" Raine repeated. "Even though the lawyer who would have drafted that will for her was also murdered and all of his records regarding Ms. Pruitt were stolen?"

"I would propose that the reason we never found a will for Ms. Pruitt is precisely because the lawyer who drafted it was murdered and his records stolen. The will, if it ever existed, would almost certainly have been part of the records that were taken."

Raine nodded along to Kahale's answer. "The will, if it exists, might shed light on the true motive of the killer, wouldn't you agree?"

"I would very much agree," Kahale answered.

Raine took a moment then asked, "You'd like to have that will, wouldn't you, Detective Kahale?"

Kahale tipped her head slightly. "I would very much like to have that will, Mr. Raine."

Raine smiled and leaned onto the counter in front of the witness stand. "If I were to tell you of a secure location where a secret copy of that will is located, would you be willing to meet me there tonight and finish your testimony tomorrow?"

"What?" Judge Brenner boomed from the bench.

"Objection!" Scarborough screeched from the prosecution table.

"Absolutely," Kahale answered from the witness stand.

Raine ignored Scarborough and looked up at Brenner.

"The defense moves to adjourn until tomorrow morning. There's a piece of evidence we need to have marked."

Brenner was so taken aback that he didn't have an answer ready.

"The State objects to any adjournment, Your Honor," Scarborough put in. "This is highly irregular. We should just proceed with the trial. Not interrupt testimony with empty promises and wild goose chases."

"Look, Your Honor." Raine decided to just be real and lay it on the line. "If I really wanted to, I could fill up the rest of the day with ridiculous questions for this witness. Hours of examination about every last fiber of the last carpet in every last room in both residences. It's what I do. Or we could call it a day, let the detective do her job, and maybe, just maybe, we will be able to get closer to the truth in this case. And isn't that what we want? The truth?"

"It's what I want," Kahale called out from the witness stand.

Brenner took a moment, then sighed very loudly. Raine knew that meant he had won.

"Fine," the judge said. "We will adjourn for the day. I'm curious about what's going to happen tomorrow, counsel."

Raine was far more curious about what was going to happen that night.

36

There wasn't much time to prepare. Sommers met with Fiona, and Raine met with Kahale. Fiona needed to get the word to Caroline, Julia, and Ernest about what had happened in court. Kahale needed to understand the entire plan. She wanted to be partners with Raine. Be careful what you wish for. Then they needed to wait until dusk again for the drive to Fall City.

Raine wasn't interested in fracturing any more ribs, so after court he parked his car on the street instead of the garage and left early to pick up Sommers. He thought a car might be following him, but it was hard to tell on the busy downtown street. Everybody in Seattle seemed to drive some version of a white Subaru; they tended to blur together after a while.

Sommers was waiting on the sidewalk when he pulled up by the three-minute 'passenger load only' sign, which was good since there were no parking spots anywhere in sight. She hopped in and Raine headed toward the freeway, Interstate-90 eastbound again.

"You think this will work?" she asked.

"I think it has to," Raine answered. "Everybody is desperate at this point. If we get our hands on the will, someone will be exposed as the real killer. And if we don't, Meredith is going to be convicted and sentenced to life in prison."

"Big stakes." Sommers whistled.

Raine smiled. "That's why we play the game."

THE FALL CITY post office was located at the western edge of the old downtown, two blocks from the Snoqualmie River and an eight-minute drive from the Preston exit from Interstate-90. It was the same exit they had taken to get to Alexandra's cabin, but instead of turning right on that unnamed gravel road, Raine kept the car on Preston-Fall City Road and followed it all the way into town. So did the white Subaru that had been behind them the entire way. And the silver Toyota SUV following the Subaru.

Raine had realized the brass key from Alexandra's office was too small to go into an actual door. He thought it might be for a personal lock box, but the chest in Alexandra's wardrobe didn't have a lock. That left a more institutional setting, like a safety deposit box, a post office box, or even a bus station locker. Raine suspected that if Alexandra kept her most secret possession in her cabin, far away from her life in Seattle, she might also keep a back-up copy of her will there too.

A little research confirmed that the one bank in Fall City didn't offer safety deposit boxes, and there no bus station in town either. That left the post office. By the time they got there, the sun was setting again and the post office was closed. Just as Raine had planned. He pulled his car into the empty parking lot and waited for the others to arrive. He hoped Timmy would stay in his car.

The Subaru arrived first. Upon seeing Raine and Sommers standing outside their vehicle, the Subaru driver pretended to be just driving past, but then did a U-turn at the next intersection and doubled back. It wasn't as if they hadn't already been seen. The car parked on the opposite end of the parking lot and, after a moment, Randall Newberry stepped out of the driver's seat. He had driven himself. Raine felt his ribs relax. But Newberry wasn't alone. Caitlin Kennedy emerged from the front passenger seat. Raine wasn't completely unsurprised, but he was gratified. So far, things were going according to plan. Or at least according to suspicion and hope.

The silver Toyota that had been behind the Subaru came around the corner next. The driver didn't hesitate to pull into the driveway and park in the nearest spot. Julia Kim exited the driver's door; Caroline Howard stepped out from the front passenger side. Fiona Mendoza appeared from the back seat. Raine waited a beat, but Ernest wasn't in the car with them. That was too bad. If anyone deserved what was about to happen, it was Ernest.

Ungermann was also absent, which was just smart. She had a bar license to worry about. Her client would fill her in on whatever she might need to know. Or he might not. Either way, she was billing her hours and climbing her ladder. Her road to the top didn't go through Fall City.

Raine pushed off his car and started walking to a central spot in the parking lot where the three groups were converging. He threw his arms wide in greeting. "You're probably wondering why I've gathered you all here this evening."

"Cut the crap, Raine," Newberry responded. "You're not in charge here. Where's the detective? Did she find the will?"

Raine looked at his wrist, although he had stopped wearing a watch years ago. His phone told him what time it was. Nevertheless, it was still a universally recognized gesture. "I thought she would be here by now. Maybe she's not coming after all."

"Why are we at a post office in Fall City?" Caroline demanded. "It's not even open. Is this some sort of joke?"

"It's no joke," Sommers spoke up to address her colleague. "We found a key hidden in Alexandra's office. We think it might go to a post office box. A post office box she didn't want anyone else to know about."

"Might?" Julia replied. "You mean you don't know. Do you even know if Alexandra's will is in there?"

"And again," Caroline interjected, "why are we in Fall City? Shouldn't we at least be at the cabin?"

"There's nothing in the cabin," Sommers answered. "We already looked."

"Just like Caitlin and Mr. Newberry did." Raine nodded toward them. "Isn't that right, Newberry?"

Fiona looked between Raine, who was smiling, and Newberry, who definitely was not. "What's going on?"

"Do you want to tell them, Caitlin?" Raine asked. "Or should I?"

"Te-tell them what?" Caitlin stammered. She was a lot less confident than when she had lied on the stand earlier.

"G. Pruitt," Raine replied. "Dozens of envelopes. All addressed to G. Pruitt. In your handwriting." Raine pointed at Newberry. "When did he tell you? Years ago, when you were a little girl, or just in the last year when you demanded to know the truth?"

"What truth?" Julia stepped forward. "What's going on, Caitlin? Is there something you're keeping from everyone?"

"Oh, definitely," Raine answered the question. "I just don't know if you told Alexandra before or after you got the job as her personal assistant. Did you tell her to get the job, or did you get the job so you could tell her? Or did you never tell her at all?"

"Tell her what?" Fiona asked.

"It goes back to that address, G. Pruitt," Raine explained. "I have to admit that took me a while to figure out. It didn't make sense that the letters would be mailed to Alexandra, but using the wrong first initial. That meant it had to be something other than an initial. It was a title. Like 'Mr.' or 'Ms.' Or 'Dr.' Only I couldn't think of any professional titles that start with 'G'. But there are several family titles that do, isn't that right, Caitlin?"

Caitlin didn't answer, so Raine continued.

"G. Pruitt," Raine repeated. "Grandma Pruitt. You aren't the only one who lost a child, Fiona. That's why Alexandra took pity on you. But her child didn't die. She abandoned it."

"She did not abandon her child!" Newberry boomed. "She wasn't ready to be a mother, but she didn't just leave the child on the firehouse steps. She gave her to a trusted friend to raise as his own family."

"You?" Julia's jaw dropped open. "You and Alexandra had a baby together?"

"What?" Newberry recoiled at the accusation. "No, of course not. The father was some worthless piece of trash who ran away as soon as he heard Alexandra was pregnant. She never heard from him again. But Alexandra and I grew up together. We used to steal apples from the orchard on the other side of the river. My mom stepped up and we took Alexandra's baby in as our own."

Raine watched the others start doing the math in their head. "That baby grew up and had a baby of her own. Where's your mom now, Caitlin? Is she part of this, or is she gone as well?"

"She died of cancer when I was seven," Caitlin practically growled. "Uncle Randy raised me after that. He told me I came from better people. Rich people. People who owed me."

"People like your grandma," Raine said. "But then she was going to give it all away to strangers."

"Hey!" Sommers smacked his arm.

"Not strangers," Raine corrected, "but not family. There would be nothing left for you if she brought on the Fab Five as partners to take over the business."

"And you would have known that was her plan," Sommers explained, "because you were her personal assistant. You would have seen all the documents. Hell, you probably typed them up."

"I did," Caitlin confirmed. "And I couldn't believe she would do that."

"Did you type up her will, too?" Raine asked. "Or did you just read it and see there was nothing for a long-lost granddaughter?"

"Don't say any more," Newberry cautioned. "This is all rank speculation. It makes no sense."

"It makes no sense if there was a will that left everything to someone else," Raine countered. "But it makes perfect sense if that will went missing."

"If the only person who signed the partnership agreement couldn't take over the business because she was convicted of murdering Alexandra," Sommers picked up the explanation, recounting Raine's explanation of intestate inheritance law, "and there was no will to transfer her assets to someone she designated, then it would all be forfeited to the state, unless..."

"Unless Alexandra's one and only living relative suddenly stepped forward to claim the entire fortune," Raine concluded.

Caitlin looked to Newberry.

Newberry shook his head at her, a warning to be quiet.

"There was no loan, was there, Newberry?" Raine challenged. "That was just a ruse to flush out Alexandra's will, if anyone had a copy you hadn't gotten rid of."

Newberry didn't answer.

"It doesn't matter," Raine continued. "Now that we all know the truth, the cops are going to get all the evidence they need to convict you, Caitlin. They can examine Alexandra's computers and isolate every keystroke you made on them. They'll pull a lot more of that surveillance video than just the section you had cued up and ready for them. Hell, they can probably even trace the cyanide to the apple seeds from that orchard over there. It's not like you can buy cyanide on the internet. I never understood how Meredith was supposed to have gotten her hands on that, but I can certainly believe an abandoned granddaughter with dreams of entitled riches could learn how to turn apple seeds into poison."

"You can't prove any of this," Caitlin screeched. "You don't even have her will. It's not in some stupid post office box. Those are for mail, not valuables. Do you think she'd be stupid enough to keep it there?"

"No, but I thought you might be stupid enough to keep it at your apartment." Raine pointed behind her at the approaching police car.

Caitlin's face blanched.

"You let it slip that you were living at least part of the time in Preston," Raine explained. "The reason we came here so late wasn't because we didn't know what time the post office closed. It was so Detective Kahale could get a warrant for your apartment. Here she comes now. If the copy of Alexandra's will you stole from Duncan's house was in your apartment, she has it now."

Caitlin's eyes flashed wide.

"You could try to run," Raine said, "but I bet they'd catch you. There's nowhere to go up here."

The police car rushed to a stop next to the assembled group and Detective Kahale jumped from the passenger seat, cuffs in one hand, her firearm at the low-ready in the other. "Caitlin Kennedy, you are under arrest for the murders of Alexandra Pruitt and Duncan Chenoweth."

Caitlin didn't run. In fact, she seemed frozen to the spot. Tears began to roll out from under her glasses and she raised her face to Newberry. "I'm sorry, Uncle Randy. I'm so, so sorry. I thought I'd thought of everything. I thought it would work."

Newberry wrapped his arms around her. "Don't worry, honey. We're going to get you the best lawyers."

"Not likely," Sommers called out and slapped a hand onto Raine's shoulder. "He's already taken."

EPILOGUE

"Ernest got everything?" Sommers smiled. "That's wonderful. That's what Alexandra would have wanted."

"I would agree," Raine replied, "considering that's what she put in her will."

They were back in Raine's office the next afternoon. Meredith had been released from custody and her cases dismissed. Raine had hoped Scarborough would find it painful to admit defeat, but he accepted the new information in his usual dispassionate, ministerial self. Dismissal was the obvious course of action. He drafted the orders in record time and Brenner seemed happy to sign them, and appropriately so. He had avoided putting an innocent person in prison.

"They really did love each other," Sommers went on. She had her afternoon latte in her hand. Raine was wondering if it was early enough yet for a slightly harder celebratory drink. "Honestly, I'm not sure what she saw in him, but he was devoted to her."

"That is probably exactly what she saw in him," Raine opined. "She'd seen what the opposite of that looked like, then lived her life avoiding any relationships at all until she met Ernest. She couldn't quite trust him enough to marry him, but she knew how to take care of him, even in death."

"So that mailbox key was just a mailbox key?" Sommers asked. "Why hide it?"

"Because the only mail she got at that address was from her secret granddaughter," Raine theorized. "Ernest didn't even know. If he had, I'm sure he would have told anyone who would listen."

"And Meredith's signature on the partnership agreement?" Sommers asked. "Do you think Caitlin found a copy of her signature on some other document and copied it?"

"Maybe." Raine shrugged. "Or Caitlin really did show it to her, and she really did sign it first, and she just couldn't admit that lie to us. But given her position in the criminal trial, she can hardly claim it was a valid contract, after all. She's stuck with what she told us and what I told the jury, whether it was true or not."

"That's just as well," Sommers said. "Alexandra will rest easier knowing her final wishes were properly put into effect."

Raine looked at his bottle of very non-alcoholic water. "Hold that thought."

He walked over to the cabinet on the other side of his office and extracted a half-full bottle of bourbon and two glasses that probably had a layer of dust at the bottom. He ignored the potential dust and poured them each a small shot of the brown liquid.

He handed a glass to Sommers and raised his own. "To Alexandra and Ernest," he said.

Sommers clinked her glass to his and they each took a sip. It was smooth, aged ten years. The good stuff.

Sommers raised her glass again. "And here's to another successful case. We make quite the team, Dan Raine."

Raine happily tapped his glass against hers. "I'll drink to that."

WE HOPE YOU ENJOYED THIS BOOK

If you could spend a moment to write an honest review on Amazon, no matter how short, we would be extremely grateful. They really do help readers discover new authors.

ALSO BY STEPHEN PENNER

Rain City Legal Thriller Series

Burden of Proof

Trial By Jury

The Survival Rule

Double Jeopardy

Prime Suspects

Made in United States
Troutdale, OR
12/27/2024

27268100R00181